FORGOTTEN TALES:

A Phoenix Dream

DARREN ARQUETTE

authorHOUSE®

AuthorHouse™
1663 Liberty Drive
Bloomington, IN 47403
www.authorhouse.com
Phone: 1-800-839-8640

Published by AuthorHouse   05/31/2012

ISBN: 978-1-4678-8360-3 (sc)
ISBN: 978-1-4678-8361-0 (e)

CONTENTS

Chapter 1

This World

"THE YEAR WAS 2210. After years of economic decline and war across the globe, the Earth's economy is finally rising once more.

In the early days of the 23rd century, 2203, one of the eight most powerful nations in the world took to war against a young nation deeming it a war of 'Peace.'
However the true purpose of this war was the acquisition of oil, the last of the planets reserve.

Over the coming years, the peoples of the young nation rose to fight back their invaders.
It took a further four years for the more powerful nation to overcome the weaker nation.

A year or more later, 2206, the war had ended but with it a rebel group sabotaged the nation's oil fields. The cost of oil rose and with it the people of the planet began to panic, buying fuel for their vehicles, causing the cost to rise even more.

But in 2209, 'The Wars are over'.

There were a number of reasons for war, but there is no longer a reason to fight just for fossil fuels. This was because of a new source of fuel, which gives off masses of energy.

Entire cities are being built for the soul use of this new fuel. The fuel is named PHOENIX, because of its colour when burnt, and its ability to burn so long.

It's no longer used as a way to life.

It's the only way to survive."

The voice stops, to search for more words to say.

A young man, who the voice belongs to, is sitting in a darkroom.

Only one light resides in the room with him and a rattling machine. The light is small and slowly blinking as the machine continues rattling.

He sits there and begins to breathe deeply. He then stares into the red blinking light and begins to speak once again.

"I'm getting off track here . . . This is our journey, from the beginning. In the year of 2259.

The year that the world changed once more."

Light from the dawning sun is shining into a room, a Childs room.

A young blonde haired boy awakens from a nightmare in his bed. The room is neat and organised, there are many toys in the room, but are organised into four piles, each in a corner of the room. The owner of this neat room is Varin Vargon, a seven year old boy with blonde spiked hair and blue eyes.

His room remains dark; his eyes are yet to adjust to what light there is.

He idly rolls over to look at his alarm clock; it is six in the morning.

Varin slowly folds back his blue bed quilt, even his sheets and pillow case are blue. He then begins to lower himself out of his single sized bed, which is a foot bigger than him.

He begins to stagger as he finds his legs, he yawns and stretches, feeling the blue carpet between his toes. His blue and white stripped pajama sleeves fall down towards his shoulders, his clothes are two sizes too big.

Varin looked at his small cabinet, upon it was the alarm clock and a necklace.

The necklace was created by Varin's Father, who also made a similar one for Varin's older brother.

This is the Vargon Family Crest. Varin places it around his neck and begins to wake more as his Father begins to yell up stairs.

'Varin you awake? Come down for your breakfast.'

The Vargon family live in the Green Sector of the mega-city known as Karves City.

Their Father believes the centre is too polluted for them to live anywhere near it so instead they live in the outskirts of the city as protection for his children, but even on the outskirts of these mega-cities' the air is still polluted.

"I remember well why each mega-city, such as Karves and the neighbouring town of Shenma City, are split into five sections: Green, Yellow, Blue, Orange and Red.

They say that the zone Green and Yellow, are the safest for being less polluted, but the real reason is for this sectors isn't Health, it's the one thing that makes the world turn . . .

Money.

Green, Yellow and Blue are mostly the residential areas of the city. However the truth is, these are the areas in which, what the rich, like Diamond Hillweller call 'Trash', the people who have next to nothing.

Orange and Red are owned by the wealthy, which can afford to life in the skyscrapers, high above the smog in these high pollution areas.

The Green sectors are for the poorest. In the case of Karves, this sector isn't owned by any Mayor, Politian, or even the nation but by Loan Sharks. Money hungry thugs who like to push people down and aren't afraid to take another life, just to improve their own."

Varin slowly walks towards his bedroom door. Opening his door cautiously.

He begins to stumble out of the door, stepping out onto the burgundy carpet.

Varin looks to his right and sees his older brother's room. The door stands wide open.

He continues on towards the bathroom, just across the hall, noticing the cream coloured wallpaper with a simple pattern running down it, a woman's touch has been placed here.

He walks past an old photograph in a wooden frame.

The photograph is of his pregnant Mother, his older brother and his Father. All laughing and smiling in a big green park sitting on a checkered picnic blanket surrounded by multi-coloured flowers during the summer, this was obviously their family photo.

Varin continues past the narrow staircase, he begins to look down cautiously, quickly remembering a nightmare before shaking it out of his head.

He passes the staircase and now approaches his parent's room, his Father's room.

The door was a jar by a foot, which almost dared him to enter.

He has never seen the room. His older brother, Drogun, would tell him tall tales of what it looked like inside, Varin never believed him, it sounded too good to be true.

'I'll look tomorrow' he always thought to himself, but he never dared to ever enter.

As he walked past he tried to see inside but no luck. It's only open enough to see the wallpaper, a peach colour with a red rose pattern on it.

Just next to his Father's room is the bathroom.

He steps into the bathroom quickly, closers the door behind him and steps into the walk in shower. He then pulls the curtain across

Downstairs his Father is cooking breakfast in the kitchen.

Drogun, Varin's older brother, is in the kitchen also, playing with his now cold fried egg and sausage.

A sudden thought strikes Drogun, he begins to think as he stares down at his food and comes up with a trick to play on Varin when he arrives.

He's done this before, a few times in fact and Varin has fallen for it every time.

Varin doesn't know why he does it; maybe for a laugh or just out of boredom.

Who knows?

Back up stairs.

Varin steps out from his room wearing a clean pair of pyjamas, they are exactly the same as his other pair white with blue stripes, they're maybe a few years older and slightly more worn at the knees but practically the same.

He begins to make his way down the narrow stairs to the small boxed kitchen. As he gets closer towards the kitchen, the air begins to thicken with the smell of fried eggs and sausage.

Drogun is the first to say morning to him.

'Morning sleepyhead . . . how's my little bro today?'
'. . . Morning D . . . Drogun' replies Varin with a yawn.

Drogun is the oldest of the Vargon brothers; his hair is short, bowl shaped but sometimes gets in his blue eyes. He uses a red tattered bandanna given to him by his father to keep the hair out of his eyes.

His hair colour is purple which he dyes once a week in an attempt to look like his father when he was going through his punk phase in 2221.

To Varin, Drogun seems kind of strange because of his clothing. Always wearing black denim jeans, which have a tear at the knees.

Drogun also seems to always wear the same black t-shirt.

Varin once had the courage to brave an adventure into his brother's messy room, his quest was to see if he had more black t-shirts, although almost getting lost in piles upon piles of mess, Varin discovered that Drogun has ten similar black t-shirts.

Varin took up a seat across from Drogun on the squared breakfast table. The old cooker was now turned off and their Father turned to give Varin his fried breakfast.

'Here you go Varin'
Varin then politely says 'Thank you dad'

Their father is nothing like either Drogun or Varin. He has long black hair leading to his shoulders, although his clothes do seem similar, black jeans, old and over used, he is also wearing a grey dirty t-shirt, dirty white trainers. And to Varin, he sees his father as tall, taller than any mountain, and when picked up and placed upon his shoulders, Varin feels like he's on top of the world.

Over the years their father began to not care about his appearance, he looked older than he actually was because of this.

Many of his hairs turned grey before their time.

Varin's Father doesn't work; he has tried on a number of occasions to get a job but no such luck, over many years he tried to take any job he could, even working at a fast food restaurant, anything to put bread onto the table. Oddly though he rejected any offer he got from the SPARK Corporation facility, in the centre of the city.

Varin begins to stare at his meal; something seems to be wrong. Varin looks down at his meal and catches ever so quickly a smile across Drogun's face. Their Father turns round to clean the pots and the cooker with the brown murky water coming from the tap.

'He's done it again hasn't he, Drogun's swapped my meal again . . . I'll swap it back while he's not looking.'

Varin then pointed at something out of the window while murmuring words.

Drogun didn't catch what Varin had murmured and although confused, wasn't expecting something so looked towards to the window following the line lead by Varin's finger.

Meanwhile quickly and quietly Varin swapped the meals.

Drogun looked back, just as Varin put everything back in its place. Giving his brother a stare, while thinking to himself 'idiot' and while still keeping an eye on Varin, he picked up his fork after giving his brother one more foolish boy look before stabbing the sausage on his plate and taking a bite.

Varin smiled.

The look of disgust instantly appeared upon on Drogun's face, he silently spat his food into the nearby bin and began to scrap the taste out of his mouth.

Secretly from his Father's view, he scrubs the remaining food off his plate and into the bin. Varin was now chuckling to himself, placing a hand over his mouth trying to remain quiet. After emptying the plate Drogun places it back, their Father turns around. Varin quickly lowers his hands and acts like he's been eating his breakfast all along.

'Wow . . . you must be really hungry Drogun—' said their father, then continuing by asking '—would you like seconds?'

Drogun jumps out of his seat rubbing his stomach.
'No thanks, I don't think I can handle anymore . . . Varin can! I'm going to have a shower.'

Drogun quickly runs out of the room and goes up stairs; Varin begins to chuckle once again.

A couple minutes later Varin finishes his breakfast.

'Varin why don't you go get dressed, but be quick, we need to set off for the train soon.'

Their Father always walks his two sons to school, but on this cold and dark day they won't be going to school, for the first time in seven years, they intend to go on holiday, somewhere far away from the polluted cities of today.
Like most people that live in the green sectors of these mega-cities, money is their problem.
Varin nods and rushes from the kitchen, making short work of the narrow staircase by climbing it on all fours.
He enters the room, opens the curtains and rushes to the small cupboard that contains all of his cloths, across from his bed, and opens the doors. He notices a wrapped present before even thinking about it or reading the card, he rips open the present.
They were gifts from his father, a sky blue hooded top and dark blue denim jeans and old twentieth century brown

leather shoes. He quickly puts on all the new clothes and takes one quick look in the mirror and yet again decided not to brush his hair.

Varin never brushes his hair mainly because he likes it messy, the other is because his grandparents once thought he was a girl when he was younger since he had long blonde curly hair and so now he keeps it short, but long enough to spike.

Varin took one step out of his room but suddenly hears the sound of the shower going in the background, but it wasn't that which court his attention. It was a loud noise coming from the roof, he smiles to himself and decides to make his way onto the roof.

It was his naive nature to go and investigate, maybe it was his imagination that caused him to have a look as well, after all he did once dream of an air balloon crashing onto his roof that will take him away from this city to live on a paradise island.

He ran into Drogun's room and towards the window almost tripping over Drogun's clothes scatted all over the floor. He raised and climbed out of the window. Stepping out onto the ledge and stood up straight, hugging against the wall. He reached over for the old rusty copper drain pipe that lingered close to the window.

The fear of heights and the flimsy feel of the drain pipe soon left his mind, this was after all his twentieth or so time of climbing to the roof.

He would often climb to the rooftop to look at the stars and think about his mother and his future.

Often however he climbed up to join the girl next door, Emily. She sometimes comes onto the roof to also look at the stars and think about her future, perhaps this is where he got the inspiration of thinking about such things.

Emily is the same age as Varin, they both have the same likes and dislikes, they also go to the same school; the only difference between the two is that Emily already knows what she wants to do with her life when she grows older.

Varin and Emily became friends when she was younger. At the age of four she moved to Karves Primary School and so she soon began to be bullied for being new and for having ginger hair. However Varin, although friendless himself, stood up for her and made her feel welcome.

He looked out for her as the years passed but as they grew older she began to learn how to look after herself and those close to her.

Varin finally made it to the roof with a few missing or broken tiles, Varin looks over the top of the drainpipe as he drags himself over the side, he smiled at the young girl on the roof that was staring into the rising sun, not noticing that he was there.

'H . . . hello Emily, what are you doing here?' asked Varin acting like he didn't realise it would be her.

Emily replied while still looking at the sunrise. 'Oh . . . hey Varin. I'm just thinking . . . wait how come you're up so early?'

Varin sat down next to her.
'Well we, we have to get the train station, so we can go on a holiday.'
'Oooh. Where are you going?' she asked
'Not too far, just to the ocean for a week I think.'
'Nice.'

'So eh, anyway how come you're up here? Thinking about your future again? About becoming a Police Officer still?' asked Varin.

Emily replied quickly 'Yep, plus—', she looked away from the sunrise for the first time and looked at Varin '—I couldn't sleep. I'm just kinda excited you know, the future is so far ahead of us but so close, you know? Like three more years and then I'll be able to apply as a trainee Officer. I just can't wait to begin. How about you?'

'Me? Well sure I can't wait either, I just can't stop thinking of i—' An image of a women quickly popped into his head '—my mom . . . I wonder what she was like, and . . .'

He went silent.

'I know how you feel Varin, I feel the same way about my dad. He ran out on us when I was 1 . . . I kinda want to know what he was like but at the same time, because he ran out on us. I don't want to know him.'

Varin goes to say something, to comfort her but he stops talking as Emily continues to stare at him, feeling almost sad now he looks down at the tiles, as the sun light changes colour from a burning red/orange to a tinted polluted green/orange.

He continues to imagine what she was like, a kind caring person and was she independent and all those attributes that makes a strong person, just like his father.

'Drogun, Varin come on, we'll miss the train.'

Barely hearing him Varin looked at Emily.
'He said it's time to go' she said before he could speak
'See you at school Emily . . . when we get back?'

Emily smiled and nodded as Varin climbed back down back into Drogun's.

Drogun was just leaving his room after grabbing a black jacket also new from their Father just like Varin's blue hoodie. Varin and Drogun both ran down to the front door fully dressed, Varin slightly dirty because of the roof.

The TV suddenly came on and was clearly heard coming from the front room.

'A high speed chase has just broken out in down town Karves City, the speeders are unknown but they are driving two . . . cars from 253 years ago, it's amazing old cars like that can still run' said the News Anchor looking confused.

The TV suddenly turned off as Drogun and Varin came to the ground floor, their father walked out of the front room and smiled to both of them, the first smile that Varin has seen in a long time.

Their father also put on his jacket; placing one hand in the sleeve and using the free hand to open the front door.

He stepped out in front of Drogun and Varin to lead them to the Train Station putting his second arm into the sleeve of the jacket and fastening it up.

The Train Station itself, is only a cross the road, which was empty because of the time of day and the entrance to the building being around the other side, facing the nearby park.

Their Father took the lead but not only to show them the way but to also protect them from whomever may have the guts or the desperation to get money, one way or another.

It was a hard time for anyone to make money to pay the bills especially those who lived in the Green Sectors.

He began to look round almost every second, as if he was expecting someone.

The brothers followed in the shadow of their towering Father, allowing him to lead them to the front entrance overlooking the park.

As they came to the park Varin noticed something about the park, he never realised until now that this is where the Vargon family picture was taken, all those years ago. However the park's plants now have become overgrown, with some weeds taking over in areas and rubbish littering the whole area.

They quickly reached the front of the building; the park was cordoned off by a small white picket fence.

The fence and streets of the Green Sector were just as unclean and broken as the park.

As they came closer to the door, Varin could smell the sweet scent of the nearby flowers close to the entrance of the underground train station, the smell reminded Varin of something from his childhood but he couldn't quite put his finger on it. There was also a faint smell of something burnt coming from behind them Their father grabbed the doors that lead to the underground station allowing Drogun and Varin to enter first and proceed down the stairs; he closed the door behind himself and took the lead once again.

Outside, a Shadowy Figure watched them enter the building; he wore a long leather black jacket with a hood covering his face. The Shadowy Figure looked transparent almost like he was a ghost fading in and out of this world but as he began to fade in and out of this reality, the stranger made his way towards the building.

The Vargon family stopped, their Father gave them gum and candy to eat as they waited patiently for a few minutes.

The smile on his face disappeared but suddenly, and only, reappeared when either of the boys looked up at him.

'Father—' said Varin, his father turned to him beginning to smile '—Where is your bag?'

'I forgot it . . . I'll just have to get a new one when we get there' he replied

'Why don't we go back now and get it? I'm sure we won't miss the train'

'It doesn't matter Varin, I don't need it.'

'But . . .'

'WE DON'T NEED IT!' he says, yelling at Varin.

As he raised his voice, the train slowly pulled into the station.

'I . . . I'm sorry Varin—' he crouched down to come to eye level with Varin '—Sorry I didn't mean to yell . . . but please cheer up we're on holiday now . . .'

He smiles at Varin as the train comes to a complete stop.

'Go put your chewing gum in the bin we'll wait right her and then we'll jump onto the train eh, what do you say?—'

Varin, nods and smiles.

'—There's a good boy.' He says with a smile.

He stands up and takes Drogun by the hand as Varin turned and ran to the nearest bin, pushing his way past a few people on their way to the train.

Drogun looked at Varin with that foolish boy look on his face again.

Their Father smiled, as a small tear began to trickle down his cheek. Annoyed and ashamed he raised his voice to his son for no reason.

Varin easily found a bin, he decides to quickly finish getting the flavour from the gum, places it in the wrapper and threw it into the bin. He turns to his family, but he sees something.

Something just out of the corner of his eye, he turns to face it and notices something in the background standing near a newspaper stand, a Shadowy Figure, the same Shadowy Figure from outside.

Beginning to worry now, their Father calls for Varin, as both he and Drogun just stood trying to see. Varin almost seemed like he couldn't hear anything right now, nothing other than his own breathe and heartbeat. The room began to spin.

Slightly annoyed by the wait, Drogun lets go of his Father's hand to get Varin.

As he lets go, a bright light flashed through the underground tunnel, reaching the Station causing the lighting on the ceiling above to flicker.

Darkness fell.

Panic amongst the passengers quickly immersed the station.

The darkness was just as quickly followed by a loud echo of explosions with metal and rock falling and crashing to the ground. The noise seemed to get closer.

As the tunnel flashed the stranger looked no longer transparent but solid. Oddly however he also seemed to disappear in the flash, both at the same time.

A force hit Varin, which throw him back two hundred yards, he hit his head on something he quickly assumed it was the wall.

Whatever it was winded him in that instant.

It help him regain his hearing but slowly, as he heard the screams, yells, cries and tears of those around him in the darkness each asking for help.

The pain in his head slowly began to fade away, but at the same time he felt as though the world around him was beginning to become darker and silent once more.

As he began to lose conscious all he heard was now the sound of faint screams and the feel of ember from a nearby fire touching his fingers.

His breathe began to slow . . .

Becoming cold . . .

The world around him became engulfed by darkness and silence once more.

CHAPTER 2

Where the Dream Begins

VARIN BEGAN TO slowly awaken.

Although he didn't open his eyes, he knew he was in bed. He could feel the soft duvet upon the skin of his hands, with his arms snuggled beneath the covers, he rubbed his head further into the big comfy pillow.

All that just happened was a dream; the Station, being yelled at by his Father, the explosion destroying the station and the appearance, or was it a reappearance, of the Shadowy Figure. All of it nothing more than just a dream.

He snuggled more into his comfy, warm bed.

He heard the gentle and almost calming chirp of birds outside his window, as the faint smell of cooking bacon wondered into his room. 'Fathers cooking' he thought.

He faded back off into a dream.

This dream, was unlike any other dream he ever had, a dream that he knew would never come true but enjoyed it all none the less.

A dream of his Mom; Hinal Vargon.

She was beautiful, an angel in his eyes. Wavy brunette hair, brown eyes, the kindest person on earth. He had this dream many a time, thinking of what she would be like but it always started the same.

The Vargon family in the park, a picnic on a nice summer's day. The sky was blue and clear, the grass green with no litter, a gentle breeze filled the air.

He began to run, and so he did towards his mother who always welcomed him with a smile and an enormous embrace, as she hugged him he smiled and smelt her perfume, she smelt like strawberries.

Suddenly Drogun came in and hugged her as well, it wasn't the Drogun that Varin knew, this was almost a completely different person. His hair was brown, not purple, he wore colourful cloths and smiled, this was almost alien to Varin but he enjoyed it none the less. His father then joined them bring with him food for the picnic and balls to play catch with.

'Varin—' said his Father '—want to play football?'

Varin nodded and ran a little away, his Father passed the ball and made a goal post out of their jackets.

'Alright Varin, you'll have to get it passed me'

Varin smiled and began to play with his Father.

A few minutes had passed but everyone was still so happy, eventually he tried running passed his Father but he grabbed Varin and began tickling him. This was his happiest moment, having fun with his family.

But it all seemed to change in an instant, the skies turned red and cloudy, like a storm suddenly erupted. The ground beneath Varin's feet began to shake as the grass seemed to wither and die. In the distance, it was like something big had exploded, a massive roar swept across the park knocking over trees, and throwing cars along the way. People began to run for their life, except the Vargon family.

'Varin!—' yelled Hinal '—Come here'
She had already embraced Drogun, protecting him in her arms, she opened the other for Varin as he ran towards her.
Their Father stood in front of them.
'H&%*' she called out their Father's name to bring him in as well but he didn't he stood there with his back to them.

The world seemed to blink with a light and he was gone but Varin saw in the distance that Shadowy Figure again, walking towards them and with every flash of light got closer and closer. Until he suddenly stood where their Father was, with arm reached out towards him saying . . .

'Varin! The phoenix will rise . . . WAKE UP!'

It shook him awake but his eyes were still closed, feeling save and at home again he didn't need to open his eyes, until he heard a clanging of metal from outside. Almost like someone was fighting.
His eyes slowly opened as the gentle sun light danced across his face, sitting up he finds himself instead of being at home, he's in a tent.
The tent is a lot bigger than most tents, it's almost the size of a small cottage.
He looked around the room and from the corner of his eye, something caught his attention, he turned to face it, a man now was staring at him, confused as he was, he could tell the man was easily in his late teens, and oddly looked

a lot like Varin, blue eyes, blonde hair. He even carried the Vargon family necklace around his neck, but he then noticed something else, what he was staring at, a mirror resting on a small wooden box.

The mirror reflected to him that he was no longer the youthful seven year old Varin Vargon, he had grown to be a man . . . but had no idea what his true age is.

The tent's door blew open slightly from a gentle breeze.

He could see a dense forest beyond it, he soon realised the timber from the forest was used to support the tent and that wild animal skins was used to keep the room heated slightly; it was also used as his quilt and pillow.

Panic and confusion began to quickly take over, he quickly rose, in shock from the bed.

The bed now beneath his feet was nothing more than hay. He looked around franticly spotting two haemic beds in the corner set up like a buck bed.

Looking around more, he saw a small metal stove using wood as its fuel in the opposite corner.

Now in full shot of the mirror, he noticed the clothes he was wearing, different clothing from what he last can remember, a light blue t-shirt, baggy black trousers which is held up by a black belt with a gold buckle and on his wrists two light brown leather wristbands. His hair was also different, it's no longer the shaggy spiked up look that he once had, this new style was similar to a Mohawk but only at the front, the fringe came down near his left eye as the rest of it blended together further along his head.

Suddenly the clanging sound of metal came from outside, a memory of the Shadowy Figure suddenly hit him but not a memory of before the incident at the station but it was a memory after.

As he walked past many of the rooms, he overheard people's murmured voice about the recent attack, people interviewing someone for something. A TV news report flicking in the background, just few doors down from the a room.

He entered the room, no one else was in the room.

It was dark, a few old bashed lockers just to the left of the door were slightly a jar. The two windows, providing little light through the shut blinds. Three old wooden chairs and two brown leather couches were the only objects in the room for sitting.

Varin sat on the leather couch furthest to the right of the room; opposite him is the second leather couch.

His eyes begin to feel heavy, without meaning to he closed them and he slowly went to sleep. For a brief fleeting second he was asleep but this was interrupted by the sound of the blinds suddenly blowing in the wind, banging against the open window.

He opened his eyes to see a man in the room sitting down on the leather couch in front of him, it was the same Shadowy Figure he saw back in the Train Station all those years ago.

The Shadowy Figure looked the same even though many years have passed since the Karves Incident . . .

'That was right, the explosion at the Station that day was late called the Karves Incident' he thought to himself.

But still Varin could not see his face apart from the Shadowy Figure's mouth. His face was hidden in dark shadow cast by his hood. Varin in shock, opens his mouth to say something but is stopped by the Shadowy Figure.

'Quiet *&%@, it's been a long time since we last saw each other'

Varin with a curious look on his face replied 'Who are you!?'

The man then spoke again 'Like I already said. I am your *%@^—' urgency then entered his voice '—You must leave this building quickly!'

'Well, perhaps you can tell me what's about to happen?' replied Varin with a sarcastic tone in his voice

The Stranger smirked, 'Let's just say the phoenix will rise'

As the Stranger finished speaking someone knocked on the door, Varin quickly looked at the door, the wind blew once again, he then turned back to the where the Shadowy Figure was sitting but he was gone.

The rustling of gravel with grunts of two men battling each other, soon followed as did slight movement in the forest.

'What the hell is happening to me?' Varin asked himself

He heard more grunts and the clanging of metal from outside, he cautiously moved and raised his hand towards the tent's door, pushing the fabric to one side as to leave the tent.

Something else suddenly popped into his head, a memory of training somewhere, a dark grey building, with twenty or so other men and women, led by an instructor named Ren.

'As a part of &@^* you will need basic skills of survival, and what a better way to survive without being seen.

Stealth will be the key to many of your daily lives and the continuation of your friends, your family, our way of living, the human race and the destruction of @&*^'

Remembering some of this training, he bends his legs, to lighten his footsteps, and holds his hands out in front of him, although not sure why and feeling as if something is missing. He slowly moved to the end of the tent.

Now, clearly in view, Varin noticed he was in a clearing near a fast moving river, he peeked out a little more and saw two men standing wide legged ready to fight, atop of a massive dirt patch. As he looked round the area, the two men spoke as they continued their battle.

'Come on brother, you can do better!' said the older of the two.

His weapon of choice shone brightly in the sun light, a double edge bladed long staff with a red ribbon tied in the centre, it seemed to stand out even more as Varin noticed that his man's hair was also red, a dark muddy red but still red none the less.

The red haired man wore a dark navy t-shirt with the collar being so long that it came up to and covered his mouth, around his forehead was orange bandana. As he moved around his 'foe' Varin saw his a little clearer, he strangely wore a belt tied over the top of his shirt just below his waist and this man also wore brown faded trousers and light brown boots.

As he prepared to attack his 'foe' once again, Varin could see he worse fabric wrist bands, brown he thought, these were like the ones he had around his own wrists but those that the red haired man wore, were once a lighter colour, maybe changed by mud from years since past. They have now become brown as the earth.

Along with this man's attire was a brown leather bag that would hold his weapon, he wore this using an older piece of leather across his chest as the strap, the bag was used as a sort of clip to hold the weapon into place no matter what he did.

The two men lunged at each other, both blocking each other's attack and swapped sides in the process, now the youngest of the two spoke and was in Varin's clear view.

'Don't worry I'll . . . ARGH' but before he finished, he lunged at his brother to try and catch him off guard.

Upon seeing the younger of the two, Varin realised the new clothing he now wears had once belong to these two men.

The youngest man had long blonde hair, he wore a long sleeved top which was a dull yellow and was slightly longer than his arms were, the top covered most of his hands but Varin could see that he too was wearing a wristband like the oldest, these were a dingy red colour.

He also wore a dark blue bandana tired loosely around his neck. This one wore a similar belt at the same place as his brother, the trousers once again were like those Varin was wearing but was a light grey accompanied with dark brown boots.

His weapon was similar to a butterfly swords except slightly wider in width. He held two of these, one in each hand, and each sword had a red ribbon tied to the bottom.

The cases which he used to carry the swords across his back, were tied by strings across his chest and left thigh. One case for each sword, so each hand could pull out a weapon at the hint of any nearby danger.

The clanging from their swords was heard once more as the youngest lunged towards the oldest, the oldest managed to reflect the attack back and was about to unleash a counter attack as his opponent regained his stance. The oldest blinked for a second but from the corner of his eye he court a quick glimpse of Varin.

Each time they lunged Varin peeked around the tent further and further, somewhat awe stricken by the way they fight. Something, almost like an instinct told him to watch these men, to study them, as he may need to fight them to escape.

The oldest lowered his weapons and said 'Brother look, the stranger is awake'

'Oh no. I'm not falling for that . . . again' said the youngest with a cocky tone in his voice

The youngest once again tried to attack but the oldest just side stepped him and said with a serious tone in his voice, 'Yal, please I am not deceiving you this time. Look'

The youngest brother, Yal, then turned to see what his brother was talking about. Looking expecting to see nothing, he quickly saw Varin, attempting to hide once being noticed.

'Oh so he is awake'

Varin realised hiding was no longer any good. The youngest began to run towards Varin, as he got closer to Varin noticed that the youngest brother has a scar vertically down his left eye shaped almost like an S.

Adrenaline began to build up as Varin's muscles became tense, he was prepared for something, even if he didn't know what exactly but his body knew. But it never happened.

'Morning, what's your name?' said the youngest

Varin remain quiet.

The oldest brother then ran over, he to had a scar but it was instead over the opposite eye, the right eye in a shape of an S.

The oldest then spoke with a welcoming, pleasant tone; 'Morning I'm Talon and this is my twin but younger brother, Yal. What's your name?'

Again Varin said nothing.

Talon continued 'You know, you should count yourself truly lucky that we found you, or else you'll be undoubtedly dead by now.'

Talon then saw the confused look on Varin's face and so he continued and explained what he meant by this, 'We found you . . . No, let me start from the beginning. Four days ago, Yal and I were fishing further up the stream near the Crossroads of Attina . . .'

Four days ago, at Crossroads of Attina—where the four waterfalls meet the river.

Two adventures with strong fishing rods in hand, carrying a small metallic box by its handle to place their captured food, walked along the river although being careful to not be too close.

Yal looked into the river to see their reason, a number of fish which will later be their food cashed by one huge fiend of a fish known as Golossus. Getting any closer now might make the creature lunge for them. They knew what to do if it were to attack but still, they thought it was always best to avoid needless confrontation, especially one that will no doubt lure the more dangerous fiends of forest.

'We'll set up here' said Talon

Some time passed, they had collected a number of small fish for food although not as much as they would of liked. At least there was no trouble from the Golossus.

'Seems to be a lot more Golossus here than near our old camp' said Yal
'True, although you know why we move around though? Right?' asked Talon
'Yes. I remember, it's to find . . . him.'

Suddenly a booming sound interrupted them.

'Thunder? But it's a clear day' said Talon looking towards the sky
'Brother, the fish . . . they're leaving'

As they looked into the river, they saw the fish lead by Golossus swimming away almost as if something bigger had arrived in the water.

'Yal look—' Talon pointed towards four waterfalls, '—there's someone in the water'

Yal began to run alongside the river to get closer to this person floating down the river. Talon was soon following him.

~∞∞∞~

'And that's when Yal dived in after you and we brought you back to our camp'
'You were breathing, just drifting along with the current in some old clothing tattered clothing, ya.'
'And so we thought you may just need rest.—'
'So we gave you a bed and some of our clothing' said Yal
'—We didn't realise you'd be out for this long' continued Talon.
'The river but I . . .—' Varin paused for a second '—but I was in . . . Karves. No Shenma and then'
Varin was cut off by Yal 'What? You're from Shenma!?'
'. . . I . . . I don't know, I don't remember'

The brothers then looked at each other with looks of worry upon their face, they've heard of this before and have come across it many times before. But they try to forget about it for now, it's still too early to tell if it is indeed symptoms of . . . they shake it out of their minds.

'What's the problem?' asked Varin
'Shenma is basically a fortress, right? So it would have been impossible for you to leave' replied Talon.
'You must of banged your head ya?' said Yal

'I don't think so . . . but I'm sure I came from Shenma City'

'It's impossible; the city has been a huge fortified fortress, protected by an Electromagnetic Shield, powered by PHOENIX. It's a dangerous place to live at, let alone be anywhere near.' replied Talon

'What do you mean?' asked Varin

Yal then gave a little laugh and asked while taping on Varin's head

'You must of really knock your head hard? PHOENIX is unstable and well because of its energy many towns ordered PHOENIX from SPARK Corporation and well about forty years later the PHOENIX blew up along with the cities.'

'Many believe that it is because of PHOENIX, that the world is as it is today—' said Talon '—Most of that happened three-hundred years ago.'

CHAPTER 3

𝕷𝖔𝖘𝖙 & 𝕬𝖑𝖔𝖓𝖊

'WHAT!? THREE HUNDRED years ago? But PHOENIX is just a new substance!' said Varin

Yal begins to laugh uncontrollably, which quickly turn into tears of laughter which crawl down his face, 'New! Ha ha ha, it's been three hundred and forty years since it was first used.'

Talon folds his arms and raises his left hand towards his chin trying to hide his whispers to Yal 'Perhaps he's had a PHOENIX DREAM?'

Yal notices Varin's look of confusion shown on his face;

'Nothing to worry about for now, you should get some rest, ya? Maybe? You don't look so good' said Yal

He was right, Varin felt dizzy.

'Perhaps it's the physical strain on your body, you have been laid up for the past few days' said Talon

Yal and Talon begin to help him back into the tent by supporting him, placing his arms over their shoulders. They take him back into the tent and place him atop of the hay of the bed and place the covers over him. The room finally stops spinning as Varin thinks to himself that the two brothers are only joking about the year.

Still feeling too ill to get back up, he simply closes his eyes allowing himself to fade off into sleep.

He feels a cold breeze creep into the tent and surround him, it begins to get worse and worse, almost feeling his own breathe turn to ice. But like most of his sleeps recently, this isn't real and once again his sleep is disturbed by a dream. The cold finally stops as he realises he's on that rooftop, deep within the heart of Shenma City along with a man, a man he recognises has never see before, yet he knows his name; Commander Hobson or CoHobson as he's known in his group.

In the distance there is nothing but a gentle glow, as though something is on fire lighting up the sky. Beyond that the two are surrounded by darkness. The only thing visible is everything on the rooftop, the door down the emergency stairs, the vents and other electrical equipment but oddly it all looks like it was made of ice but Varin could feel no coldness from it but he could feel guilt as Co. Hobson's voice echoed of what he had said on that rooftop in Shenma all those years ago in 2269.

'2259 The great town of Karves City was totally destroyed only one hundred people survived out of a population of three thousand and the same thing will now happen to Shenma! The deaths of all these people will be on your shoulders!'

Varin's thoughts begin to echo as if he had screamed them 'I was seven at the time that happened . . . How can I remember that?'

'I, Co. Hobson, the leader of Trans-Gression. Will lead the world into a new order, the onus is mine, and mine alone and I will not allow some trainee cop, wannabe hero! Stop me'

Suddenly a loud yell and the sound of flames echoed in this empty abyss.

'BROTHER? FATHER? WHERE ARE YOU?' said a young Varin

'It was Trans-Gression, they're to blame. YOU DESTORIED KARVES CITY!' yelled Varin

Another voice echoed the area but the voice did not belong to Varin.

'Quiet brother. It's been a long time since we last saw each other—'

Varin turned around to see a staff room, he entered the room, no one else was in the room.

It was dark, a few old bashed lockers just to the left of the door, left slightly a jar as they always were.

'How do I know this?'

The two windows, providing little light through the shut blinds.

'Why is this so familiar?'

Three old wooden chairs and two brown leather couches were the only objects in the room for sitting.

Varin sat on the leather couch furthest to the right of the room; opposite him is the second leather couch.

He looked away and then back at the couch opposite him, there sat his brother as he remembered him at the station.

Drogun smiled at him and said 'Varin WAKE UP!'

'BROTHER!' yelled Varin waking, sitting up in bed in a cold sweat.

Night has now consumed the day, the two brothers are outside of the tent sitting near where they were sparring earlier around a small camp fire. Varin could hear them speaking but he couldn't make out their words. He ever so slowly and quietly moved towards the fabric wall attempting to listen to what Yal and Talon were speaking about.

'Yal, you know how PHOENIX DREAMs are right?'

'Yeah, dreams that are created by being far too close to PHOENIX for a long time' replied Yal

'I think he may have just had another' said Talon

His brother suddenly looked straight at him and said 'Another PHOENIX DREAM? . . . But that means if he has another two he could . . .'

'Quiet! He might hear you . . .—' Talon tried to see around the tent wondering if Varin is watching them. He then continued '—Tomorrow, at the crack of dawn. We'll go to Karves and well introduce him to the others and we'll see if he remembers someone or if anyone recognises him, if not then we'll leave him there. We don't need anyone slowing us down—'

He stops as Yal nods in agreement. '—Good, we should let get some rest as well, it's getting late. I hope he doesn't suffer through the night'

'But what . . . what if they continue through the night?' asked Yal

'I guess . . . we'll have to kill him'

They begin to lay curling up next to the fire looking up towards the sky, staring at what stars they could find before going to sleep, Varin returned to his makeshift bed and quickly fell asleep soon after the brothers did.

~∾∾∾∾~

'Wake up sleepy head—' said Yal but to no avail, he shook Varin as he yelled '—WAKE UP!'

Varin awoke in a panic 'What? What? Morning already?'

'Indeed, get ready we're going to the village today' replied Talon, standing by the fabric door.

Five minutes later Varin stumbles out of the tent tying his belt around his waist keeping Yal's baggy trousers from falling. He walked other towards the brothers who were waiting for Varin.

'Thanks for the cool clothing guys'

Since most of the clothing once belonged to Yal, he was the first to reply with a smile 'No problem'o.'

'We're going to Karves, to meet the Resistance' said Talon, he began to walk off with Yal.

They managed to get a foot away before Varin said 'Wait . . . but Karves was destroyed ten years ago . . . wasn't it?'

Once again laughing at Varin's comment Yal replied 'Ten years ago, haha it was destroyed well over three hundred years ago'

Varin begins to shake his head and says in disbelieve 'Wha . . . ? No it can't be . . . how . . . IT'S NOT POSSIBLE!'

'Yo chill man, ya'

'What's today's date?'

'April 2nd, 2609' replied Yal

"If this was a joke, it's gone too far now . . . but maybe they're telling the truth. Why would they need to lie to him?"

Varin then whispered to himself '2609 . . . What the'

'Effects of a PHOENIX DREAM—' said Talon, secretly, leaning towards Yal and whispering. '—Anyway as I was saying. I and my brother are both apart of a Resistance known as the Trans-Gression . . .'

'You're from the Trans-Gression!?'

Upon hearing this Varin, stumbles backing away from them shocked by the revelation of them both being Trans-Gression members.

Varin reaches his left hand towards his thigh, where a gun would have been, as a reaction slightly remembering something from the past.

Yal gives an evil sort of smirk and raises his left hand holding something that Varin had never seen before . . . but recognised, a Volgin Mark III Pistol.

'Looking for this?—'

Varin's fist began to clench in anger preparing to attack his former saviours, as Yal then passed Varin's gun to Talon.

Yal continued to speak '—This weapon was made in a PHOENIX factory and in the casing of the bullet contains PHOENIX as it's catalyst to fire, we can't let you have it for our personal safety . . . as well as yours'

Talon then took it apart, first emptying the clip, then removing the Barrel, finally he threw the pieces in different directions as far as he could.

Now left unarmed Varin asked them with anger growing even more in his body

'What do you guys want from me!!'

"The group known as the Trans-Gression killed his family and a thousand more, why not finish him off?"

Talon took a couple steps forward, towards Varin, and spoke in a calm voice

'We want nothing . . . we wish to help you'

Varin took a couple more steps back away from the slowly approaching brother.

'I don't believe you'

Yal walked beside his brother and took a couple more steps forward and also spoke in a calm voice trying to make Varin feel better.

"Were they playing mind games with him? Was this all really a joke? Or a ploy by Trans-Gression to get him to tell them vital information? Information he no longer knew . . . Or were they really just trying to calm him down?"

'Trust us we are here to help change what happened in the past, that is and always been the Trans-Gression mission, from day one and if you don't trust us . . . here take this.'

Yal slowly took a couple more steps to Varin but he dared not to take another. He gently threw Varin an old Frontier Nickel 9mm Revolver.

As soon as Varin court the Revolver in his hand he began to study the chamber, the sight piece and the hand grip. Upon finishing his quick study Yal also handed him a small sized box of ammunition for the Revolver containing twenty bullets.

Varin took out six bullets from this and placed the rest in his pockets. He loaded the six chambers and gave it a quick spin, not sure to trust them or not he suddenly raised the gun to Yal.

An expression of shock suddenly came onto Yal's face as he said 'Whoa man, calm down ya'
'Just leave me alone, I didn't ask for your help'
'Varin!—' yelled Talon '—We are not your enemy Varin'

The trees alongside them began to rustle. Red eyes moved in the forest.

'Varin put the weapon down' commanded Talon
'What is the year?!' asked Varin cocking the hammer

'We told you.' Yal replied
'What year is it?!' demanded Varin one more.
'2609!' yelled the two brothers

The forest rustled once more and something ten foot away from behind Varin, a creature with red eyes, jumped out from the forest.

'Varin . . . watch out!'

Varin turned looking over his shoulder first before twisting the rest of his body, Yal and Talon pulled out their weapons as a sudden feeling of fear came over Varin as everything seemed to go into slow motion.

At the sight of this creature Varin himself reacted, a nervous reaction, he moved the gun away from Yal and pointed it towards the creature, prayed that this old Revolver would work and pulled the trigger as the creature lept towards him with it four claw like fingers ready to cut and tear him to pieces. Now only five feet away. It was big and fast.

The bullet hit the creature between the eyes. It made a loud thud as it hit the ground inches away from Varin's feet.

"They trusted him enough to give him a working gun with live ammo. And what did he do to repay them? He spat in their face . . . such a fool."

He began gasping for air as if the fear was strangling him. Varin asked as he slowly lowered his arm.
'W . . . what is that thing?'

Talon then said putting his weapon back in its case tied to his body and approached slowly to stand by Varin's side.

'It's known as a "Fiend", it and many others began to appear hundreds of years ago. No one knows the exact date but we do know it is a result of PHOENIX.'

'The Fiend that attacked is known as 'Sra'. This forest is full of Fiends and most are much stronger than that creature.' said Yal.

"The Sra, a vicious tribal like beast, are larger than a fully grown man, green scales almost the same appearance of a frog and with huge red eyes. If you've never seen one consider yourself lucky. The males are the worst, the stench alone is enough to knock you off your feet, if that doesn't get you their sharp claws will.

These creatures are named Sra because they chant this word constantly when amongst themselves."

'I . . . I'm sorry, for not trusting you. It's just that none of this makes sense to me. One minute I'm in 2259 at the age of 7 and then I'm suddenly in 2609 and I look like I'm twenty, it just doesn't make sense—' Said Varin collapsing to the floor '—Where the hell am I? What happened?'

'No need for apologies and I'm sorry Varin. I don't have your answers—' Talon offers a hand to Varin to help him up '—Come we must head for the village.'

The three of them begin to make their way to the nearby village, a 4 hour journey at best. Yal led Varin, with Talon covering the rear, along a narrow almost secret path through the forest. The path, it seemed, was only known by the twins.

Talon was looking cautiously around with his left hand near the weapon encase another type of Fiend was to attack them for entering its territory.

"Although begging for answers now, little did he know of the role that he would play, that destiny had set in motion for him"

CHAPTER 4

This New World

AS THEY TRAVELLED through the forest, Varin noticed the scratches of the Sra on numerous trees and broken branches but as they drew closer and closer to the village the marks began to fade away until not one tree had any sign of mark, broken branch or any other trace of a Sra being there.

They finally reached the clearing where the village could be clearly seen.

As they entered the village grounds, Varin could hear voices call out behind the large wooden wall, Talon began to ease his hand, slowly, away from his weapon with every step they took towards the village. They reached the back gate of the village. The door began to slowly swing open with each step they took closer to it.

Talon finally removed his hand away from his weapon once the gate had opened and shut safely behind them. Along the twenty foot wall was a number of guards, none official all but villagers with makeshift weaponry.

A sign stood out once they entered the village, to Varin the sign seemed to almost render him breathless as he read its engraved message.

'Welcome to Karves'

'Wha . . . ? Karves has been rebuilt' said Varin. He looked beyond the sign, looking towards the streets as if he was a child in awe of everything.

The village was split into three sections, section one was the main entrance to the village, section two was where the Bar and many public shops were and often the busiest place to be during the day. The final section, section three was the residence area and back entrance to the village. Their current position.

It wasn't the same place he remembered as a child and none of the buildings were made from the metals and glass he remembered, instead they were replaced by small houses made from wood and lined with straw roofs but there was something about this place.

It made him feel like he was home again.

'They're here, the Ninjas of Raiden!' cried out a women.

Before he even realised it, the group were surround by the villagers, mainly the women and children. Some even bore gifts of food, clothing and a number of other items as gestures of thanks.

'Mr. Talon when I grow up I wanna be just like you, look I've been practising'

The boy suddenly strikes a pose, try to impersonate Talon

'Heheh nice, you reminded me of well me—' he says as he messes the kids hair '—but never impersonate people, never live a proxy life, find your true self and live the way you want, okay?'

The boy nodded and ran off towards his friends.

'I touched Talon, how cool am I?'

'Erm . . . brother—' said Yal, while signing something for a fan '—Wh . . . What does proxy mean?'

'Hm, it means; a person authorized to act for another.' he replied before another person offered him gifts

'Talon please accept these gifts and please watch over my brother and husband when you fight SPARK.'

'Please great ninjas accept this food for your journey.'

'Ninjas of Radien, please take this equipment with you and watch my son.'

'Thank you but—' Talon begins to raise his voice so the crowd can hear him '—Thank you, all, but we cannot accept these gifts.'

'But you saved the village from the Fiends.'

'We may of helped this village a number times from the Fiends we never asked for a reward and we still don't want one' replied Yal

The crowd disappointed that they could not repay their saviours or give the gifts as their upcoming journey began. The crowd turned to return to their homes.

'Wait . . .—' called out Yal '—Does anyone know this man'

Pointing towards Varin, the villagers turned as he smiled back nervously, they all shook their heads and went about their business.

The twins returned to Varin's side as they continued their walk deeper into the village, while occasionally nodding and smiling to the villagers as they welcomed the brothers return to the village.

'Varin, do you see that thing there?—' asked Yal pointing towards a pile of rusted metal in the distance. '—It's a memorial, go take a look.'

As he stepped closer and closer to the rusted metal, he realised this wasn't any old scrap, it once was metal from a building from his time, parts of it had been remoulded into a shape of a bird flying from the ashes. A piece of metal had words carved into it.

'In Memory of those who died during
The Beginning of Chaos
2259

Karves, Rebuilt in the year 2399,
After being destroyed by PHOENIX in the year 2259'

'. . . I once lived in Karves until 2259—' said Varin muttering to himself '—When I was only seven, when I lost my family . . . Trans-Gression . . . they were blamed for the incident, not PHOENIX . . . right?—' Varin then began speaking to himself '—Is this a dream? Please tell me it's a dream, this can't be real . . . please allow me to wake up. Back home please . . . please' said Varin

"He wasn't speaking to anyone in particular, just talking so that maybe someone would answer him"

'Talon . . . you think, he could possibly be from the past?' whispered Yal

Talon didn't reply to Yal's question.

'I think we should go to that Bar. The others will be here shortly. I hope.'
Saying this snapped Varin from his thoughts.

'But wait . . . why was the village rebuilt in 2399? Why? Why not sooner?'
'Because that was the year the PHOENIX stopped destroying—' replied Talon with a heavy sigh '—Many towns and cities were destroyed. 2399 was when it all, finally, stopped. From that day on it was known as; "The end to the chaos, the day the world was whole once more."' Talon paused for a second as Yal took over.
'We, as the human race, relied too heavily on the fuel and so in 2259, it had its revenge and destroyed every town, city and country on the planet.'
'As a species we had to start again, using mother nature as our shelter and food source, while at the same time remembering the past to not make the same mistakes—' spoke Talon, smiling as Varin grabbed onto each of his words '—Only one city still uses PHOENIX, while the rest have been turned to rubble because of it.'
'Is Shenma the last city?' asked Varin.
'Indeed, the power behind PHOENIX and the ones that some say once ruled the world, SPARK, are nothing but a shadow of their former self. However in a way they

still do rule the world as they're the only town, city, nation with an Army. The people are powerless; we all are within the might of SPARK—' Talon stopped himself from ranting any further.

'—. . . Out leader will explain more late, for now that brief history lesson is over. Perhaps we should meet the others at the Bar'

Varin nodded in agreement, more wanting to meet their leader about PHOENIX, perhaps they have more answers that could help Varin.

They began to walk towards Section Two, a short ten minute walk brought them to the inner wall dividing the sections from one another. If he had to make a guess as to the purpose of this, he would be right, it's to protect each section of the village from the Fiends. If the guard were to be outnumbered they could fall back to the next section to defend it from the enemy.

Before he even realised it they had already came within sight of the Bar in section two, from the distance Varin spotted a sign in the front of the Bar stating.

'BAR: 0700-2300
INN: First floor.
Now playing here TODAY ONLY, Sylvia'.

Yal and Talon entered first, walking up to the Bar man. They began to ask if the other TG members arrived yet.

Varin entered and stood close by the door, he was trying to not get in the way of anyone else in the Bar, however standing in the door entrance with many people coming and going he soon was.

The Bar its self was dark although hanging from the ceiling are three chandeliers, each with a number of candles to light the room. Lingering in the air was smoke from its regulars and locals smoking on their pipes.

The feel of the place was that of busyness as a number of small groups of people talked and laughed wildly to themselves, every now and again they would turn to Varin, look at him and then get back to whatever they were doing.

It made him feel un-welcome.

Across the eight foot room, from the entrance, was the stairs leading to the rooms used as an Inn for travellers or those that had too much to drink the night before.

Just to the left of the stairs was the six foot long Bar in the twelve foot long room, behind the Bar was a number of pumps and two workers who were the land lords, both looked like no nonsense people.

One of the landlords was talking to the Twins about something, something that made them glance over to Varin a number of times.

'Talon, good to see you my old friend' said Yaris the Bar man

'Indeed it is old friend . . .—' Talon grinned at the man before continuing '—How's the Professor?'

'He's good, kooky as always but well you know what he's like'

'Indeed, I was wondering if you could ask the Professor something for me. Our friend there, his name is Varin Vargon and claims to be from the past'

'The past you say?—' Yaris looks over Talon's shoulder to look at Varin '—You know how to attract the crazy ones don't cha'

'I was wondering if the Professor could dig through any old records that he has that might prove it one way or another who he might be and where he came from'

A look of slight worry came over the Bar man's face.

'You'd know I love to kid, but the Professor? You know I don't like going near that PHOENIX generator of his. Can't you just ask around town to see if anyone knows him?'
'It's not running on PHOENIX, he's told you this a number of times. And we've tried, no one seems to recognise him. So can you do this for me please?'

Talon holds out his hand, resting on his palm lays blonde hair and a badge.

'Okay I'll see what I can do for ya'
The Bar man takes the items from Talon's hand and places them under the bar.

'Thank you Yaris' said Talon with a bow of his head

To the left of the Bar was a fire place which was always burning the logs of wood at steady constant flame to keep the place warm, creating enough light to brighten the room just enough to see some of the wooden furniture placed around the bar.
However it was something to the right of the stairs, catching his attention upon the stage or rather a slightly raised area for performances.
A young woman was preparing the stage for the show, placing a tall stool to sit on in the centre and bringing out a large wooden instrument a double bass.

She was cooping fine with the process by herself and by the looks of the men in the room no one would help her either way.

Her long brown hair glistened in what sun light dared to enter the Bar. Something about her stood out, maybe it was her green eyes, but Varin couldn't quite put his finger on what stuck out about her. She was the same height as him, if not a little taller than Varin was.

It might even be the elegant dress, made of only three colours, white, pink and purple, that she wore. The dress seemed old but was still in good condition, it did resemble something Varin once learnt at the school about the ninetieth century, perhaps it came from the 1880's, he thought to himself.

He approached the woman.

'Hi, can I help you?' he asked

'No it's okay, but thank you for asking' she replied with a smile before it quickly faded

'Are you sure? That looks quite heavy'

'It's okay, thank you, I've got it'

He walked away, slightly hurt because he was just trying to be nice, but no matter he thought, and then continued to Yal and Talon who had just finished speaking to the Bar man.

'So when is your leader meant to get here?' asked Varin

'Quiet Varin—' said Talon '—Not everyone is a TG supporter, there may be spies amongst us working for SPARK'

'Why would SPARK still be after TG? Haven't you guys won? Everyone knows PHOENIX is dangerous'

'Because they still want power' replied Talon

'Which means they want to control the world' said Yal

'Why?' asked Varin.

Yal and Talon looked at each other, not sure what to say.

'That's the one thing we still don't know, why would a business owner want to control the world?' said Talon.

They're conversation was then broken by a man wearing an expensive suit, pushing past them to get to Yaris.

'Same again there mack' said the man

The Yaris handed the man his drink and he went back to the group of men sitting directly in front of the Bar, on the first table in the front row. Four men sat around the table, each wearing expensive suits, he handed the smallest one in the group a drink as he demanded them to get him another, he seemed to be their leader.

On the table behind the four men were two men with blank expressions upon their face, these two kept a close eye on the four in front almost as if they never blinked.

Varin turned back to face the Twins but as he did, he saw out of the corner of his eye, at the every back of the room were two long tables, on the table furthest away from the fire place a stranger sat in the corner with a hood covering his face in shadow.

"A haunting memory came back to him, a man of mystery he's seen a number of occasions in his life . . . yet he couldn't

quite put his finger on those events . . . but it couldn't be! Could it?"

This was the same stranger that has Varin has seen over the many years, the Shadowy Figure, but something about him looked slightly different.

Either way Varin stormed up to the Stranger and said
'You!—' barked Varin '—. . . How the hell did you get here!? What are you doing here!?—' this time he slammed his fist down on the table '—Who the hell are you!?'
'HEY—' yelled Yaris '—We'll have none of that in hear, take it outside if you must'
'Sorry, you have the wrong person my friend' the Stranger replied

Not once did the Stranger make eye contact instead, he just kept looking forward whilst smoking from his pipe.

'No, I know you, I've seen you a number of times all throughout my life, like you've been haunting me all my life'
'Must be someone else, I've heard black cloaks are in this season'

Yal came up behind Varin and whispered
'Calm down Varin, we're not here to cause trouble ya'
'No Yal I know this man but I want to know why'

Varin turned to face the Stranger, who continued to look forward trying to ignore Varin until something court this eye, in Varin's haste to turn his necklace fell from under his shirt revealing the insignia of the Vargon family crest. The Stranger stared at it.

'Tell me my friend, where did you get that?' he asked as he continued to stare

'It's my families crest' replied Varin

'Hmph . . . fate it seems, although without a sense of irony' said the Stranger.

He smiled to himself and stood up, as he did so the Stranger lowered his hood to revival his face. The first thing that Varin was drawn to, this person had dark purple hair and a similar hair cut to what someone he once knew had.

'Brother!?' said Varin

'What this guy is your brother?' asked Yal

'I am indeed his brother, I am Drogun Vargon . . . It has been a long time my little brother'

A woman walked onto the stage, as she did everyone's attention seemed to automatically draw to her, the candle light of the bar began to dim as she took to the stool.

Varin's mind was still racing though not once noticing the stage with his attention still on his brother, finally after all these years he found his brother, question after question popped into his mind before he finally asked 'But how yo-?'

Drogun cut him off 'Quiet the show is starting.'

Silence fell over the Bar, a muttering silence perhaps but even the rowdy men in the front became quiet as the lights continued to go down, even the fire's flickering flames slowed and stopped as if the atmosphere demanded it.

A light seemed to suddenly shine down onto the empty stage, it drew and grabbed everyone's attention upon the figure in dark.

A woman stepped into the light, the room now completely silent, a young woman, the same woman in fact that was setting up the equipment, the little known singer;

Sylvia Arow.

She seemed to be slightly nervous as she stepped into the light but none of the less the show began. She tried to speak but the words didn't seem to want to leave her throat, she instead sat upon the stool and pulled the double bass from her side to stand in front of her. She took in a deep breath, closed her eyes and began to play. She didn't play the best she thought she could, perhaps it was the nervous that got the best of her every time she hit a wrong note, but she played none of the less.

There was something about her that commanded their attention as she played. She began to sing with it and again the nerves got the best of her.

But not one person looked away.

The song was filled with emotion, of love, lose and regrets, no one cried, but to Varin this made his eyes tear up, something about the past that he couldn't quite put his finger on . . . something to do with the girl next door.

The two men in front of Drogun's table stood up, blocking the view of the show from the group. The two then began to make their way towards the four rowdy men at the front.

'Hey! Sit down! You're blocking my view!' yelled Drogun.

They ignored him, he stood up and once again yelled at them.

The small fire began to rise again.

This time the two men finally turned to face him, but did something no one expected.

They began to tear at their own flesh.

'They're either crazy or they're . . .'

'Assassination Droids!' yelled Yaris as he dived under the Bar.

The Bar suddenly erupted into panic, as the Droids revealed themselves. The people within the Bar, even the two landlords fled for the exits as the four mobsters on the front row hid under their table.

The signer, Sylvia, casually walked out of the back exit, grabbing some of her stuff on the way out.

Almost smiling Drogun, held out his right hand to the side and revealed his weapon, a sword, as if by magic. With this in hand, Drogun jumped upon the table and charged towards the two Droids, running along the table yelling and finally jumping at the end of the table.

As he charged the Droids transformed their arms into guns and tried to take aim at Drogun but he was moving too fast for them.

As he came down from above them he swung his sword. Not one person left in the bar could count how many times he struck both of them, his arms and movement became so fast and blurred, what must have been a handful of seconds to Drogun was all but one to everyone else.

They stood still, still processing what happened to them.

The Droid suddenly moved, but not as a solid object, they fell as pieces of scrap metal, crashing to the wooden floor, almost breaking the floor with their heavy remains.

Their now exposed wires laid there sparking uncontrollably with fluids leaking out onto the floor. They crashed before Drogun had even landed, their sparking remains now started a small fire when Drogun finally landed on the floor. As he did his right knee buckled and give away under him, it took him with surprise.

He looked at the fluid from the Droids and touched it with his finger before smelling it, it confirmed his fears.

'PHOENIX' he whispered to himself.

Drogun rose slowly back to his feet.

Yal, Talon and Varin sat dazed by Drogun's actions. He defeated the two Droids before the group even left their seats.

The small fire now spread to the ripped clothing of the Droids, Drogun stared deep into the flames.

It suddenly died down.

'Who are you?' asked Yal

Drogun turned to face Varin and the Twins;

'I am Drogun Vargon, also known as Rýnadaer, from the elvish lands of Windor'

CHAPTER 5

Let the Show Begin

'THANK YOU, I thought I was a goner there. You saved my life—' said a voice from under a table

Turning to the face the voice, the fire finally extinguished, Drogun saw three men standing a couple of feet away from him, no one's lips moving as the voice continued.

'—You have no idea how long I've been worrying about those droids being on my back for'

Looking down he sees the fourth mobster, the leader of the group. A short man, no taller than his waist stood there in a pin striped suit with a pencil moustache and a tall fedora hat, to more than make up for his size.

'I wasn't saving anyone's life. I just wanted to watch the show' Drogun replied

The little man spoke again 'Nonetheless you saved my life, and perhaps I could interest you gentlemen in some well-paid work?'

'Not interested' replied Drogun.

'Names Amras—' He held out his hand to shake, but Drogun to offer his. He quickly retracted it and straightened up his suit '—Don of the Newen Mafia and these are my boys. Meany, Dicky, Tricky and Bob'

'He's our leader' said Bob with a arrogant smirk on his face.

'Thank you Bob, he's my wife's godchild, not to bright . . . few crayons short of the box if you know what I mean. I didn't catch your or your friends name's kid, who are you?'

Varin rose from his seat and stood next to Drogun.

'I am Varin and these . . .'

'As I said earlier—' spoke Drogun cutting off Varin '—I'm not interested'

'Elvish Lands? Right? You're not an elf are you?'

Drogun takes a threatening step towards Amras, 'Why? You got a problem against elves?'

'No, no I was just wondering—' replied Amras with a nervous look on his face.

Drogun turned once more with his back now to Amras.

'And the answer to your question is no, I was brought up by the elves . . . they are my closest thing to a family'.

'What about the necklace?' asked Varin as he stepped closer to Drogun.

Drogun turned his head slightly and replied, 'What?'

Varin then takes another step, 'The family crest necklace'

Drogun then turns his head away from Varin 'I lost it'

Amras bored by Varin and Drogun's conversation speaks, 'I hate to interrupt this little family trip to memory lane, but can we get down to business now?'

'Sure' spoke Yal
Talon looked at him 'YAL!'
'What . . . we could kill some time this way' he said to Talon
'Okay, great. I need some tough guys, like yourselves, to get us a secret item that . . .'
'Not interested' said Drogun, suddenly cutting Amras off.
Drogun then makes his way for the door as the mobster thinks quickly on his feet.

'Perhaps one hundred Gillian will change your mind'
It does what the mobster wanted, stop him in his tracks but instead of just accepting, Drogun instead replies 'A thousand Gillian'
'A thousand Gillian, you're mad! That's more than we're getting to do this eh . . . request'
'Then why do you need us?'
Amras unwillingly says, 'Alright, alright, you're twisting my arm here. There's this Fiend protecting a jewel and we are unable to go near it . . . that's why we need you guys. Just to defeat this one Fiend'
Drogun turns to face the group and asks 'What do we get out of this?'
'Well . . . you'll won't be able to keep the item of course, that's for us, but . . . eh . . . perhaps two hundred Gillian will do you fine?—' Drogun doesn't say a thing as Amras begins to panic '—Okay . . . Okay . . . three hundred'

'A thousand Gillian' replied Drogun.

The mob boss turned to the others, Varin couldn't quite make out what they were saying but he saw a lot of frantic hand movement and a lot of mumbling.

'Fine, a thousand Gillian it is . . . you better be worth it, kid.'

'Perhaps we should get moving then—' said Talon to the group, he looked over to Yal and continued '—the others won't be here until tomorrow at the earliest if they've been held up'

Yal smiles to himself and begins to rub his hands together.

Amras and his mob, lead the group towards the back of the Bar, the place now belonging to them with everyone else gone.

Varin stops to see that Drogun limping towards the seat he once sat in.

'Are you coming Drogun?'

Drogun then says while putting up his right leg on the table.

'I'm afraid I can't go. It's my knee. An old injury, I'll just slow you and the others down. You go on ahead I'll see you all when you get back. We have a lot of catching up to do.'

"What kind of brother would do that? Demanded payment and then let his younger brother do the work . . . actually that sounds just like an older brother . . ."

Varin nods and gives a smile before stepping outside. To his left he sees Talon wave him towards an alley around the back of the Bar.

Every one stood around a man-hole cover leading to the sewers below. Amras' men walked over towards the man-hole cover and lifted it with their bare hands as the rest watched.

As the man hole was opened Amras explained that they would need to go through the sewer to collect the item which he required, something he only described as a 'Shiny Jewel.'

'What!? We got to go through the sewer to get there?' asked Yal

'Unfortunately for you guys . . . Yes.' Said Amras with a smile

'Who cares? Do you have a map?' asked Varin

'No we don't but my men were down there earlier, they blocked off areas of the sewer and all that's left should lead you to the location of the Crysta . . . I mean Jewel—' said Amras as Yal and Talon entered the sewers. '—Hey kid . . . as a warning. They're certain blockades that might have been destroy by some Fiends which lead to some even bigger dangerous Fiends, so be careful. Oh and another thing near the end there is a two way junction, you want to go left. Right you got that?'

Varin replied with a nod and so he too jumped down into the sewer.

Amras' men then closed off the sewer, 'Let's go boys, we'll tell the boss of our progress.'

The smell overwhelmed Varin, the sewer was dark and damp, little dots of light from other man-hole covers shone into the darkness every couple feet. They began to make their way through the sewer with Varin taking charge, stomping their way through the murky water around their shins.

'On we go then eh?' said Varin

First entering the darkness, their eyes yet to adjust, they could hear the faint sound of movement but they could not be sure where from with the echoing of these walls. The further they entered the darkness, the noises grew louder but not of their steps but of echoing growls and movements in the surrounding sewers by Fiends.

It sounded like they were all around them, getting closer with heavy footsteps.

Yal and Talon nodded to each other and began inching their hands closer to their weaponry, with Yal watching their back. The group began to quicken their paces also.

Their silence only helped echo each step they took, further and further into the sewer until finally one of them spoke.

'So that was your brother ya?' asked Yal

Varin nodded 'Yes, I'd recognise him anywhere'

'But you're from 2269 right? So . . . how did he get here?'

'That's what I want to know'

'Varin, perhaps something bigger is at play here?' said Talon

'What do you mean?'

'A destiny'

'Destiny? I don't care about that, all I ever wanted was to see my family again, now that I know Drogun is in this time, that means our Father must be here as well and I intend to find him'

'Yeah Talon, destiny seems a bit grandeur at the moment with no proof that he is actually from the past ya . . . no offense Varin'

'None taken'

"If only he knew."

Finally light emerged at the end of the sewer, it stung their eyes but at least they now knew they nearing the end as the sounds got louder, almost as if the creatures were standing right next to them or rushing them from behind it made them all paranoid until they couldn't take it any longer.

'Sounds like they're trying to surround us' said Talon

'They won't be able to right? They're in a different sewer, all the entrances are blocked off right?'

'That's what Armas said' replied Yal

'But he also said some of the Fiends may of broken their blockades' said Talon

The echoes seemed to stop for a second and then rush from their side towards where they came from.

'They've found a way in' said Varin

'. . . Let's keep moving' said Talon

'No . . . run. RUN' screamed Yal

A sudden thunderous noise came from the sewer they had just walked, the Fiends had indeed found their way into the same system as the group. Although the group couldn't see what the creatures in the darkness they did make out its outline, from what they did see, the creatures was bipedal with a long tail. After that they didn't stop to look back.

The group was not far from the exit when they began to run but these Fiends were fast for their size, they were tall, taller than even the sewer itself so they had to hunch slightly running towards their three delicious meals.

Varin cold almost feel the Fiends breathe upon his neck as it seemed as every step he took, they took three. He looked behind the group frequently, and saw with each turn the Fiends getting closer and closer like a horrible game of Red Light/Green Light.

He stopped looking, hoping they would get no closer until he heard the faint fast footsteps come behind them and suddenly stopped, looked and saw a young Fiend in mid-air leaping towards him. Snout and jaw wide open.

Yal suddenly grabbed it around its head and with the thrust of his blade in his other hand stabs the creature, killing it and discarding it to the floor. All the other Fiends kept on running past the carcass of their fallen brethren, except one, the biggest of them, scars and tribal symbols marked this creatures body, it alone stopped and checked the body of its child. It lowered to one knee and snuggled the child with its long snout but it didn't move. It let out a deafening roar and began to run again. They just pissed off the Alpha.

Finally the group reached the end of the sewer, they heard the yell and turned to see how far away their enemy was.

'Oh shete, we've really angered them' said Yal

'I think you killed their child' said Varin

'HEY, if you two aren't busy you might want to help out here' yelled Talon

Talon was standing outside of the metallic room, inside was a number of locked small boxes. Yal and Varin rushed outside to help shut the large steel door. It moved slowly even with all three of them pushing, the creatures drew closer as the Alpha pushed any of them out of its way, it's mouth now watering as it grew closer. It entered the room and charged towards them with its tribe behind it. It reached out its hand and just then they shut the door and span the metallic handle to lock the vault.

'Wait . . . a vault. Where are we?' asked Varin

Varin turned and saw where they ended up looked familiar.

'What the hell is this place?' asked Yal
'Karves City?' replied Varin
'The old decayed ruins of Karves City'

Varin began to look around seeing old broken wall tiles some still hanging to and from the walls and ceiling, he moved a head of the twins but then recognised that one spot where he once laid.

'The old Subway Station' said Varin, finally seeing the place for what it once was.
'Do you know this place?' asked Yal, now standing next to Varin.

Varin took a couple steps forward towards the spot. The events of that day seemed to echo in his head.

'We found someone, over here—' said a man '—He's still breathing, help me out over here.'

"Varin was found unconscious shortly after the accident by a few survivors from other parts of the city. He was near a smouldering fire and close to death.
Drogun and their Father were never found."

As the earth beneath Karves began to shake and roar almost with the sound of pain, Emily turned on the TV just after the incident. The TV began to flicker; the power was beginning to fade away. She quickly scanned the channels and found a news broadcast that reported almost immediately about the incident.

'A disaster has occurred in the centre of Karves City. For an unknown reason, the main factory of the SPARK Corporation has exploded leaving most of the city in ruins.
At this time many believe the armed uprising group, Trans-Gression, are to blame for this incident . . .'

The TV went off, what power was left had been used. Emily sat in darkness shocked by what happened.

"There were only few survivors that fled to
the neighbouring city, Shenma City . . .

The factory, where the explosion accord, was the housing facility for SPARK's fuel, PHOENIX. People don't know what they could expect any more for the origin or ingredients of PHOENIX are unknown.

The people were powerless within the might of SPARK.

The incident was soon forgotten, as well as any further dangers that may lie in PHOENIX."

'Yes, this is where my brother and father disappeared, this is the place I last saw them . . . and she survived.'

'She?' asked Talon

'Sounds like Varin had a girl back home ya'

'Wasn't like that . . . I think, ggrr I can remember parts now what happened after 2259 but . . .'

He couldn't finish his sentence, the events of that day, the same events now repeating in his head seemed to replay right in front of him.

"One reality faded, into a dream, everything faded into the memories of that day. Ghostly and slow"

He saw his young self, staring off into the distance, off at the Shadowy Figure. Varin moved closer to try and see the figure clearly.

'Varin! Come on!'

This time he clearly heard his younger brother, Drogun, call him.

Drogun let go off his Fathers hand and stepped off the train. And then the flash, but this time it came towards him slowly, the flash seemed to illuminate the Shadowy Figures face.

Varin tried to see but could not recognize the face of the figure. He quickly made a mental note, 'Dark hair, small black beard on his chin and dark blue eyes.'

The flash grew closer to the figure, Varin saw that the figure was now no longer transparent as he saw in the past but became solid; the figure began to run, running straight towards Varin's younger self.

As quick as the figure began to run towards the young Varin, something court the dreaming Varin's eyes, a large piece of the ceiling began to fall, directly above his younger self. Uncontrollably, his legs demanded he run to save his younger self, and so he did.

The Shadowy Figure was a mere second ahead of the blinding light, but still seemed to run in slow motion, even to himself Varin was running slow, but that piece from the ceiling was going faster, getting closer towards the young Varin.

Now a few feet away from the young Varin, the figure and himself dived towards the child.

As the older Varin was about to grab the young, the figure suddenly came out of nowhere and grabbed him, pushing the young Varin away from the heavy ceiling piece, into safety.

Varin suddenly felt like he was speeded up, he hit the wall, winding him.

CHAPTER 6

The Elementals

REALITY RETURNED TO him like a punch to the gut, forcing him to gasp for air as the twin brothers approached him. Now panting for air, a cold sweat drizzled down his face.

The brothers, although concerned, seemed to be running slow towards him, even as they spoke, they seemed to be in slow motion.

'V-a-r-i-n-!' called out Yal

'A second PHOENIX DREAM? We need to get him to a d-o-c-t-o-r-'

'We can't just exactly l-e-a-v-e—right now ya, with the amount of fiends around here we'd be d-e-f-e-n-c-l-e-s-s—carrying him'

'There must be a high concentration of P-H-O-E-N-I-X—here, maybe that's why the fiends are collected around here?'

They lifted him back to his feet.

'I . . . I'm okay, really. Let me go.' pleaded Varin

And so they did, before their hands even left his arm he dropped back to the floor again.

'We should turn back.' said Talon
'No, we came this . . . far, we should con . . . tinue onwards.'
'But we don't even know where to find this Jewel, Crystal thing he was on about' replied Yal
'It does seem we've been led on a goose chase . . . but we should continue, we need to find another way out and a place to rest for Varin'

Yal nodded in agreement, wrapping Varin's arm over his shoulders once more, unknowing which way to go they decided to follow the tunnel.

'No, wait . . . stairs, go up the stairs . . . That'll lead us to the street'
'The street of Karves Village?'
'No . . . the city, and . . . my house.'

Almost dragging Varin, they reached the top of the stairs and the now broken, shattered door, that once lead to the subway station. They passed through staring upon what remains of the park, a dark place, no sun, no light. The plants, trees and grass that once bloomed here died years ago, nothing remains, nothing but old ash and dust.

Unknowing where to go the brothers turned to Varin, who pointed them in the direction of his old home as there was no other place to go, each street was blocked by rubble from one building or another.

The streets were cracked and broken from the incident, needing them to have a running start to jump most of the tears in the streets.

Something asked Varin not to look at this house as they attempted to go past but his young curiosity told him to turn and look.

"A world of destruction, buildings all around destroyed, except for that one."

There stood in the middle of the row of houses, the Vargon home, not one part of it was destroyed or even damaged due to the incident. As if it was the only one spared.

Something then began to beckon him to enter the building. He could see in his mind, him reaching towards the building, opening the front door, seeing his brother and Father giving him strength once more.

But something, something far off into the distance a ray of light glistened.

Something was shining and reflecting the light.

'Let me go, I . . . I feel okay now' said Varin

And so the brothers did slowly, thinking he may collapse once more, but he didn't he stood strong on his two feet.

The three of them began to make their way towards the light thinking it could possibly be this "Jewel" they are looking for or at least an exit.

~∞∞∞∞∞~

After some time they finally arrived at a large clearing in the centre of the clearing, laid a crater. A powerful blast had accrued here some time ago.

"The location of where the SPARK Corp. building once stood, the building that blew in 2259. Thanks to him . . ."

In the centre of the crater was a pedestal, holding a blue crystal the size of a snooker ball.

'Guess it wasn't a wild goose chase after all' said Yal
'We must be careful, it looks like it's been here for some time. Perhaps we should take it to the Professor to analyse it.'

Without saying a word Varin dropped the foot tall crater and alone dared enter the crater, as the others looked on.

'Slowly Varin, that Fiend Amras warned us could be around'
He slowly approached the pedestal cautiously as the others looked on dreading the moment something might go wrong, Varin now entered the ray of light shining from above.

'Is this it?' asked Varin

He slowly moved his hand towards it slowly, he suddenly raised it from the pedestal with great haste but nothing happened.
The twins came up to him as he smiling, cockily strutted towards them.

'Easy money'

The ground begins to violently shake. Almost forcing them down to the ground, as walls begin to rise from the ground around them to create a dome twenty feet around the pedestal, trapping them inside. The walls closed off the light, yet it wasn't dark enough to not see.

Yal and Talon began to attack one of the walls in hopes of breaking it down, two loud roars echo around the dome along with a banshee scream also. With the sound now bouncing off the walls, the group cover their ears.

Three creatures rise from the floor, one created of water.

'To claim this crystal yours, you must be one of pure heart.'

Another made of Earth begins to rise.

'If you are not one of pure heart . . .'

'These must be guardians of this thing . . . the rumours must be true' spoke Talon

'What . . . ?' asked Varin as another Guardian rose from the floor, the Fire Guardian.

'YOU WILL DIE!'

The Water Guardian then screamed like a banshee once more and began to flood the area as the two other Guardians disappeared.

Now Yal furiously attacked the wall with all of his might until the water quickly took him off his feet. He tried once more kicking and punching it, anything he could to try and break that damn wall.

The water rose so quickly, it now almost touched the ceiling, forcing them to take in their last breath.

"Knowing they were trapped, I couldn't stand back any more, I pierced the shell of the dome, cutting a hole into the wall. As they tumbled out along with the roaring water, I hid back into the shadows."

Coughing and gasping for air the group got back to their feet and fled, unknowing of the stranger in the shadows. The Water Guardian once again unleashed a tidal wave, which now stalked them as they fled for their lives. The dome itself collapsed under the pressure causing an even bigger tidal wave to chase after them.

They ran back past the Vargon home, the water slowing a bit to fill the cracks but it remained right behind them. Almost at the station, Varin turned to see his once proud home fall to the crashing tide, which was still coming at them.

They finally ran into the station itself seeing the water leak in from the roof above, or what was left of it. They stopped to catch their breath, now wet and tired of running.

'W . . . why is it always . . . something chasing us today?' asked Yal gasping for air.

Until the sound of the wave heading down the tunnel towards them echoed in.

Shocked in horror with only one place to run they decided to run towards the sewers hoping to escape that way, but the other Guardians had other plans for them.

The Earth Guardian raised another wall blocking their exit. Quickly changing their direction, they now ran down the remaining train tunnel, towards another sewer system still being chased by the Water Guardian and still with the crystal in hand.

They arrived at another sewer system, closed off by a metal grate. Talon quickly grabbed his weapon and swiped the grate. It fell to the ground with a rusty clank.

Yal dived into the pipe, followed by Varin, followed by Talon. They began to crawl their way through this small one man pipe as fast as they could, they begin to see daylight at the end of the tunnel as the water began to fill the pipe. The tidal wave stormed by with some water forcing its way into the pipe, the wave finally court up to them and now forced them towards the light, pushing them at an uncontrollable speed.

The pipe over looked an ocean, but it won't be the ocean that would pose a threat, it'll be gravity. A two mile drop to the smashing rocks and pounding ocean below.

Yal is the first to be forced from the pipe, closely followed by Varin and Talon.

With his back to the water below, looking towards the others, Yal nods and looks down to the waves below. Realising he will not survive unless he did something quickly, he quickly thinks of something, he moves his hands towards his swords, pulling out one of them.

'Varin . . . catch!'

Throwing the sword forcing it upwards towards Varin, quickly with his one spare hand Varin grabs the blade, with the other hand still a hold of the crystal. Yal then reached for his other sword and grabbed a hold of it with both arms, raising the arms above his head. Hoping it would disturb the water enough for him to make a safe landing. Talon pulls out his weapon with arms out stretched towards the water. Yal hits the water with a powerful crash, closely followed by Varin and Talon, each landing a good meter or two apart in deep dark water.

Yal is the first to rise from the water in pain but alive, closely followed by Talon who is much the same. He waits a seconded . . .

'Whe . . . Where's Varin?' asked Yal coughing, almost winded from the fall.

Varin was nowhere in sight.

They both dived under the water. They see him not far away but unconscious, still with the crystal in hand.

They dived further towards Varin and noticed the crystal began to glow.

They reach out to grab Varin when suddenly the Water Guardian, forces them away, she wraps her fish like limbs around him, she seems to be protecting him. She stares at Yal and Talon briefly with a growl, she turns to Varin and whispers something softly into his ear.

Yal and Talon approach, drawing their weapons, the Water Guardian sees them but continues to whisper something. She finally releases Varin and disappears into the misty ocean. They grab a hold of Varin and rush to the surface.

"What she said still, surprises . . . and confuses me . . . 'We are not meant to be kings of our fate, but I must define my own future, there is no fate but what I make' . . .

But this is why I and my brother, Drogun, are doing these recording in hopes of remembering our past on this journey so far . . . and remembering those that have died because of this journey.

They shall never be forgotten.—"

CHAPTER 7

Defending the Once Great

YAL AND TALON drag Varin's body onto the beach, just a short way from the rising tide, they remove the Crystal from his tight grip and begin CPR (cardiopulmonary resuscitation).

"—I once heard 'building the future and keeping the past alive are one and the same thing.' After my journey I fully believe this. I choose to carry on fighting in the memory of my loved ones and all those that died. I will have revenge for them."

Varin begins to breath once more with a cough, he rolls to his side with as gasp, spitting out water and takes in a deep cold breathe as Yal and Talon sigh with relieve.

'Thought you were a goner for a second there buddy' said Yal
'What did she say to you?' asked Talon

'Who?'

'The Water Guardian, she was whispering something to you as you were under the water' spoke Talon.

'I don't remember, last thing I do remember was . . . the fall and that's it'

"I lied."

'We should get back to the Bar, it's getting dark, and we have a good three hour walk ahead of us.' said Talon

They grab Varin, picking him up and placing him around their shoulders once more.

'I hope this isn't a regular thing for you, ya'

Some time passes, Varin regains his legs and walks on fine again still with the Crystal in hand.

'This is intriguing' spoke Talon
'What is?' asked Varin
'The sun is setting'
'Ya, it does that all the time' said Yal
'But where are the Fiends?'
'What do you mean?' asked Varin
'Sunset is their most active time and we're deep within a Sra forest at present, yet where are they?'

A sudden rustle of a nearby bush stops their conversation.

'You get what you wished for ya'
'It's too dark to see into the trees' said Varin

Talon picks up a stick and rips part of his t-shirt, wrapping it around the end of the stick before setting the fabric a light. They slowly approached the bush, with Yal and Varin drawing their weapons.

They move the bust aside to see a family of Sra starring back at them but not with anger or rage but with fear as the light from the torch reflected off their eyes.

'They're scared . . .' said Talon
'Of the light?' asked Varin
'No. The Crystal. We need to see the Professor'

And with that they continued on towards Karves Village now at a jog.

They soon returned to the Bar, although still wet and now very cold.

Many of the villagers are still shopping even now, picking up various items such as fruit and vegetables.

The sun was almost gone now, yet a little remained to obscure Varin's eyes as the silhouettes of a group in the distance walked towards them. Varin held on tighter to the crystal

The group approaching them held a small pouch. Now within one hundred yards of Varin, the smallest grabbed the pouch which seemed to almost grow in size and became a lot heavier. He and his men, blocked the path of Varin, Yal and Talon from walking any further.

The group smiled.

'You've done well boys—' said the small man, almost struggling to get his words out with the weight of the pouch, '—but we'll be taking that now!'

He suddenly dropped the pouch, the contents were nothing but potatoes, luckily his men were fast as at the same time his men drew their guns, weapons similar to what Varin once used and pulled their triggers.

However they weren't as fast as the Twin Brothers, who pulled out their weapons at the same time and blocked each bullet. The crowd around them now ran for cover, some dropping their possessions.

The smallest of the group grabbed at the Crystal snatching it from Varin and hid amongst the crowd, he disappeared once more. But as he did this he blocked the sun to reveal himself, Amras—Don of the Newen Mafia. Amras and his gang fled as Varin, Yal and Talon began to give chase.

The villagers ran for their lives, all of them scattering and running in all different directions, bumping into one another, blocking Varin and the Twins as they gave chase. But the villagers didn't worry about them.

Ducking and weaving amongst the crowd Varin got a good view of Amras with his men far ahead of him. Varin sprinted towards him with the twins not far behind. Suddenly a shadow over took Varin and the others. It began to catch up with Amras, the shadow belonging to someone running on the roof top. The shadow ran to the edge of the building and jumped off landing a top of Amras, standing back up he grabs a hold of Amras and raises him to eye level, as his men continue to run.

He then throws back his hood with his other hand, Drogun. Varin, Yal and Talon run up to Drogun.

'W . . . Where . . . did you . . . come from . . . ?' asked Varin out of breathe

'I heard all the commotion from the Bar's Inn, I climbed to the roof to see what the problem was, much like you used to do if I remember correctly' he said with a smirk

Yal then says sarcastically 'You act like your some kind of hero'

'Force of habit, I suppose I won't need to now—' They stare at Drogun but he still is facing Amras, '—I'll explain a little later—' Drogun shakes Amras and continues, '—I suggest you and your buddies leave town, never to return and never to trick me again . . . but first I'll take that'

Drogun grabs the Crystal, from Amras' feeble grip, steam began to rise from Drogun's hand as he quickly places it into his pocket. With one arm still a hold, Amras wriggled and kicked to escape from Drogun's grasp. He lands to the floor with a thud but on his feet, he turns to run as Drogun goes to grab Amras but suddenly village bell rang.

The Villagers that were still around rushed even more franticly, this time with far more terror in their hearts as people in armour and holding various weapons took posts around the main gate of the village.

The bell continued to ring.

'Here they come!' yells one of the Fighters on top of a lookout tower.

Something begins to bang on the city gate as a villager yells, 'Run!'

There was another bang against the gate, wood and metal began to crumble away from the gate. The sound was of something big running into the gate.

'What? No already?'

'What is it Talon?' asks Varin

'This happens once a month, it's one of the reasons why Yal and I stayed in Karves so long'

'What is!?'

'Fiends' said Drogun

The gate finally gives way and splinters open, knocking a few of the Fighters and Warriors back as the Fiends launch their way into the village.

'Yal, you and Varin will go and protect the villagers, I will help in other parts of the village and Drogun, you . . . where did he go?'

While Talon was talking, Drogun rushed into battle to defend the front gate using his sword. The sword was a lot more elegant than Varin thought it would be, it seemed to be made from pure silver, wrapped around the hilt of the blade was purple dyed leather, crissing and crossing each stand. The blade itself was a little odd to Varin with it being almost completely straight but having a slight curve towards the tip, as the light reflected off, it seemed sting his eyes a little. Amongst the elves the blade is known as "Tur-anion" meaning "Patriot."

Drogun ran towards the gate as fast as he could and as he ran flames seem to appear from his hand traveling down the blade until it was entirely covered in flames. As he grew closer and closer to the nearest Fiend, Drogun began to lower the blade towards the floor until he was dragging the flaming blade along the floor trailing dust and flames behind him as he went. One Fiend saw him coming closer, a Boar like creature known as a Matoro, it began a charge towards Drogun.

Now two steps away from the Fiend he used a technique that he learned from his master, this technique was simply called "Shift". As he performed "Shift" it seemed like he went through the Fiend causing it to stop in its tracks, when it stopped Drogun was down, leaning on his left knee and his left hand with his right leg out in front of him.

Holding him up, while his right arm, with sword in hand, was behind his back pointing upwards.

The Fiend stood still as if it had seen a ghost or had been turned to stone. A streak of fire began leading from where Drogun first began "Shift" leading up to his left foot, where it ended, once the fire was complete the Fiend split in half as Drogun moved onto the a next Fiend.

Varin looked on, unable to comprehend what Drogun just did.

'What the hell was that . . . how did he do that?'

Yal grabbed Varin and dragged him away from the front gate to protect the other parts the village.

'I don't know Varin but we got to move' said Yal

More Fiends made it past the gate than what they thought. They split up to defend different areas of the village. East was protected by Talon, West by Yal, South by Varin and North by Drogun and the village Warriors.

The East sector was full of Fiends and most villagers were already in doors, except one family whom were stopped and surrounded by three Matoros. Two Matoros stopped them from running into a house as the third began to walk towards them. From Talon's position he could see that he could easily take out the two at the back giving the family chance to run.

He got a hold of his weapon, took a second and then threw his weapon towards the first Matoro on the families right hand side. It easily impaled the first, the force of the throw caused it to die instantly and fly towards the second one, the second one was hit by the lifeless Matoro against the wooden wall with the force alone causing the double edged staff to impale the second Matoro. It too died.

The family quickly ran into the house as Talon came running towards them, the Matoro jumped at him. He quickly pulled the staff from the wall and used it to block the mouth of the Matoro. He forced it back and to the floor which he then impaled as it struggled to get back on all four of it's legs. He then heard a yell from another nearby villager and off he went.

The South was probably the safest part of the village since most of the Fiends could not make it past the North gate let alone the other sections, but a couple Fiends did make their way to the South sector where Varin was waiting for them. Unfortunately for him seven Matoro made it to the South sector.

Five rounds were left in his gun.

They began to charge towards him. He fired.

'One down,—'

'—Two down,—'

'—Three,—'

'—Four.'

One bullet left, three Matoro still standing.

They began to surround him; he was uneager to fire first and use his last remaining bullet. They now had him in a triangle position, the bottom left and the top one quickly lunched towards Varin. He aimed for the bottom left one with his gun.

'Better not shoot' he thought to himself.

He kicked the Matoro from under its jaw forcing it to launch into the air, flipping head over heels, the second was already in the air by its own accord to maul Varin. While still having his gun aimed at the rising Matoro, quickly hit the second with a roundhouse kick forcing it to fly towards a corner of a building, its body bent around the corner back first. The third stayed where it was as the other Matoro began its decent. He saw it from the corner of his eye, it came level with his head. He spun round and used the hand grip of his revolver to strike it upon its head, forcing it to fall five foot away, dead.

Varin quickly aimed the gun at the third and final Matoro, but it didn't move. The Matoro was sat on its hind legs and began to look scared and shake if a cold wind suddenly blew in the middle of winter.

It then seemed to faint onto the floor. Varin checked its pulse, it was dead. Its green discoloured flesh felt cold. He rose back to his feet and began to put his gun away until he heard a wild scream coming from the West sector.

"It was up to Yal to defend the West sector of the village and he was doing fine until three 'new' Fiends showed up. Yal and Talon have never came across these 'new' species of Fiends. But still . . . Yal didn't back down."

Yal stood at the bottom of a street, surrounded by lifeless Matoros and out of breath. Just to his left were a family of three, cowering from the Matoros.

'Go—' said Yal, '—get home quickly, its safe for now but won't be for long.'

The parents grabbed their ten year old daughter by the hand, said their thank yous and began to make their way to the nearest house. Reaching the door the little girl tore hands free from her parents and ran back to Yal with her arms wide open.

He dropped to his knees and hugged her back as she whispered, 'Thank you Ninja' into his ear. She let go and ran back to the house.

He stood back up, paused to place his weapons away and turned to check the area was clear. He saw three Fiends at the top of the street, three hundred yards away, snarling and staring at him.

The Fiends looked a lot like a Silver backed Gorillas except for its colours, which was just pure black with red parts on its arms and knees, it's size was much bigger than a normal gorilla. It almost was the same size of the houses lining the street.

Yal hesitated for a second, there stare was like they were looking into his soul, he flicked his wrist to get his swords out once again. The Fiends instantly reacted letting out a hollowing yell and began to run towards Yal, two of them took to the rooftops one on each side of the street. They roared as they approached.

Yal pulled out both his blades and began to run, in the opposite direction of the Fiends.

He ran for his life, the Fiends were quick and soon reached the end of the street as Yal managed to turn down another street that was no further than fifty yards from where he stood, one fiend court up with him. He suddenly stopped in his tracks as it lunged from behind, he trusted his blades towards the creature, it couldn't stop in time causing it to impale itself on his sharp blades.

The two other fiends jumped from the rooftops towards him. Yal launched himself off the dead Fiend, jumping from its large chest to narrowly avoid a swipe from the second fiend as it dived towards him from atop the roof. The third however was in mid-air diving towards him but wasn't ready to attack, as Yal passed it he struck it with his blades. It fell towards the ground it fell to pieces landing in two, near the other dead Fiend.

The third and final Fiend, looked at its fallen brothers. It nuzzled close to them both, shaking them slightly with its head, checking them if they were still alive. It seemed saddened by this; it looked at Yal as he landed on the ground 100 yards away. It let out a mighty growl, the anger burned in its eyes as it stared at Yal. It began to move slowly towards Yal, stepping through the pool of blood that its fallen brethren had oozed onto the floor, it noticed it the cold and checked its hand.

Something unexpected happened, not even Yal was aware that this was possible. The Fiend suddenly stood up straight, as it began to change, mutate almost. It quickly grew bigger, its fur and skin seem to melt away and fall away, as its muscles enlarged and became its new skin. The colours of the beast also changed to dark red, dark like blood.

Once it finished changing, it began to bash its chest and roar so loud Yal covered his ears, the Fiend was so loud the entire village heard its war cry. It stared once more back at Yal and began to charge towards him.

Yal stood his ground this time, although more out of fear than bravery. He gripped his weapons tight the closer it got as he prepared for its attack.

Aloud noise echoed from down the street where Yal had once came; the Fiend tried to continue its charge. Yal looked up from the Fiend, noticing the wound in its head, as Varin begun to lower his weapon. The Fiend slowly tried to get to Yal as its life began to leave it. It finally dropped to the floor in front of Yal, landing at his feet. It looked at him one last time while resting on its knees, it was now the same height as Yal, as it stared into his eyes. It roared one last time. Yal swung his blades. Its head disconnected from its body.

'Now we're even' grinned Varin.

Something caught their eyes, a figure jumping onto the roof. Standing on the roof above them was Talon.

'Nice to you both in one piece, we need to get back to the front'

CHAPTER 8

The Great Tournament

YAL, TALON AND Varin began to make their way back to the front as fast as they could. By the time they got there Drogun and the Fighters were killing the last of the Matoro Fiends. The last one fell by Drogun's hand as they arrived.

'Th . . . That was . . . fu . . . fun,' said Varin out of breathe.

He, Yal and Talon began to take in deep breathes, as the villagers once again returned to the streets.

'Excuse me son' said elderly man to Varin, the man seemed to be no older than sixty and wore a black robe.
'Yes sir?'
'Please call me father'
'S . . . sorry father . . . I meant no disrespect'
'None taken, son. I just wanted to thank you boys—' he takes a look at Varin, Drogun, Yal and Talon, '—for saving our lives. So thank you'

As he looked at Drogun, his eyes seem to spark. He turns and begins to slowly walk away holding one arm behind, supporting his back.

'Father wait'
'What could I do for you?'
'I was just wondering if this normally happens.'
'What? Attacked by fiends, yes it does. But lucky we have you guys, the Trans-Gression, here to protect us,' he then walked off.

"The old man was the new local Priest for the village, he often resided in the Church. None of the villagers knew his true name so they just called him 'Priest'."

The Priest disappeared into the crowed, which quickly formed to thank those that exterminated the Fiends.

'That's kinda funny, you still have religion' said Varin turning to Yal and Talon
'Why is that funny?' said Yal
'Just in my time religion is pretty much a minority' replied Varin
'Is that a problem for you?' asked Talon
'No, not at all. Just kinda funny, when the world went to hell because of PHOENIX, they turn to something to comfort themselves'
'Truth be told, this is the first church I've seen in a while' said Yal
'It's new in town, he only opened three days ago, I wonder where he came from' said Talon

As the others talked among themselves Drogun tried to look for the Priest, something about his eyes unnerved him. But he was nowhere to be seen.

Drogun turned to face the group as he saw a man aged twenty five standing right in his face. In a large crowd the man would stand out anywhere with him have a ginger Mohawk. Drogun took a few steps back and saw the man in full, wearing old worn out dirty, cut denim jeans, his t-shirt was the same, dirty white cloth with cuts, tears and rips. Holes and dirt everywhere even his denim jacket was the same with its two sleeves removed.

'Hey, I saw you fighting those fiends and well I was quite impressed. Did you know there's a local tournament starting in a few minutes. I don't mean to toot my own horn but I'm the local Champion and I was hoping that you guys would enter the tournament.—' he spoke so fast almost not giving the others a chance to speak, '—The sign up booth is just over there—' he pointed over his shoulder to a small looking house just across from the gate, '—Cya round, the names J.C by the way.'

He then almost disappeared into the crowd, only his ginger Mohawk could be seen amongst the crowd, like a sharks fin in the ocean. Eventually Yal, Talon and Varin made their way out of the crowd to see around the other side of the Inn, where the town square resides, a tournament was begin prepared. In the centre of the town was a wrestling ring with ropes and everything that Varin can remember watching wrestling on TV when his Father wasn't home. Around the ring was plenty of elevated seating, more than enough room for the entire village. The entire area looked like a party was going to happen, with flags on string decorating the area.

On the wall of the Inn stood a billboard attached to its wall, pieces of paper littered it asking for brave adventures to find or hunt rare plants or Fiends. But the biggest piece of paper had the prizes for competing in this tournament.

'Third place G1,000 in cash, second place a top of the line weapon (worth G1,500) band first place a VIP ticket to the newly built town (worth G3,590)' read Yal

'A ticket out of town? Doesn't seem like much for a top prize' said Varin

'I guess it's to get across the channel between Karves and that new town . . . erm, what's it called again?' replied Yal

'Skyspear' said Talon.

'Hey, where did Drogun go?' asked Varin.

They began to look around to see Drogun but no luck.

'He does that a lot, ya?' said Yal

'He did that as a child as well' replied Varin.

'Let's take a look around the square, the others should be in the next hour or two' said Talon

'Ya, taking part will be a perfect way to kill some time' said Yal

'Shouldn't they cancel this tournament? I mean the village was just attacked, people were injured if not killed' asked Varin

'Isn't that a good reason to continue the tournament? These attacks by Fiends happen all the time, that's one of

the reasons Yal and I came here, to defend this village.'
replied Talon

'One of the reasons? What are the others?' asked Varin

Talon ignored his question and continued 'And if they
feel like getting on with their lives after that shouldn't
they?'

'Yes but aren't they just bottling up their feelings? Just
brushing it under the rug like nothing happened, that's no
way to be'

'No, you're right but for them, Varin, this is right ya.
Life is a struggle but we can't give up and that's why we
have to power on, remember the fallen but continue on
regardless knowing they're in our memory.'

An Announcer begins to read out the rules for the
tournament.

'Come on we'll go take a closer look at the tournament'
said Talon.

'No weapons, what so ever shall be used, anyone court
using one will be disqualified. First man to be knocked out or
thrown from the ring will be eliminated from the tournament
by any means necessary. Round One . . . Begin.'

First to fight is the current Champion, J.C.—the man
with the Mohawk which they met earlier.

The bell rang.

To J.C the bell meant the beginning of a boxing match.
When that bell rang it was like the man changed, his stance,
arms and face changed from a welcome open jolly man to
a man closed and serious. Within seconds he was in the
face of his opponent. He swung a right, a left and then an

uppercut. His opponent stumbles backwards stunned from the punch, the sheer force alone caused the man to stumble so far back with his head tilted up, he soon falls out of the ring. The Announcer immediately stands with a cheers and declares J.C.

'Winner and new record holder, for the quickest knock out in less than thirty seconds, J.C!'

The square quickly rumbled with cheers, by now it looked like most of the village had turned out and were supporting J.C. There must have been more than a hundred people watching and cheering, with more coming as the minutes went by.

'Quite a turn out' said Varin
'Yeah, Hm . . . it's starting to get dark' replied Talon
'Free entertainment when you can get it though, ya?' said Yal
'We should really see about getting a room to rent rather than partake in this'
'Where's ya sense of fun Varin?' asked Yal
'Fun? Today has been the longest day of my life. I've woken up in a new place essentially, got chased by tidal waves created by creatures that never existed in my time, fought creatures known as Fiends and saved your life . . . I could do with a break'
'Was fun though wasn't it?'
'Yal. Give him a break, he has been through a lot today, more than enough for a normal person'
'Ya, I was foolish to think he could keep up with us' said Yal with a smile to Varin.

Varin knew exactly what Yal was trying to do . . . but he bit the bait anyway.

'Alright Yal, I'll sign up. I like a challenge anyway, and when I win then we'll see we can keep up with who.'

They quickly signed up and were led into a house nearby to prepare for their bouts. Twenty minutes had passed, Varin was sitting in the corner trying to prepare but it was difficult. His body was already feeling the effects from the day, his muscles were tired and tight from running, bruises and cuts had begun to show and he was exhausted.

Finally someone came to get Varin from the back. Yal and Talon gave him a nod as Varin left the house, it was now night time as torches lit most of the town as he drew closer to the square, he could see torches now light the square full with a lot more people—now it did seem the full village turned out.

He heard the mumbling of the Announcer, '. . . and his opponent will be Varin Vargon'

His opponent was a cocky one, upon seeing Varin bruised and weary he yelled out to the crowd waving his arms in the air, 'I've already won this fight'

He continued to trash talk, which seemed to get the crowd behind him but Varin tried not to pay him to much attention, he's dealt with school bullies before a number of times . . . even the same person a number of times.

'What was his name . . . ?'

The bell rung. Snapping Varin from his day dream, as his opponent rushed from his side of the ring to give Varin a right jab. Another memory flooded his mind from the days of him training in that empty hanger again. What Ren said that day echoed in his mind but he noticed something else, someone else a girl with red hair and another guy, that bully.

Varin dodged the punch by ducking under it, as he did Varin thrust his elbow into the ribs, winding his opponent he then struck him on the back of the neck. Hard and Swift. Which causing Varin's opponent to be pass out as he collapsed within the confines of the ring. Everyone, including the Announcer, looked on in amazement.

No one cheered they all stared in silence at Varin looked at the clock that now resigned on the wall, brightly stating the length of each match.

'Ten seconds . . . N . . . new record holder Varin Vargon' spoke the Announcer.

Now the crowd reacted and cheered for Varin, cheering his name as he left the ring to walk back to the house.

Upon returning to the house, Varin saw the Ninja Twins making their way towards him.

'Congratulations Varin.—' said Talon, Yal didn't say a thing but he gave Varin a pat on the back, while looking angry about something. Talon noticed Varin's concern, '—We're up next, Yal and I, we must fight each other.'

'Barely enough signed up for there to be a tournament, apparently. So we must face each other' added Yal.

'Shame really, in our fights. I always win' said Talon before leaving the house. Before the door can fully close the sound of the crowd cheering and the announcer filled the room.

'They like him more' said Yal

Varin place a hand on Yal's shoulder and said, 'I believe in you Yal, you can do it.'

With that he regained some of his former energy. Varin decided he didn't want to miss this fight and so decided to follow behind Yal.

Yal breathed in deep and stepped out the door, expecting people to be quiet or boo him, instead they cheered him. Now he felt that rush of energy and cheer he once had back in him.

That little girl from before was there and in her hand was a doll made to look like Yal. She thanked him one last time and wished him luck as the Announcer called out his name. He entered the ring as Varin took a seat near were Yal's biggest fan, the little girl, now sat with her family.

'May the best man win' spoke Talon getting into his fighting stance

'Don't worry I will'

The bell rung and in that second the two brothers never held back, they charged each other and began to constantly counter each other's attacks or block each shot. The crowd quickly began to grow bored.

Suddenly Talon staggered back, and almost as if he couldn't believe it Yal stood shocked and Talon raised a hand to his chin. Yal then started to parade round like he had already won, but Talon realised this was Yal's weakest time. Yal tried once again to land the same punch but this time Talon was expecting it and so he dodged it by ducking to the right of Yal's left fist, in that split second he grabbed Yal's arm flipped him over with his own momentum. Yal's smile quickly turned into a realization of terror when he saw Talon's boot raise up as he fell. The boot landed on his chest forcing him to fly into the crowd surrounding the ring.

People began to help Yal up as the Announcer quickly gave Talon the victory as the crowd roared into cheer. The little girl wasn't happy.

'Your arrogance is your weakness, you need more training.' Talon spoke over the cheering crowd, he then bowed as did Yal back on his feet. He then went and joined Varin.

The Announcer then chimed in again stating that the next match will between Talon and the local champion. J.C. Talon took to standing in the corner, meditating while J.C came out, entering the square as hero would, confetti and band marching behind him. He paraded around the ring first tagging people's hands as he made his way round.

J.C finally entered the ring.

He turned and yelled across the ring, 'This is the semi-final, you ready?'

Talon just stood there with his eyes closed, still meditating. The Announcer raised his arm up to bring the small hammer down onto the metal bell to begin the match when Talon turned and stepped out of the ring.

Yal was the first to react, 'What . . . what is he doing?'

The crowd began to boo him as Yal ran up to his brother and asked that.

Talon replied, 'He had already won, he was the better fighter. There was no need for a match to prove it.'

J.C began to paraded around once again, now yelling people are afraid of him. The Announcer quickly called Varin over for the final match.

He jumped into the ring and as soon as he did the bell quickly rung, giving no chance for Varin to be ready or possibly leave the ring.

He turned to see J.C already in front of him and suddenly volley of hooks, jabs and kicks were landing on him. He did manage to block or dodge most but a few hit. He hit hard but was a little slower than Varin, giving him enough time to dodge J.C's attacks.

Dodging the attacks seemed to annoy J.C more and more.

'Stop running away coward'

Varin dodged one wild swing from J.C and then delivered a uppercut of his own to J.C knocking him to the ground. He quickly got up and got even more angry, again Varin blocked and dodged all of his punches and kicks causing J.C to become even more infuriated. Varin again knocked him to the floor, this eventually began to amuse the crowd and soon brought them to laugher.

J.C was not amused by this, again his rage rose and seemed to reach a new limit. His rage began to physically transform him into a sort of demon; he grew twice size bigger than what he once was.

His skin changed into a dark purple and the Mohawk seemed to grow down his back as a tail emerged, his face and nose became a snout as his nails began to turn into claws and his teeth became fangs. It's mind however was still on winning the match, it swung and hit Varin forcing him to fly into the turnbuckles of the ring, winding him and knocking him to the floor. Began to strike down wards to the downed Varin.

People began to run from the square as the Announcer waved in a bunch of guys with restraints and a tranquilliser to stop the beast.

The men with restraints managed to hook themselves around the demon's neck but it quickly swung them off with a roar. One managed to hit it with a tranquilliser it seemed to not affect it. Varin got back to his feet while it was distracted.

'Varin, get down!' yelled Talon.

Both Yal and Talon jumped from the nearby crowd stands towards the demon, delivering a flying kick to the demon. They hit it, but it was like hitting a break wall, although it did begin to fall it whipped them away with its arm causing them to land in the stands. He ring under the monsters weight broke as Varin ducked down. And finally it seemed the tranq began to take effect—as it fell it began to shrink back into human form. It crashed through the wooden stands causing broken bits of wood and dust into the air. Once the dust and cleared, amongst the wood laid the naked still breathing body of J.C.

'Winner! Varin Vargon—' yelled the Announcer, one person still in the crowd claps, '—For transforming during the match J.C has been disqualified and anything that happened after the transformation has been null and void, crowning Varin Vargon the new Champion.'

Whomever stuck around cheered and clapped for Varin as the Announcer handed him the title and the first place prize.

Varin looked down at the title, 'I don't deserve this.'

He walked over to J.C and placed the title on him, as he now was waking up with people throwing robes upon him.

'You're pretty good, if you kept a cool head and the fight continued . . . you'd would have won. I'll be asking for a rematch someday. J.C, you just work on that'

He then walked over to Talon and Yal, whom were smiling to themselves, as the Announcer looked on shocked once more.

'That was an honourable thing you did Varin' said Talon
'I know. I wish my brother was around to see it though—' They left the tournament area, '—He used to look out for me all the time and then I use to look out for . . .'

". . . Emily."

CHAPTER 9

Shadows of The Past

'They should have been here by now' said Yal

'They must of set up camp now, it'll be too dark and dangerous to go traveling now' replied Talon

'Dangerous? Why? I'm sure a large group of Trans-Gression could take on a few Fiends' said Varin

'Indeed they could during the day, but upon night fall Fiends grow stronger and the most dangerous ones come out at night, mostly'

'Stronger? Even the Fiends we've already faced? How?'

'Something to do with the moon, ya. They even say the Fiends come from the moon'

'Which is just silly I assure you Yal—' said Talon '—Come, we're retire to the Inn for the night.'

The group return to the Inn and stay the night.

Although now finally laying down to rest after the exhausting day, Varin couldn't get to sleep—his mind was too busy wondering what may of happed to Emily and who that bully was that he can't quite seem to remember.

～◦◦◦～

Varin eventually got some sleep but he didn't care, his mind was elsewhere with the thoughts of his past. The soon left the Inn to find Drogun standing in the middle of the street.

"My brother was midway through a sentence when he noticed me."

'. . . Drogun, where the hell did you go?'

"I knew he was thinking of Emily at the time. His face turned from a glorious smile into an expression of pity, wondering about those that he had left behind."

Drogun goes to speak but is stopped by Talon.

'They're here' he announced, pointing towards people approaching from the distance.
'Trans-Gression?' asked Varin
'Yaha' replied Yal as he too ran off.

Drogun turned to see them, Varin was about to join Yal and Talon as Drogun grabbed him.

'Myradi. (Little Brother) It's our little friends, there's only three of them. Where are the others?'

Amras and three others from his mafia ran towards Varin and Drogun. Amras throws himself at their feet and begins to beg.

'Y . . . you got to help us our . . .'

Drogun cut him off, 'Why should we help you?'

'There is no reason why you guys should help us, but please, we beg of you our Ex-boss has sent someone to kill us.'

Drogun then turns his back to the group and says, 'Everywhere I turn, there's somebody who wants to destroy me, don't turn your problems into my problems'

Drogun then begins to walk off as Amras says 'Our boss knows you guys have the crystal and he'll want it back, once the assassin is done with us he'll be looking for you guys.'

Drogun continued walking. 'Well he can come get it.'

'BOSS! HERE HE COMES!!'

They all turn around including Drogun. Even Yal and Talon heard the mafia member yell and came running over to join Drogun and Varin. Off in the distance, the sight of a small one manned helicopter like carrier. Talon then takes one step forward beside Yal,

'Yal it's him—' Yal pulls out his weapons and jumps towards the Assassin, '—don't worry guys we'll take care of him' said Talon.

The approaching Assassin wore a brown leather jacket, in fact most of the other items of clothing he wore where brown leather, in any other village he probably wouldn't of stood out as much.

As Yal approaches the Assassin's carrier, the Assassin jumps from his craft holding a metal staff. He blocks Yal's attack and flicks him away, causing Yal to land in the square near the gate.

The Assassin falls towards Talon, he pulls out his weapon. Talon blocks the Assassin's attack with the Assassin's staff landing atop of Talon's.

'Nice to see you again' said Talon.

The Assassin smiles, he then throws the Assassin towards Yal. Yal places one of his swords out and prepares the swing the other to finish the Assassin, but the Assassin saw this coming. As he flew towards Yal, he turned around to face Yal. This shocked Yal for a brief moment allowing the Assassin to jump up onto Yal's first blade, he then ran along it and jumped off as Yal swung his other, missing. The Assassin flipped over the head of Yal swings his staff forcing Yal to be thrown into a side of a building as Talon now rushed over to fight him.

Talon slid to take out the Assassin's feet but again he was prepared for this and jumped over as Talon came to a stop. He quickly rose to his feet as Yal joined him by his side. The Assassin landed but a few feet away from them gracefully with his back towards them.

They both attacked together, attacking low and high but the Assassin blocked each individual attack, they both paused for a quick second and attacked at the same time, one high one low. The Assassin stopped their attack and threw them back, causing them to be put off balance, he quickly struck Talon with a kick, forcing him to take a few steps back with sharp inhales. Yal retaliated striking with a quick attack, the Assassin blocked the strike but it caused the metal staff to break.

He smiles at the Assassin, the Assassin smiled back.

The metal staff now in both his hands, began to separate more revealing it to also act as a whip. The Assassin began to flail his whips everywhere kicking up dust and bits of the ground as Yal performed back flips away as the Assassin swung the whips around him. He grabbed Yal's foot with one whip and lifted him over head before finally launching him to the floor, forcing him to land painfully on the ground.

The Assassin smiled but only for a second upon noticing the many Trans-Gression members now entering the village and making their way towards him. The Assassin smiles once more, giving one last look at the twin brothers and jumps into the air, his lands on his carrier and flies away. Talon stopped next to Yal and helped him up as the TG members came over.

Drogun suddenly picks Amras up and asks 'Who the hell was that guy? And what does your boss want with these crystals'

'You mean there's more than one?' asked Amras, Drogun responds by shaking him. 'Fine he . . .—' something happened, pain crossed Amras' face as he tried to continue, '—wa . . . nts . . . to . . . be . . . come . . . a . . . G . . . O'

Amras' head fell down to his shoulders as Drogun saw the other lifeless bodies of the other mafia members. From a nearby rooftop laughter was echoing throughout the village.

'Ha-ha. I'm not returning without first completing the mission. You both require more training, I see you never learnt anything from me, see you some other time. My sons!'

The Assassin then disappeared from view once more.

'Who was that guy?' asked Varin.

'Their father, Raiden' replied an old familiar voice.

Varin turns to face the familiar voice, Commander Hobson.

'You!' Varin reaches for his gun.

Drogun grabs his arm, 'Cool it brother, he's not our enemy'

'He maybe not yours, but he is mine' Varin shakes his arm free and takes aim.

'Don't Varin—' Drogun holds his blade to the neck of Varin, '—What happened in the past, happened in the past. You were a cop now you're a civilian, a citizen of this world, a normal person'

'Much like you then?'

'No—' He lowers his sword, '—I am Rýnadaer of the elvish lands of Windor'

'Rýnadaer?'

'It means Fist of Fire, I am a Mage'

"Drogun spoke this almost as if he believed it himself, at the time I didn't believe a word of it. This is no final fantasy."

'A Mage? Ha, this is the real world there is no such thing as Mages'

Drogun lowers his blade and walks past Co Hobson.

'I hate to agree with anyone but he's right, there are Mages. Only a few but there are some' said Co Hobson

Varin once again raised his gun as other TG member came closer, helping Yal and Talon.

'Varin! Lower your weapon!' yelled Talon
'But this man is a terrorist, he and his group caused the destruction of Karves City . . .—' Varin takes in a deep breath and remembers something '—and the loss of three hundred good men and women, each with a family, at the Shenma City Police Department'

"When did that happen?"

'No. That was a cover up by SPARK CORP. they caused the destruction of Karves City' said Yal
'What about the SCPD?'
'We had no involvement in that and as far as we know neither did SPARK' spoke Co Hobson taking a few steps forward, raising his hands in the air.
'Why would SPARK harm those that swore to protect it!?'
'Easy there hero. I don't know, but if you want we can help you. Help you find the true course of why it happened.'

Varin begins to search for words, he lowers his gun.

'How . . . how did you arrive, if that's the correct word, in this time?'
'Shortly after the fall of the SCPD, I finally managed to run into the main office of SPARK Corporation. We quickly found a secret area where we found the owners frozen in these things. There was four of these pods in all.

In one of them I could clearly see had the Mr Hillweller, the owner of SPARK, and the other, who I assume was his son. The third however had two life forms in them but I could not see who they were. The last remaining pod was spare, I guess that was for their servant or something. We couldn't damage the machines, we couldn't switch them off, SPARK was already falling but I couldn't let it go to waste just so these little pricks could begin again. So I jumped in and set it a year earlier then the owners so I could continue with the fall of SPARK'

'Why, why didn't you just kill them there and then? To end it all'

'I may be known as a terrorist, but I'm no murderer.'

'So they're not out yet?' asked Talon regaining his posture

'This is true but they will be very soon'

'So why don't we plan for a massive attack?' asked Yal also regaining his posture

'Later.—' replied Co Hobson, '—For now is not the time and by the looks of things you both still need a rest. I suggest you meet up at HQ in a few days, for now go to Skyspear, no doubt your father will hunt down hero and enigma here in his search for you two.'

'The 'hero' has a name, its Varin by the way and the 'enigma' is my brother, Drogun'

'Okay. See you around . . . Varin, take care Yal, Talon 'n' Drogun'

Co Hobson walks off with the other members of TG.

'Let's get going.' said Talon

Yal led the way to the transport system with a limp, Talon stays where he was as a strange feeling washes over him, someone watching.

'Father . . . if we meet again you will die by my hand.'

Talon begins to walk towards the others, slowly catching them up. Raiden, Yal & Talon's father, is still standing on the building rooftop watching them, he heard Talon's threat. A look of rage and anger forms in Raiden's eyes, he turns away as his long brown leather jacket blows in the wind.

'Over here, ya'

He pointed towards a sky tram, a sky tram full to the brim.

'Tram's a bit full' said Varin
'They're mainly rich people passing through this hell hole of a town, this entire tram is VIP only' said Drogun.

He steps on with Yal, Talon and Varin closely behind him. Yal and Talon quickly pushed and elbowed to the back, while Varin and Drogun were stuck near the now closing door.

'This is where we came from. We were born here'
'That city was destroyed. This is a new town built on top of the old. It's nothing more than mankind trying to hide their mistakes.'

The tram begins to move, climbing up the long metal wires heading over the village's wooden walls. Beyond the village are miles and miles of wilderness, nothing but over grown grass and forests lined the way from the village to the shore. In the long grass Varin could make out the faint outline of numerous Fiends, hiding or hunting other Fiends for food. The tram soon reaches the shore and is now a good three mile above the water level, Fiends even roam in the waters of this world.

'Karves is no longer apart of the once proud continent it once was. Karves is now on an island of its own, it's big but it's cut off from the main continent—' Varin looks towards Drogun as Drogun continues to speak, '—From what I've learnt, the waters rose in 2294. Global warming was to blame as well as PHOENIX. Shortly after Karves City was destroyed, other towns and cities went, which in turn led to the warming of the planet. The polar ice caps melt, and the tides rise. Leading to this dead and decaying world.'

Yal pushes his way to the brothers.

'Hey, isn't that the singer from the Bar?'
'Yes it is, the Bar owner must of given her a ticket as payment or something' replied Drogun

Sylvia, the singer from the Bar, looks over towards Drogun and smiles, she then waves. Varin smiles in return as Drogun turns away.

An hour soon passes on board the packed tram. They finally arrive at Skyspear, Talon is the first one off the tram he then begins to look round and ask people for directions, he approaches an old man.

'Excuse me, kind sir, but could you point me and my companions in the direction of the local inn?'

The old man continues to walk, 'Fucking tourists.'

'You may have to be ruder than that, sometimes—' says Drogun as he approaches Talon with Yal and Varin. Drogun then turns to a young man, '—HEY!, which way is the inn?'

'Over there' the young man then continues walking.

Drogun begins to walk in the direction the young man pointed towards. Yal, Talon and Varin being to walk slowly behind Drogun as he led the way to the inn. He reached for the door as someone stormed out; she bumped into him causing her to drop her bag filled with paper, along with her suitcase.

He crouches down to help pick up her stuff as she mumbled in embarrassment her apologises and anger about the inn. He placed the paper back into hands and stood up; he was shocked to see her, as he stared into the dazzling green eyes of the singer from the Bar once again. She smiled at him as he passed her possessions. He apologises and then steps to one side to let her pass.

Before leaving she quietly says, 'I hope to run into you again one day.'

"She said that as she walked past me, now that I think about it maybe I should have said something in return . . . if only I knew the future."

He begins to watch her as she walks down the street searching for something. He couldn't take his eyes off her until Varin stepped in front of him.

'Thanks for waiting, even held the door open for us'

Varin, Yal and Talon then walk past as Drogun brings his attention back to inn and his face slowly turning red.

Talon walks up to the main reception desk and says, 'Two rooms please'

'Sorry the inn is full you'll have to come back some other time' replied the receptionist replies

He then leans over the desk and quietly says something to the receptionist; he then stands back as the receptionist says 'We have two rooms, prepared. Free of charge.'

'Thank you—' Talon then turns back towards the others, who are standing by the stairs, '—We're all set.'

Shocked and amazed by what just happened Varin asks 'What did you say to her?'

Talon then turns to Varin as they incline the stairs to the two rooms, 'I told her I'm a member of the Trans-Gression'

'So you just tell them that and they give you free stuff?'

'No. Only this place allows you to stay for free; the founder once was a Trans-Gression member ya see.' adds Yal

Talon hands Varin the key for his and Drogun's room. Varin and Talon were unlocking the room as Talon spoke. 'We'll have a little break for now—' Talon unlocked the room allowing Yal to enter as he continued to talk to Varin,

'—Meet up in our room a bit later so we can plan for tomorrow'

Varin nodded and entered his own room closing the door behind Drogun.

"I did nothing for the rest of the evening; I slept the remainder of the day. I could have, and probably should of asked Drogun about how he got here to . . . but I guess I felt save with him around.

Gee the past 48 hours . . . that day was the weirdest thing I've ever experienced, it's hard to believe such things happened or even could happen.

Drogun tells me he also slept, but I saw him at one point looking outside of the window, watching as the people walking through the town during the heavy down pour of rain.

Sun down soon came and I was awoken by Drogun to speak to Yal and Talon to discuss the 'action' plan for tomorrow."

'In the morning Yal and I will go to meet up with some fellow TG members and see when this attack on SPARK is. Drogun obviously you are more skilled then I or Yal, so I think it would be wise if you protect that Crystal.

However the TG knows of a PHOENIX Professor, rumour has it he helped develop it into shields for SPARK. His name is Professor Valiant Shirriff. He'll be in the nearby forest. He's experienced with PHOENIX and should soon work out why this crystallised form of PHOENIX is important to those mafia guys.'

'Can he be trusted—' Drogun turns away from the window to speak to Talon, rain drops now beating down on the window, '—Is he still on the SPARK payroll or does he work for the TG?'

'SPARK once tried to kill him, we offered protection obviously he accepted.'

'That's all I need to know.' Drogun began to make his way towards the door.

'Your leaving now?' asked Yal

'I work best in the cover of darkness' he opens the door as Varin turns

'Don't you need a torch?'

'I already have one.'

With a blink of an eye he disappeared as the door suddenly closed by itself. The faint smell of burning wood was left behind as Varin turned back to Yal and Talon.

'What about me?'

'Have fun ya, while we're gone.' said Yal

Talon then stands up

'Try some shops to get some more ammo for your gun, get some food as well you haven't had something since we left camp. Here—' Talon throws a small bag towards Varin, containing one thousand Gillians, '—Yes, well I think now we should get some rest for tomorrow. It could be more . . . eventful.'

Varin returns to his room. He opens the door and sees there's a note on the floor. He slowly lowers himself down to pick up the folded piece of paper.

'I wish to thank you for what you did back in Karves.

Please meet with me tonight by the water tower,
I wish to thank you in person.

PS. Thank you for helping me earlier . . .'

The rest of the letter is wet and the writing is smudged and impossible to read. Varin stands back up, with the note in hand, and closes the door behind him. He places it onto a table close to the door. He strolls towards the bed but suddenly a thought entered his head, one word, five letters.

He runs back over to the note. The hand writing . . . it looks similar to hers, could it be?

"The first thought that crossed my mind was that she had also appeared in this time, my mind was suddenly plagued with thoughts of he. Thoughts about the good times we had together."

Varin ran towards the door to meet up with the writer of the letter, hoping it was Emily.

CHAPTER 10

Fall of SPARK

HE QUIETLY SHUTS the door behind him, it locks itself as he makes his way down the stairs to the entrance of the inn as each wooden step creaks under his feet. As he draws closer he begins to hear the receptionist, asleep at her desk. He moves even more quietly now on the ground floor as again each wooden floor board creaks as he heads towards the door.

Even the doors itself creaked as Varin began to slowly open it. He dared not open it any more in case the receptionist was to awake, he slipped through the small gap and ran down the mud path to reach the water tower. The rain now beats down harder, glistening in the moonlight of the night.

Varin comes to the cross road ten foot steps away from the Inn. One way, to the north, leads to a graveyard and an exit leading to a nearby forest town. Another, to the east, leads to the exit of the town, the third, to the south, leads back to the Inn and the final road, to the west, leads to the centre of the town and the water tower.

The area is used as the main of town, where the town hall and most stores reside, this town is much bigger that of Karves Village.

Varin begins to make his way down to this road to reach the water tower, making a mental note of the shops along the way.

As he finally arrives at the town hall, he sees that the water tower is hidden in shadow from the town hall, although off the ground by a good seven feet, isn't much of a tower at all, more of an over grown water barrel.

Walking in and now almost soaked he stands underneath the tower Varin stands under to the tower, almost walking into one of the towers four legs in the dark.

Ten minutes soon pass and nothing yet, not even the sound of roaming pets or worse Fiends, but suddenly he hears footsteps behind him. He quickly turns around. All he sees is a silhouette of a female walking towards him, one name instantly pops into his name. Emily.

He goes to call her name but suddenly he's kissed by her before he can even open his mouth. She opens her eyes as a flash of light begins to shine from the distance, the light reveals Varin's face to her. She instantly stops and begins to back off.

The women spurts out the words, 'Oh no.'

Shocked by what she has just done, whilst holding her hand over her mouth, she turns and runs flees. Varin opens his eyes once more shocked by what just happened simply because he wasn't expecting it, but that doesn't mean he wasn't enjoying it. He sees the silhouette run off into the distance, now revealed by the moonlight, who she is,

'Sylvia?'

Varin just looks on confused and wondering why would she run off like that, so suddenly. He decides to return to the Inn.

The next day, Varin wakes up, still fully dressed, lying on his bed in the Inn's room. He gives out a yawn and raises his head to find Drogun, looking out of the window once more. Varin then notices something shine from the corner of his eye, to his left a box of ammo and the blue PHOENIX crystal upon his chest. It begins to shine brighter but with no daylight shining upon it. Varin begins to stare at it almost hypnotically as if it is alive. The crystal suddenly stops shining as Drogun turns, 'Morning.'

Drogun then looks back out of the window.

'Morning . . . what you doing up?'
'Just admiring the weather.'

The room then lights up from a flash of lighting closely followed by the sound of thunder. Varin begins to rise from his bed now fully awaken with the crystal in hand. The sound of heavy rain pounding down on the tin rooftops.
Varin asks, 'It's still raining? Thought that would of stopped by now.'

He stands by Drogun, both look out of the window as Drogun replies, 'That's what Skyspear is famous for . . .—'Drogun then turns away from the window and walks towards the door, '—its rain.'

He opens the door with a loud creak, Varin turns and asks, 'Drogun, where are you going?'

Drogun pulls up the hood of his long coat and says, 'I'm off to find Yal and Talon, they've been gone for far too long.'
'I'll come with you.'

"As we stepped out from the inn, the skies seemed to open up, the rain quickly become much heavier, with every drop it felt like someone knocking on your head asking if someone was home, luckily it suddenly stopped. And I noticed someone in the graveyard, Sylvia."

Sylvia entered the graveyard to pay her respects; she lowered to place some flowers as she kneelt before a grave and lowered her head.
A Fiend slowly entered the town limits and began to stalk towards Sylvia, quietly as it possibly could.

Varin turned to Drogun to say, 'Drogun look!'

But before Varin had a chance to, Drogun was already running towards the graveyard. Varin then began to follow.

"I was reminded of someone as I ran towards the graveyard, I wanted to save Sylvia because . . . because she seemed like no one else I'd met before, with all my might I ran as fast as I could."

'Stand back!' yelled Drogun to Sylvia, she couldn't hear.

Varin suddenly stopped in his tracks as he saw the Fiend ready to attack her, they wouldn't make it in time, he drew his gun to attempt a shot, but it was too dangerous. Either Drogun or Sylvia would be shot from that distance. Drogun was twenty foot from her and lying in front of him was a waist high brick wall with a metal spiked railing making it a foot higher. He jumps the wall with ease.

He can now see the Fiend clearly, a Tri-han, a wolf like creature with a much larger head, taller shoulders bones and a poisonous bite. He was now ten foot away.

Sylvia finally stopped paying her respects, some tears crawling down her face. She casually stands up, wiping the tears from her check. She opened her eyes and raised her head. Her face turned from sorrow to rage as she turned to face the Tri-han, revealing her weapon a folded up staff from behind her back, she held it out with one hand and it instantly folded out to reveal its true form, a deadly Scythe.

With one mighty swing, the Tri-han's head was disconnected from its body. It still attempted to attack, now headless. The head flew towards Drogun, he stopped in his tracks and raised his sword cutting the head in half. The Fiend now lay in three pieces as Drogun lowered his weapon.

Sylvia then refolded the Scythe back into a stick and placed it into the sleeve of her dress.

'Thanks for your help but I can look after my—'
The Fiend's headless body had enough strength for one last attack, it reached out it's leg and sharp claws to attack

Sylvia. Instantly thinking, Drogun raised his weapon once more and grabbed a hold of Sylvia. He span her around his back swinging the sword while doing so. The creature now laid, dead, in four pieces.

'—self.' said Sylvia finishing her sentence.

'Maybe with a little more training.'

Drogun then put his sword away, he gave her a little nod and walked out of the small graveyard, Varin finally reached the entrance.

'W . . . What happened? Is it gone?'
'Yeah it's been dealt with'
'What about her, maybe she could join us? We are going somewhere else after this right? We could do some training on the way there' said Varin

Drogun stared at his brother and replied, 'We have better things to do.'

'It's okay, I'm off to find someone . . . so I'll be on my way, thanks guys. Bye.'

She then walks past Varin and Drogun. Towards the north exit of the town.

"Drogun then muttered something to himself as she walked away, I never asked him what he said that day."

"Bye is forever. Later is later."

'There you two are—' spoke Yal, '—we've been looking for you.'
'We came looking for you as well.' replied Varin

'We're gonna make our way to Shenma City, the TG are going to attack the main factory there.' said Talon.

Drogun then stood surprised by this announcement, 'Shenma City? That place is surrounded by Hunters and no one leaves which means no one gets in.'

Talon then takes one step forward and places his left hand on Drogun's shoulder, 'We've found away . . . but first we must meet with the others and then the attack can begin. However we brought you here to meet someone Varin.—' he removed his hand from Drogun's shoulder and turned towards Varin, '—Hopefully you would find someone you knew, and that person turned out to be your brother, although I would like to know truly where you are from, it's now up to you if you wish to join us.'

Yal and Talon begin to walk towards the north exit, leading to the powerful Shenma City. Varin stood in the graveyard contemplating, he turned to Drogun. Before he could speak Drogun spoke while staring into nothingness, 'Go . . .'

Varin was puzzled his quick comment. He then run and quickly court up with Yal and Talon. Drogun remained there at the graveyard entrance, he removed his hood and looked up into the sky to feel the rain, now beginning again, land onto his face.

'This isn't a part of my mission . . . but I suppose I could do with a little more training. I hope you'll still watch over me master.'

He pulled the hood back up as he lowered his head down and begins to take a one step forward when suddenly he hears a noise from behind him, he quickly looks behind him. He sees nothing, just the exit out of town; he turns back and begins to walk towards the direction of the others.

Not long after him, Sylvia climbs from behind the small wall and begins follow them from a distance.

'We'll keep to the main path, it may take an hour or so longer to reach Shenma but it would be much safer than going through the forest.'

Drogun said nothing, Varin nodded with agreement after getting a few supplies.

'Keep up, ya.'

They ran off, heading to the north away from the town. Drogun and Varin began to follow. They soon left the area of rain hanging over Skyspear, four miles away from the town, twelve more to go to the rendezvous.

'Yal We'll take a break here.' said Talon
'Why? we're two miles away the rendezvous.'
'For Varin.'

They sat down by the side of the road, leaning against the trees for some shade. Drogun shortly arrived and sat next to Yal whom offered a drink of water. Varin arrived a minute later, tired and dragging his feet.

"But he kept walking, not for a second did he think about stopping. He never spoke as he passed us. His actions spoke louder than words."

The group looked on as he passed and decided to continue and march forth like him.

Thirty minutes later, they arrived at a cross roads. Straight on and another six miles would lead them to the outer edge of Shenma City.

'Straight on will lead directly to Shenma City, we don't want that. Keep a look out for a red ribbon.' said Talon.

'But . . . I . . . I thought—' spoke Varin still panting for air '—we wanted to go . . . th . . . there.'

'Indeed we do, but if we go any closer we may be picked up by Hunters.'

'Hunters?'

'Machines, much like those robots back at the Bar. Only less human, more pain, more death.' spoke Drogun.

'Over here! I found a ribbon they lead into the forest.' yelled Yal.

Another hour or so walk following reds ribbons led them to a clearing, deep within the forest. Many members of the Trans-Gression were already there sitting against the trees, on the ground or on fallen tree logs, their leader Co Hobson was stood in front of them all. His mind, fixed upon the speech he was about to give. Varin fell to the floor to take a seat on the ground, Yal sat in front of him and Talon remained near the back also sitting on the ground. Drogun remained stood up, leaning against a tree. Co Hobson began to walk back and forth as the members began to fall quiet now that the group had finally arrived.

He finally stopped and faced them, 'Brothers, sisters. We now have a way to stop SPARK from destroying this once great planet. Many of you will think that there is no safe passage to or from Shenma City because of the Hunters and the PHOENIX Shield, but let me tell you . . . there is. In the year 2268 I and a handful of others attacked the SPARK Corp Generator in Gade City. But we were stopped—' Co Hobson takes a look at Varin before continuing, '—by a hero and thus we had failed to stop that generator supplying Shenma City with enough power for SPARK's own person defence machines in areas of the city. Had we knocked that generator offline, SPARK would have ended there.—' The members of the TG began to slowly smile. '—I think you're all catching on now. We attack the Gade City generator.'

Voices of the members began to rise, Varin became lost within his own thoughts.

"Is this world my fault? What if I . . . I . . . no we, we stopped them. My fault?"

'Yes that's it. If we destroy it or at least take it offline then the PHOENIX Shield in Shenma City will shut down along with the defensive capabilities and their precious machines, allowing us to gain entry and exit of Shenma City. Now to do this we all will need to go to Gade City to destroy the generator. One group will have to leave as soon as its offline to enter the city while the other remain to fight off any guards or whatever they send to turn it back online—'

He turns away from the members for a second and turns to face them once more, sorrow now seemed to be trembling in his voice.

'—some of you may not return, but know this, on this day SPARK will fall and today will always be remembered as the fall of SPARK!'

They cheer once more but silence falls over the clearing once more, although the smiles of many stay.

'Sir, how will enter Shenma? If we're all in Gade City an hour or so away.' asked Yal.

'We will be air lifted into the city and we'll attack from two areas, the main lobby entrance and the rooftop. Lieutenant Talon, you and your team along with me will begin the attack from the main entrance to the building. Lieutenants Marko, you will enter from the rooftop along with your team. Any further questions?' No one spoke or moved until Co Hobson yelled to the members 'Okay dismissed.'

All the members began to raise to their feet, picking up their backpacks and weapons before setting off towards Gade City.

'Marko, Talon can you bring your team over here please.'

Four people, including Marko walked towards Co Hobson. The other TG members were already heading towards Gade City, Varin looked round and saw no one else around.

'Varin, Drogun. Sorry I never asked but I hoped you both would be in my team.' said Talon

'Fine with me.' replied Drogun

Varin smiled and they both began to walk towards Co Hobson, whom led them to a random area, filled with trees, a short distance away from the clearing.

'Marko begin flight preparations. Varin, I think you will remember this.'

Co Hobson reached into his jacket pocket and removed a small thumb sized controller, upon this controller was one circular button. He pressed the button, the area around them almost seemed to dissolve, revealing that this thick area of trees is actually a clearing. Which in the location is a Helicopter from 2268.

'It's the Apache that chased me, Craig and . . . Emily.' said Varin

"Craig . . . that was his name. If this world is my fault, are their deaths also my burden?"

Varin then begins to remember that mission but more importantly Emily, flash backs of her. Flash backs of their last night together as a couple. The night of the prom.

2266,
Five months before Varin enrols into the Police Training Centre (PTC).

It's the farewell Prom for Varin's school, Shenma Comprehensive School. Varin is still the relationship with Emily.

Within the hall of the school is the prom, many people are enjoying themselves, laughing amongst friends, dancing, enjoying the atmosphere of the event, except one.

Varin sat alone in the corner of the hall. Everyone else is up on the dance floor. His thoughts have been plaguing him recently. Today is the remembrance day of the Karves Incident.

His thoughts concerned his future and his past. The death of his family, the destruction of his home town. The job he wishes to have. He has in front of him an unfolded piece of paper, his exam results. All his grades for each of his subjects are D's or at most a single C.

"The choice was mine alone; I didn't know what I needed to be done at the time until Emily came to speak to me."

'Varin, we need to talk.'

She grabs his hand and drags him from the hall, to the outside to talk. She starts to become upset at what she is about to say, 'Varin . . . . over the last year you've kept me away from knowing the real you. I became a great friend to know you better but still you kept to yourself, and I've tried so many times . . . but you kept pushing me away from you.

I'm your girlfriend and yet still you, you push me away. I'm here for you.—' she pauses expecting an answer from Varin, he says nothing and so she continues, '—For a long time you wouldn't even allow me to see your room at the Orphanage. Every other child's room was filled with bright beautiful colours but yours, yours was like a prisoner's room and you even had news clippings of the incident—' Emily begins to cry, Varin attempts to speak but doesn't know what to say, he instead places his arms around her, she pushes him away, '—even now, you feel so distant. You need to stop living in the past Varin and move one but right now you're not and you're taking me with you.'

'Emily, I'm sorry but what . . . what are you trying to say Emily?'

'I think we should break up.'

Emily's eyes now flooded with tears. She lets go of Varin and makes her way back inside to be with her friends. Varin remained outside, stunned and heartbroken. He then begins to walk off towards his home Karves City, twenty four miles away. Varin begins to walk off in tears.

CHAPTER 11

The Storming of Gade

'IT LOOKS LIKE you've modified the Apache—' said Drogun, snapping Varin from his day dream, '—you've combined it with a Hind D or vice versa it seems. What does this thing run on?'

Co Hobson takes a couple of steps along the chopper, 'Yes we did, its purpose now is to carry our men around faster to help defeat SPARK. The chopper runs off diesel.'

'But all fossil fuels were used up back in 2210.'

'True, but we managed to collect the fuel from around the world. It's the same with the other vehicles really, it took us years to get enough to run his thing, most of its fuel we used back in 2268.' replied Co Hobson as he began to wipe the chopper with a cloth.

'Other vehicles?'

'Yes, we have three early 20th century cars known back then as "Sport Cars." We've modified them also, to run on PHOENIX fuel—' he pauses for a second, '—of course these things are still dangerous because of the PHOENIX but at least if they were to blow, it won't be as strong as an atom bomb.'

'But you mixed them with PHOENIX, wouldn't they still pose a threat if they were to blow up?' asked Talon

'No, the PHOENIX acts like an extra boost. When heated this will give them more power thus more speed until they cool down once again. You'll be able to get from one side of this continent to the other in under an hour.—' Co Hobson throws the cloth to the floor and turns to face the group. '—Anyway the reason why I showed you this is because we will be using this thing to get into Shenma City, I wanted to warn you guys that we will be using PHOENIX in it as well. You may back out now if you wish not to take part in the main assault. We only have enough fuel for it to get us from Gade City to Shenma's SPARK Corporation building, after that it could be seconds before it decides to fail.'

'How is it going to get to Gade city to begin with?' asks Varin

Co Hobson reaches into his pocket and pulls out a small crystallised PHOENIX gem, 'With this, Crystallised PHOENIX. This PHOENIX holds more energy and is less likely to blow. In the centre of this crystal is fossilised fuel we created it using a form of fusion, we call it Solidus Fuel. We simply mixed the PHOENIX with the fossil fuel diesel to create this fuel hybrid. PHOENIX can combine with anything, even humans.'

The group look on confused, Drogun smirks slightly as Co Hobson continues with regret in his voice.

'Ten years ago, I, Marko here and a fellow member managed to get inside one of SPARK's buildings, the main one in Shenma. We purely went there just for reconnaissance. We got to the lower levels of the building to where they create, dig, house or whatever the hell they do with PHOENIX. The way we snuck into the place led us to this small one man catwalk'

Back in that room housing PHOENIX, Co Hobson remembers it well, the smell of stale air mixed with the fumes of the fuel. It was almost choking.

'What the hell is this?' said Marko

'Looks like a storage area?' replied the new guy

'Storage? I thought they would make or at least dig up the stuff here. We need to get a closer look—' he turns to the new guy, '—Hey newbie, you led us in here. Where do we go from here to get down this floor?'

'There should be a catwalk along this path that will lead us to a room with stairs which will take us down.'

Co Hobson leads the way if the other two shortly behind and come to the catwalk high above the open vats of PHOENIX. He steps onto it and it shakes.

'Okay we'll need to go one at a time space out'

He continues to step forward, this time I little more gingerly.

'The last person across was the new guy, an alarm was raised or something and we were confronted by guards on both sides. The bridge giveaway from under him as we ran and he fell into the PHOENIX, he began to drown. There was nothing we could do, two weeks later we saw him again but he changed, he was another person. He had long White hair, white as the moon.—'

Shocked, Drogun reacted to Co Hobson's words 'White as the moon . . .'

"Blood Moon."

'—He attacked us, almost killed me until he said something like "Planet, element crystals" he then disappeared and we never saw him again.'

Varin noticed the look of shock and concern on Drogun's face as Lieutenant Marko of the TG jumped into the chopper after finishing a few tests.

'What is it Drogun?'
'Huh? . . . Nothing for now, just a fear'

Co Hobson places the Solidus Fuel into the fuel tank. The engines roared to life and the blades begin to rotate.

'A fear of what?'
'Things to come'

Hobson hopped into the chopper.

'Anyway, the others will reach Gade City in two hours, you guys will be able to be air lifted to Gade along with Marko's team, and we'll prepare for the others once we get there. Hop in.'

Every member of the group entered the Chopper, but Drogun remained standing where he was. He begins to slowly back away from the chopper as if a fear fell over him. The others look on, concerned Varin yells, 'What's wrong!?'

Drogun backs up to a tree, Varin goes to speak but is distracted as Drogun suddenly dives his hands into the bushes beside the tree. He pulls and throws someone from the bushes to the floor, Sylvia.

'What are you doing here?' asked Drogun.

'I . . . I . . . followed you guys. I overheard, I . . . wished to meet with the Commander—' she replied in shock from being caught, no one normally catches her when she's sneaky. She looks up to see Co Hobson staring back at her, '—Hobson. Sir . . . I wish to . . . to become a member.'

'Meh, Drogun we gotta go' yelled Co Hobson over the roaring of the choppers blades.

'What about her? The Chopper can't carry us all'

Sylvia finally court her breath, stood up 'Commander, I wish to become a member of the Trans-Gression.'

Co Hobson nodded, 'Welcome aboard, but you'll have to walk to Gade City. Drogun lets go.'

But Drogun just stood there, 'I'll walk, it won't be correct to leave anyone behind. Besides I'm not a fan of heights.'

Varin, looked on, he seen his brother do this before, be the hero, the nice guy for no reward in return. The thought of Sylvia's kiss crossed his mind, maybe he could talk to her what that was all about?

"That's when I realised, the note wasn't meant for me, it was for Drogun."

They look cute together he thought. The Chopper began to take off.

'Wait . . . I'll walk also Hobson' called out Varin.

"I hadn't spent that much time with my brother yet, I thought the walk could do us some good."

Varin popped out of the Chopper, along with Yal & Talon.

'We'll also walk Commander.' said Talon
'Fine, we'll meet you at Gade City in two hours. Let's go, cya later hero'

The blades roared back into action, lifting it off the ground. It soon took off and was out of sight as the group began their journey to Gade City through the forest leaving the road Shenma City in the distance.

An hour had passed since the group set off, reaching the jungle surrounding Gade City. The journey until now was easy, as for each step they took, they could feel the temperature rise.

Varin walked towards the back with Yal and Talon on either side, he hadn't worked out what to speak about to Drogun yet, it's been ten years since they last spoke. Sylvia followed behind Drogun, doing a little jog every now and then to keep up to his pace. The road was quiet.

'Thank you—' spoke Sylvia, breaking the silence as she jogged to be by his side, '—for walking with me, but you didn't have to.'

'I'm sorry. I've walked a long and lonely road a number of times, it doesn't get easier' replied Drogun.

'I would have been okay on my own' said Sylvia,

Drogun stopped in his tracks, standing still as his eyes swept the jungle, 'Not in this part . . .'

They all hear something in the trees running around the group, the others stopped shortly behind Drogun.

'What is it?' asked Varin
'Ya, I don't hear . . .'
'Sssh'
The noise begins to get louder and closer. They each move their hand closer to their weapons, Drogun moves to stand next to Varin as he places his hand over the grip of the gun.

'Don't pull the trigger' Drogun whispered.

Something large, muscular, blue and loud jumps through the vines, leafs and trees in front of them, scattering the group, except for Drogun. Sylvia falls to the floor as the creature almost lands on her. It growls and snarls at the group, upon noticing Sylvia between its legs it moves in closer showing its teeth and fangs.

The twins reveal their weapons ready to attack. Varin raises his gun from its holster to aim it at the creature, Drogun then pushed Varin's aim away from the creature and begins to speak to it in a language no one understands.

It begins to calm the creature, as Drogun begins to pet it and rub his hand amongst its large fur leading to the light blue mane around its head, as I he does this it begins to purr a little.

'This Fiend is no threat, this is a Togu. We in the elvish land use the Togu to travel great distances, we could use it to reach Gade City within mere minutes.'

Drogun holds out a hand to help up Sylvia whilst keeping his eyes on the Togu, she pulls herself up as he places her hand on the brow of the creature. Varin looks on in amazement.

'Will it be able to take us all to Gade City?'

Drogun takes a second to answer Sylvia's question, but Talon cut him off before he had a chance to speak, 'My brother and I will use the trees, after all we are Ninjas.'

Talon begins to bow, his normal gesture of farewell for now, Yal rushed off into the surrounding jungle.

"Yal is such a kooky guy, here we are marching to a battle and he thought now was the best time to have a race, haha gotta love that guy sometimes."

Talon begins to stand up straight and within a blink of an eye, he too ran off, quickly catching his brother. Varin watched as they used their speed to quickly run up one of the trees and begin to leap from treetop to branch on their way to Gade City.

'That's unfair!' yelled Varin

'Varin!—' called out Drogun now sitting upon the Togu, '—They want a race, they got one'

Varin runs up to Drogun and the Togu, as Drogun turns it around. Varin jumps on from the back as Sylvia runs up to the side, Drogun offers a hand to help her, a little reluctant to accept at first but then takes Drogun's hand.

She sits in front of him as she says, 'Let's Go'

'Hold on,—Neua!'

The Togu suddenly bursts into a run leaving nothing but dust and claw prints in the ground behind them.

~~∾∾◦∾∾~~

Within ten minutes they reached the city limits of Gade City. As they got closer and closer to the City they began to hear off in the distance the sound of battle, gun fire, explosions and the Chopper.

The battle only took place near the generator, away from the civilian homes that watched the battle from the hills. Drogun stopped the Togu before they got any further.

'Draw your weapons . . . we're going to rush past them and go straight for the generator'

Varin and Sylvia nodded as they both drew their weapons. Drogun, took a second and then kicked his heels into the Togu commanding it to go as fast as it could. With a blink of an eye the Togu shot off, roaring as it ran past those trying to defend the generator. They stormed by security guards each one holding a gun, attempting to stop the TG members.

As the Togu stormed passed these men they'd try grabbing them, Drogun swiped at the ones trying to grab them or attack the Togu from the left, Sylvia was doing the same protecting the right with her Scythe.

Varin stood balancing himself upon the back of the Togu, ignoring the explosions around him to clear their path by shooting any guard that got in their way, but not to kill, to injure. Every slight bump would cause Varin from time to time hold out his hands to help him balance. Up ahead he could see one guard preparing for them, turning a lance toward them from a fallen TG member, Varin took his aim, shot injuring the man, but he remained where he was.

Varin aimed again but as he did the Togu jumped over a body of a guard, causing him to fall. Drogun raised out his left hand to grab Varin by the collar of his shirt and threw him back up as the Togu neared the guard with the lance. He took aim one last time to take out the arm of the man, he dropped the lance as the Togu now jumped over him.

At the top of the mountain range near the generator Varin could see the Chopper hovering as well as seeing Yal and Talon fighting ten guards on their own, other TG members tried to help but were easily beaten back by the ten guards, the high ranking officials of the station.

As Varin, Drogun and Sylvia rushed towards them on the Togu an explosive device went off from underneath. It sent each of them flying, Drogun off into a nearby tree hitting spine first, Varin was flung forward along the dirt road and Sylvia was pinned underneath the Togu.

Catching his breath again Drogun slowly crawled towards Sylvia to check up on her, she was alive, knocked out but still breathing—barely.

Varin slowly began to stand up slightly deaf from the exposition. Still dazed he turned to see Drogun yelling at him but couldn't make out the words until the Chopper overhead came close to see if they were okay, his hearing quickly returned. He now heard his brother calling for him, he turned back from the Chopper to see Drogun near the Togu.

'Varin! Go on a head!' shouted Drogun.

Varin nodded and began to make his way towards the generator. Drogun stayed behind to get the lifeless Togu off of Sylvia. Something from the corner of his eye, glistened the PHOENIX Crystal that was once in his pocket now laid by the paw of the Togu. He ignored it that for now continuing to try and lift the Togu off of Sylvia.

It was no easy task but it began to slowly move, but it was too heavy for him to lift. Its paw inched closer and closer to the PHOENIX Crystal. It began to sparkle wildly until its paw finally touched the Crystal.

He tried one last push as he noticed something, noticed something quite impossible. The Togu began to breathe again as its eyes opened wide. It stretched out it's legs and got up, moving away from Drogun and Sylvia.

Sylvia suddenly coughed and gasped for air, Drogun sat her up but looked at the Togu in shock, she to begin staring at the Togu.

"How did it come back to life . . . it was dead. Wasn't it?"

Varin finally reached the top to regroup with Yal and Talon, his head still ringing a little. As he approached they were no longer surround by the ten officials standing in their way, they were not surrounded by the ten officials, unconscious, laying on the ground. However one managed to close and lock the massive steel gate to the building, stopping the TG from gaining access. This one guard even managed to destroy the control panel.

Talon then pulled out a two way radio, 'Commander, can you use the rockets on that thing to blow it?'
A few seconds of quiet and then the reply, 'Clear the area!'

Varin, Yal & Talon begin to drag all the unconscious guards away from the gate as Co Hobson prepares to fire the four rockets. He first lines himself up and holds the position.

Co Hobson is prepared to fire, he then says over the radio, 'Preparing to fire, all clear?'
'All clear'
'Fox one . . .'

CHAPTER 12

Assault on SPARK

HE FIRES THE first rocket closely followed by rocket two, three and four. As the rockets hit smoke from the blast begins to crowd the area and the sound of a loud thump against the steel door, the smoke begins to lessen as the large steel doors begin to fall flat on the floor shaking the ground and picking up dust from the ground. Co Hobson lowers the Chopper as the rest of the TG group run towards the generator.

Drogun and Sylvia reach the top of the range, with Sylvia sitting upon the Togu.

'Talon, get in!' roared Co Hobson over the Chopper.

Drogun is about to join them but quickly turns to Sylvia, 'Wait here'
She then grabs his arm, 'I can go as well'

She drops down from the Togu, her ankle gives way underneath, the reason why she was on the Togu to begin with.

'Not with that ankle. Look the TG have driven back SPARK, you'll be safe for now but you need to leave as soon as possible, this is no place for you—' he then points to the Togu, '—Look after her'

He runs over to the chopper.

'I can look after myself.' she said in a sad tone.

As the Chopper lifted off many TG members, ran up not totally sure of what to do now that their leaders had gone. Sylvia rose to her feet, using her Scythe as support around her left arm.

'I'm in charge here—' she yelled '—half of you go shut down the generator and prepare to defend the main entrance. The other half, come with me!'
'Why should we listen to you?' said one of the members

Suddenly two remaining SPARK guards attack her from behind, grabbing her arms in the process, she kicks one with her right foot as she stands captured. She sweeps round knocking the other off his feet with the metal stick of her scythe, getting back to her feet she kicks him, knocking him out.
It all happened so fast even the Togu wasn't prepared by the time it snarled at them they were already unconscious on the floor.

'Any other questions?'

They break up into groups, half go into the factory as the rest begin to climb back down the hill following Sylvia. Her plan is simple, hold the line, and so they approach the houses to set up a trap for anyone that attempts to switch the generator back on. The Togu stays close to her.

Shortly afterward the shield and at Shenma shut down, the people begin to panic on the streets of Shenma City.

'The Fiends?!'
'The Fiends are attacking!'
'NO, it's the TG.'
'Erm . . . sir, excuse me sir.'
'Yes I know, servant—' spoke Diamond Hillweller, residing in his office at the SPARK HQ overlooking the streets below, '—send fourth one hundred of my men to protect the city.'
'And the other three hundred sir?'
'Turn on the Gade City generator.'
'Very well sir'
'Oh . . . one last thing servant, prepare to awaken my son.'

Old 20th century busses and vans left from the SPARK Corp. main building carrying Diamond Hilweller's private army known as FOX (Fouilleur Of X-tal.) Created by his son for the soul purpose to defeat the Trans-Gression and unlike the them, FOX carry and use weapons to kill. FOX members are supplied with Sub-machine guns and wear protective clothing similar to the 20th century British special forces counter-terrorism group the SAS. Kevlar shin guards, Kevlar bullet proof vests and Kevlar helmets.

The busses and vans divide up amongst the streets of the city, keeping order in the city stopping any riots that may occur while the other three hundred men in their busses had one destination, one mission in mind. To restart that generator in Gade City.

Over head the chopper passed by.

Diamond saw it approaching the city limits, nothing could stop it, but he simply smiled.

'Fools.'

He walks away from the window and enters the other room.

'Okay this is it. Prepare for war.' said Co Hobson to the group.

Marko landed the chopper onto the street in front of the main entrance and allowed them to get out before rising to the roof for his team to attack.

Co Hobson led the way into the building, followed closely by Talon, Yal, Drogun and Varin.

'Do not pull out your weapons unless absolutely necessary.' said Talon

'Stop right there,—' said a security guard, with his arm out baring their entrance '—I'll need you to leave. The building is experiencing technical problems'

"At least that's what the guy would have said if Co Hobson allowed him to continue after uttering the words 'The building'"

Co Hobson grabbed the man's right arm with his left and give a sharp punch into the guards rips before flipping him over to the ground.

"CQC. Kinda made me smile knowing that my former enemy knew the same technique as me."

They continued onward and upward, receiving little to no resistance.

Marko's men on the other hand received most of the attention from the guards, who were armed with submachine guns. The chopper barely landed before it was sprayed with bullets from five armed guards. The TG members sneaked out the side, the five guards smiled as their clips emptied assuming the TG members were dead.

They began to even laugh until the side door was kicked down by one of the TG members, Marko himself, revealing a chain gun. Marko smiled.

Each of the guards threw down their weapons and began to beg for their lives, the other TG members quickly tied them up. The TG members removed their weapons and ammunition then stood behind Marko once more. He opened fire, bullet shells were thrown from the chain gun spitting out onto the floor, all the bullets however were blanks as the TG members and Marko began to laugh.

'Rebels, but not murders'

Two members of his team stayed behind to watch the guards as the others now equipped with weapons to defend themselves went down two floors to confront the owners of SPARK.

They soon arrived on the floor where they'll find the Hillweller's grand office. They quickly approached the rooms double doors, however noticing the plastic sheet lying from the door to the other side of the hall and up the wall, they ignore it, behind the door is the owners without a doubt, they decided to proceed without Co Hobson. Marko kicked up the door as the other flanked in behind, no one was in sight other than a white cloud of steam.

The room begins to feel cold as if they walked into a freezer. It begins to clear as standing right in front of them a twenty-ish year old man with his hand on the hilt of a weapon, the steam was still hiding his face and weapon.

'Halt. Who are you? What are you doing here?' asks Marko raising his gun along with the other TG members.

'Are you threatening me?' asks the stranger.

'Who are you?' Marko asks again.

'It's treason then?'

'What?!'

The strange reaches for this sword and before Marko and his team realise he is standing behind them. He places his blade back away into his case. When he slams the blade into the case Marko and his team fall to the floor dead and in pieces. He returns to the room.

'Marko we're on the floor now, what is your current location?—' asks Co Hobson over a radio, no response, '—Marko . . . come in'

'Trouble?' says Varin

'We'll press on. That's what we're set on doing here right? We knew there would be deaths' says Talon to Co Hobson.

Walking up a more steps of the stairs, they come to the hallway, Hobson checks to see the way is clear, his face suddenly turns to shock, disgust and rage as he sees the remains of the team lying in the hallway on the plastic sheet. Suddenly the sheet is dragged into the room.

At the very thought that his team members, his friends, may of been killed stunned Co Hobson but by seeing their lifeless bodies in pieces. His anger took over.

'ALRIGHT, LETS GET THOSE FUCKERS!' roared Co Hobson with deep anger in his voice, but Drogun stepped in front of him blocking his path.

'Don't make this personal. The death of someone you know can be heart breaking, but this isn't a personal vendetta this is to save many more lives. The lives of a nation, the lives of every man, women and child on this planet. Down with SPARK Corp . . . Not death to SPARK Corp.'

'THEY NEED TO PAY FOR THIS' yelled Hobson once more.

'Then go home, we'll take over from here'

Co Hobson's anger subsided and Drogun took lead, leading them to the room. He pulled out his sword and kicked down the door. Their stood a man in a white suit, slicked back white hair and green eyes. Drogun pulled up his blade to the stranger's throat.

'Are you the owner?'

He remained quiet.

'Are you the owner?' Drogun repeated once more.
'Are you threatening me?' he replied.

Drogun removed the weapon from his throat.

'No, just looking for someone.'
The others walked in as a man from up a short flight of stairs called down, 'The owners are not here they already left, I believe they took that chopper'
'Show yourself' yelled up Co Hobson.

The man climbed down the stairs, a short, balding, overweight man reached the bottom of the stairs. He too had white hair and brown eyes.

'Are these them Hobson?' asked Varin.
'No, I don't recognise these men. What are your names?' asked Co Hobson
'I am Thorn Collina. This man is my father, Diamant Collina'
'What are you doing here?' asked Yal
'We, my son and I, intended to also kill the owners of SPARK so that our world can be saved.'
'May I join your group?—' asked Thorn '—I've always been a keen fan of the TG'

'Now is not the time for enrolment—' spoke Co Hobson, that sick thought of his friends dead once again passes through his mind '—you, did you kill my men?'

'Your men? Oh the men carrying the SMG's. My son killed them'

Yal then revealed his weapons and attacked Thorn, with every attack from Yal. Thorn managed to dodge it or block both of Yal's blades with his sword, a katana, still in its case.

He smiles as Yal stopped

'I assumed they were apart of FOX, they did not identify themselves'

'Yal, now is not the time we must leave' spoke Talon

They all turned to leave the room.

'May I join you' asked Thorn once more.

'No, you may not join Trans-Gression' replied Co Hobson

Thorn became angry, 'I must insist, I would be very . . .'

The power came back on and with it the alarm for the building quickly echoed, FOX members will be on their way. An elevator door to the side of the group disguised as a wall of books opened.

'We gotta leave. Now!' said Co Hobson

'Go to the fifth floor, there's a parking lot you can use that to escape' said Thorn

'You're still not joining us.'

The group get in and elevator doors shut. Leaving Thorn and his father still standing in the main room.

'Son, follower them. Let me and SPARK know of their plans'

Thorn nodded, he turned to leave to find five men carrying SMGs pointed at his face. FOX members.

'Identify yourselves!' demanded one of the men
'I am Primrose Hillweller.'
'And I am Diamond Hillweller.'

The men quickly lowered their weapons, almost as fast as their faces dropped. They stood to attention.

'I'm sorry Mister Chairman, I didn't know. You look so different.'

'Next time I'll cut you fucking legs off' promised Primrose, walking past the men.

The elevator door opens on the FOX Riot parking lot level B, revealing a darkened concrete level. Tire screeches could be earned echoing from levels below and above. The group walk out. Suddenly a loud siren echoes throughout the building and to every FOX members radio.

'Trans-Gression members are in the building. Shoot on sight. Parking lot level B'

They began to search the vehicles for keys. Drogun looks around the area and sees a guard post, empty, but inside hanging on the back wall. He enters and confirms it, a bunch of keys all labelled. He grabs two.

'Here.—' he throws a key to Talon, '—It's for that white mini bus'

'It can only fit four.'

'Go on without me, I'll catch up.'

They climb in and Talon starts the engine. He puts the vehicle into gear and sets off, as they move the elevator door opens as the group reach the down ramp leading to Level A of the parking lot. Members of FOX run step out from the elevator to the ramp, stand in a line, and open fire at the mini bus. Glass flies from the back windows.

At the back of Level B, Drogun is searching for the vehicles to who his key belongs to. He knows it must be an old one with the dust on the key and that's when he notices at the park a small tarp covering a vehicle. He pulls at the tarp revealing the motorcycle facing the wall, it's old but it'll do.

He quickly hops on, starts the engine and turns it around allowing the back wheel to do all the work, smoke flies from the tyre. The rev of the engine echoes through the parking lot, he heads towards the ramp. The men turn round court off guard by the motorcycle.

They raise their weapons once more to shoot the bike coming towards them, Drogun pulls a wheelie to defend himself. However the men don't shoot, the motorcycle belongs to the chairman's son, Primrose.

Drogun extends out his arm, a ball of fire appears from his hand. He lowers the motorcycle back to two wheels and throws the fire ball to the feet of the men blocking his path, they dive out of the way. He speeds past onto Level A.

The men quickly get back to their feet and begin to shoot towards him.

He cut a hard turn avoiding more gun fire, as a FOX vehicle begins to chase him. He ducks between a narrow line of cars spaced just right amount from one another as it's door opens and FOX members begin to open fire trashing the cars as they pass. He cuts another hard corner that leads to the ramp which will take him to the street but the passage is barricaded by another FOX vehicle.

He stops, turns the bike around with a screech and brings out Tur-anion, his trusty sword, grabbing by its hilt with his left hand. The previous FOX vehicle now caught up as he set of towards, it with so much torque he performed a wheelie, dragging his blade behind him. The blade was soon covered in flames again as it kicked up sparks from the asphalt.

The FOX members hanging from the left door opened fire.

Nothing seemed to hit him as he drove towards the vehicle like he was playing a game of chicken. He suddenly moved the bike to the right of the vehicle, he swing his blade and hit the front dragging his blade along the entirety of the vehicle causing it to flip and come a dazzling stop at the bottom. He raced along back up to the level, past the open views of the city, where he noticed something just out the corner of Drogun's eye, the mini bus with the others in it.

'Where's Drogun, he should be here by now?' said Varin

A sudden loud roar of the engine makes Varin in the back of the mini bus turn round, as his brother bursts through the concrete wall on Level A on the motorcycle land on the roof of another the vehicle chasing them, a 20th century yellow school bus, filled to the brim with FOX members. He drives off the roof and revs the engine more to catch up with the others.

'Talon! Talon, Head for the highway' yelled Drogun

Bullets streams past.

'But it doesn't lead anywhere' replied Talon
'FOX will be crawling round the streets, it's our only way out'

"Just as Drogun had said, FOX members were crawling the streets. It was barricade after barricade but none blocked the entrance to the highway."

They entered the highway's on ramp, nothing but two miles of former highway now leads them to the edge of the city. Drogun backed off from the side of the van as another mini bus now joined the chase.

'The defences are still off?' said Yal
'We need to go faster, just go faster' replied Co Hobson

The other mini bus got alongside there's and began to ram into the side.

'There look!—' yelled Varin, pointing to the edge of Shenma City, '—The power's still off'

The FOX vehicle opened fire on Drogun causing him to weave all over the road to dodge their bullets, getting his blade out once more, he reflected the sun light back at them to blind them.

'There the off ramp, take that' said Co Hobson.

The mini bus alongside the group gave one last ram, as they turned off onto the ramp, it hurled towards the divider and crashed blocking the off ramp for anyone else.

'Drogun!' called out Varin as he looked out the back to see the road blocked, he raced on by with the yellow bus shortly behind him.

Talon headed straight for the metal door barring their way from freedom, he pushed down harder onto the pedal, the small mini bus forced it's way through the door ripping it from the wall.

Something began to beep, Co Hobson's watch.

'The shield is powering up!'

Drogun was still on the highway unable to take the off ramp because of the carnage left behind. He had no choice but to carry on the highway that would end so shortly. The edge of Shenma began to power up, emitting a yellow glow.

'He won't make it' laughed a FOX member.

That member began to push the breaks, but they wouldn't work, he pushed again even harder. Still no response.

Drogun gave the engine one last rev before reaching the edge of the highway. He flew from the highway the device surrounding Shenma. The PHOENIX shield finally began to spurt into life once again, the shield was reactivating faster than he was travelling. He closed his eyes, flying towards the device, the shield now appeared in front of him.

Everyone that was watching, one thought popped into their heads.

He's a goner.

He opened his eyes and something seemed to surge from his body like a shield of his own. He made it through alright, but now it was the sudden stop of the ground from hundred foot up that was the next problem.

Nothing he can really do can help him now, all he can do is pray for the best.

". . . And I'm not a praying man"

CHAPTER 13

Fear Of The Unknown

THE MOTORBIKE HIT the floor with a hard thud, leaving imprints in the ground and the bike in half. Drogun on the other hand, landed on his feet but was forced to go into a roll. Hunched over he imminently reached for his right knee. The ache and pain of that old injury came back. From above, the sound of screeching tyres thundered.

Drogun quickly rose to his feet and looked up, there the yellow bus was coming towards him, falling towards him. The men inside now turned to ash by the shield filtered out from bus. The bonnet now faced the sky as the rear fell towards Drogun.

He stood there for a second, calculating something before suddenly jumping kicking his feet into the metal bonnet of the bus. He began to run up the bus towards rear of the vehicle, once reaching the rear he stood still as it, now completely vertical, hit the ground causing it to bounce.

He moved closer to the underside of the bus and it began to tip that way to the ground. He now stood underneath he vehicle as its roof hit the ground, he slammed his feet down. He flipped from the vehicle landing on the ground before taking a knee, the force once again causing his right knee to hurt. He quickly got back to his feet to see the bus flying away from him towards the forest a couple yards away. Glass and pieces of metal now littered the area.

He turns his head slightly to see the black smoke coming from the forest. Smirking he falls to the ground.

All the group, all but Co Hobson, ran from the mini bus to Drogun.

'He's . . . ?' said Varin

'. . . Unconscious, he should be fine once we get him back to a village' spoke Talon, finishing Varin's sentence

'What the hell did he do?' asked Yal

'I have no idea, he shouldn't of survived that'

The horn from the mini bus began to scream. Co Hobson's head rested on the horn, tears stream down his face.

'I promised, I promised so many that the fight would come to an end. Soo many lives lost today . . . AND FOR WHAT!—' he raises his head back up and begins to hit the steering wheel '—I failed! And in all honesty, I'm sick of this fight. So sick of making empty fake promises. I once promised to look after a man, I assumed had amnesia or something, he was the one that fell into that vat of PHOENIX, I couldn't even fulfil that promise.'

Talon approached Co Hobosn to calm him as the others lifted Drogun to his feet, dragging him towards the mini bus.

Drogun began to mumble something.

'What?' asked Varin

'. . . Take me . . . to W . . . Windor'

'The elven lands?' asked Talon

Drogun didn't respond.

'How long will it take for us to get there?' asked Varin

'Two days through the mountain range. But we need to get to Gade to help the others and this thing doesn't have enough fuel to take us to both' replied Talon

'My brother needs help now!'

'Varin I'm sorry—' spoke Co Hobson '—I cannot let any more of my brethren die'

'But it's alright for my brother to die!'

No one spoke, Varin stared at each of them one at a time, in turn they turned away from his stare. Varin lifted Drogun onto his back and began to walk off towards the mountains. Yal was about to call for him but Talon stopped him.

'Allow him to go, he needs to help his brother'

Co Hobson whispered under his breath.

'Good luck . . . hero'

Co Hobson threw the mini bus into first gear and headed as fast as they could to Gade City.

They arrived at Gade later that day, night had fallen as they find Gade now over run by FOX. The city was much similar to Karves village, except that all the buildings were at least three floors tall. To the south, near the generator, rested the FOX encampment as they patrolled the now empty village. Resting at end of the encampment laid a make shift prison of captured Trans-Gression members.

The streets were littered with the bodies of FOX members, Hunters and fellow TG members.

'I'm sorry, my brothers . . . my friends' cried Co Hobson to himself.

'Look, there!—' pointed Yal, '—a prison, ya?'

'Indeed, we'll need a distraction to get closer'

'I'll drive the car down the hill into the empty houses on the other side of the city, that should buy you enough time to get everyone out.' said Co Hobson

'Good idea Sir, but allow us to do it. We'll be able to get away, you may be captured'

'Very well, meet back up in fifteen minutes'

They nodded and with that Hobson took his leave, and begun to sneak his way towards the prison, as the Ninja Twins drove the vehicle around to the other side of the city.

Co Hobson waited not too far from the encampment among the bushes and trees. It wasn't long before it sounded like hell broke loose.

The mini bus, now of fire lighting the skies, tore through the wooden buildings, as FOX officers rushed around yelling orders to their men to get to that hill. In the commotion he snuck up to the tent of the make shift prison and cut a hole through the back, no guards were inside. He tore is it bigger and snuck in.

As he entered the entire TG group nearly roared with cheer.

'Quiet. Where's Lt . . . ?'

Before he could finish one of the members replied,

'He was killed'
'But the new member, Sylvia, took charge—' called fourth another member, '—With her in charge we prepared a trap, we managed to defeat most of their men and hold out a little longer . . . until . . .'
'The hunters?' asked Co Hobson
'No, they sent in their best men within FOX. Their special forces unit'
'FOX has a special forces unit? Where is Sylvia now?'
'I'm here—' Co Hobson turns to the tear in the makeshift prison's tent that he made to see the, covered in cuts, Sylvia with her dress now tattered and torn, '—I and a few others were just about to break everyone out, but looks like you beat us to it' she smiled.
'Thank you Sylvia for taking charge but we need to leave here at once where are the keys for their chains?'
'A FOX member has them' yelled one of the twenty men and women prisoners.
'Call him, Yal, Talon—' the twin brothers now stood by the torn entrance, a little out of breathe. Sylvia was a little shocked to see them stood behind her, '—and Sylvia make sure the exit is clear and if we get split up meet at the hideout in Karves.'

Sylvia, Yal and Talon nodded once more and took their leave as Co Hobson moved to the fabric door and waited for the FOX member. The TG members began to stage a fight, to get the attention of the guards carrying the keys.

'I'll go see what the prisons are doing'

'What about the commander?'

'He'll be too busy dealing with, whatever the hell that was I won't bother him about the prisoner's acting up'

'I'll join you, just encase, who knows what these Trans-Gression scum are up to'

The guards walk into the tent. Co Hobson waited for them both to enter. The one with the keys hung around his hip, unsuspecting of anything amiss until it was too late. Co Hobson approached from behind, tapped him on his shoulder and as he turned gave him a quick right hook knocking the man out. The other now turned with his assault rifle in hand, Co Hobson had his side to the other FOX member when he yelled, 'Freeze!'

He had Co Hobson, there was nothing he could do—unless he got closer. The member approached closer to him a little surprised that he managed to knock out his buddy but more surprised that he had captured Commander Hobson, leader of Trans-Gression by himself.

Co Hobson raised his arms in surrender. The FOX guard took a few steps closer.

He was now close enough.

Suddenly Co Hobson stretched out his arm to the gun knocking it away from him and the other TG members, he grabbed the handle of the rifle with his other hand and gave the guard a swift kick to the stomach, winding him. He crumpled to the floor as Hobson now stood above him with the rifle in hand, he hit him with the handle of the rifle knocking him out.

He quickly grabbed the keys and released the others from the steel prison. They rushed from the make shift prison's exit following Sylvia's directions to Talon and his to Yal, the safe route they made through the jungle.

Co Hobson runs up to Sylvia, 'Need any help?'
'No I'm fine' she replied.

He continues onto Talon, believing her word.

'THEY'RE ESCAPING!'

That voice sounded familiar.
Something came towards Sylvia with great speed, it seemed like a grey blur, it jumped and kicked her in the stomach. It suddenly appeared behind her, it kicked her in the back forcing her towards a clearing in the jungle, where a large group of FOX member now stood.

'Talon! Get everyone out of here and back to Karves. NOW'

Talon nodded, disappearing into the jungle. Co Hobson ran to help Sylvia but before even taking a step, he was instantly surrounded by FOX members. He raised his hands in defeat. They took him to the centre of the clearing. Lying on the group was Sylvia in extreme pain, she spat up some blood while being restraint to the ground by her attacker using his foot.

'So . . . this is the leader of the Trans-Gression. Commander Hobson, right?—' spoke a man in a suit and tie, '—FOX leave us, hunt down his team.'

The FOX members left the centre and began to run to the font of the town as fast as they could, but twelve people remained, ten others of whom also wore a suit and tie.

'And you are?'

'He's Dicembre—' said Sylvia, wiping blood from her mouth, '—leader of FOX's special forces unit. Cognition.'

'Cognition?'

'The mental process of knowing, including aspects such as awareness, perception, and judgment. In other words, knowing YOU! are the enemy. Awareness that YOU! bring death and destruction. The perception of one, SPARK CORPORATION! . . . and your judgement, DEATH!'

Co Hobson grins, 'Been practising that line much?'

The man that once was a grey blur pushes harder down onto Sylvia suddenly, causing her to let out a cry of pain. The grin is suddenly gone from Co Hobson's face

'I read your file, never realised you would have a sense of humour specially since all you do is bring death everywhere you go.—' Dicembre now grins, '—Hey. Everyone, why don't you leave us? Go and hunt down the other members. I request to have some fun with this one.'

Ten of them left without a word, except the guy still standing on Sylvia.

'Marzo! You as well'

He growled while slowly stepping off Sylvia and once again turned into a grey blur as he sped off on the hunt for

TG members. Sylvia slowly rose to her feet using her scythe and leans against a tree.

'Good to see you again Marzo. Oops I'm sorry, Sylvia Arow right?'

'Dicembre, it's been a long time . . . not long enough though'

'Oh come on, that how you greet an old friend?'

'Come a little closer and I'll greet you proper' she says holding the scythe in both hands before almost falling, she leans against the tree again.

'Never knew when to give up did you?'

'I see you found a replacement?'

With Discembre distracted by Sylvia, Hobson thought now was the best time to attack. He rushed from behind but Discembre was prepared, raising an arm he grabbed Hobson by the throat and pulled him towards his face.

'Wait your turn Commander'

He gave him a head butt and a knee to the stomach, then pushed him away as he turned back to continue talking to Sylvia.

'You were easy to replace, after all we were ALL made by the glorious, SPARK Corporation.'

'I'm not a puppet, a tool to be used'

'That's what you think'

'That's my perception, yes'

'Fine—' said Discembre, he turned to see Co Hobson stand in a fighting pose, '—This should be soo, much fun'

He stands in a fighting pose as he unbuttons his jacket and slacking off his tie a little.

'Not quite' says Sylvia.

She whistles, a sudden roar is heard. A roar of something big.

Dicembre turns to see something flying towards him, about to pounce onto him, a big blue fur ball, the Togu. The weight of the creature forces him to ground. He grins and he then turns into shadow and disappears through the ground. The Togu growls, it begins to approach Sylvia, wagging its tail in excitement to see her again. It moves over closer to her, allowing her to support properly.

'You knew them?'
'It's a long story, I'll explain later. Where's Drogun and Varin?'
'There was an incident, Varin's on his way to Windor with Drogun on his back'
'How are they going to get there?'
'Varin intends to walk'

She slowly climbs a top the Togu.

'I'll find them.'

She sets off. The city now quiet and deserted once more, only Co Hobson and Dicembre are in the city.

Varin knew his march would be deadly and treacherous, but he had to make it, for his brother. Now ten miles away from Shenma City, marching through the forest.

For the past mile now he's heard the Fiends all round him, none of come in any closer as if something is keeping them at bay but he doesn't care, there's only one thing he cares about right now.

"I must get my brother there."

Already his strength is beginning to leave him, his will power alone is the only thing still carrying Drogun.

"With every step, I am one step closer to reaching Windor. That was my one thought that was what my will was telling me."

He comes to a small pond deep within the forest. He pauses to see another path round it as it looks he noticed a clearing in the canopy of trees letting light through, it looks up to see not far away now lays the mountain range. The first ten miles of the range was a steep upwards climb leading towards snow and ice.

He knew from their that the next ten miles after that was wondering a snows equivalent of a desert, twenty miles after that was getting down from there on ice and rock and then eventually a desert that led all the way to the green Elvish lands.

He went to the right of the pond, stepping over fallen trees and ducking low branches, but with his energy quickly leaving him an accident was soon to happen. Stepping over a fallen tree, Varin tripped causing him to fall into the pond.

Varin let go of Drogun, he tried kicking to keep above the water but he just couldn't do it anymore, he stopped and began to sink to the bottom. Weighed down by his cloths.

"I stopped there, at the time I was telling myself 'I will have only a small break' but really I was considering stopping. I'm no hero, I was only trying to help my brother but I can't go on. But the crazy thing is, I did something this sort of dangers many times before and it could of easily killed me, climbing that drain pipe to the roof. Only to speak to her . . ."

'Varin!' yelled out a voice, a female voice

"Emily."

Something was moving fast through the forest. A figure quickly dived into the water grabbing both him and Drogun, for a split second he thought it was her, Emily, the girl he can't seem to stop thinking of. He smiled as she pulled them from the depths to the solid ground. He looked up not moving, unable to move. He heard her performing CPR on Drogun as a Fiend through the leaves and shade of the forest approached him and began to lick his face, the Togu.

His grin quickly changed and a panic set in.

'Drogun!?' he called out, sitting up.

Drogun quickly responded by coughing up the water but continued to lay their unmoving but breathing.

'Varin, Are you okay?' asked Sylvia, their hero.
'Sylvia? You . . . you saved us. Thank you'

'Are you okay to walk?'

'Yeah, what?' he said reaching his feet.

'I'll take Drogun on the Togu, I'll get him to Windor.'

'But I . . .'

'It's okay Varin, I'll look after him. I'll meet you again in Karves, that's where the TG are meeting up'

She struggles but manages to place Drogun onto the Togu.

'Okay but have you seen our far it is? And the terrain?'

'I'm not afraid, besides I owe him one—' she climbs up, '—take care of yourself Varin.'

She kicks the Togu and it speeds off. It quickly makes it to the mountain range and begins to jump from ledge to ledge with ease, making quick work reaching the mountain's snowy tops.

'Good luck'

He turns around and there standing in front of him was a familiar face of someone he once knew, Emily.

'Varin . . . ?' she said with tears beginning to stream down her face as her smile grows. She faints but Varin manages to catch her in his arms as she falls.

'H . . . how . . . ?' asked Varin in shock.

He raises her head slightly, wondering to himself.

'How can she be here? She died. What to do? Where should we go . . .'

He places her onto his back, raises to his feet and begins to walk once more, this time heading for Karves.

The only town he really knows in this new world.

Three hours after being freed from the prison in Gade many of the Trans-Gression have arrived in Karves, they immediately head towards the building used for their hideout. The villagers looked on somewhat scared by the state of some of the members, other villagers try to help some of them to the hideout. Yal and Talon are the last ones to enter the village, the gate closes behind them, they help any members into the hideout and close the door behind them.

'That everyone?'

No one replies, only moans are heard.

'How long do you think he will be?' asks Yal
'Co Hobson? Could be a while I suppose' replied Talon
'Or he could be dead'
'Have faith, he'll make it'
'And suppose he doesn't ya? Who will lead Trans-Gression then?'
'I suppose we could vote for leadership'
'Or we could just call it a day' said one of the members
'We could . . . We could but that would be taking the coward's way out. We made a promise to this planet, to these people to put an end to SPARK and to PHOENIX'

'That's why we fight?—' said another member '—because we made a promise to people that don't really care for our course? Us combined with the people of this planet can put an end to SPARK . . . then why don't they fight?'

'Fear' replied Talon

'Fear? Fear of what?'

'The unknown. We use PHOENIX as an energy but the people still need a energy source for everyday life. In order to raise these people to fight against SPARK, we'll need a new energy source that is just effect as PHOENIX.'

'Then our fight is useless!—' yelled another member '—how can we rally these people if we used all fossil fuels'

'Renewable energy! Solar power, tidal waves, the wind itself. Our fight isn't futile'

'Ha-yeah all we have to do is wish on a star that these people will fight' spoke another member.

Talon is left speechless as many of the members now rose back to their feet and begin to leave.

'Talon, what about Co Hobson?' asked Yal

'He won't be joining you just yet son!'

Yal and Talon turn towards the door, standing in the door way is there father. Raiden. Standing behind him is another man, but the light from outside has darkened the man, no one can see his face.

'Father!' yelled Talon

'The name's Hunter D'

CHAPTER 14

Forgotten

'KILL THEM ALL' said a familiar voice, the same voice from Gade.

The assassin now known as Hunter D, quickly turns away from his sons and then throws his coat towards them. He instantly reaches for his weapon, the metal staff, he breaks it in half to turn it into the metal whip once again and begins to make his way towards Yal and Talon. Killing anyone in his way with a quick slash to the throat or chest. Yal and Talon their weapons as the coat flies towards them, they cut it in half to see some of their brethren and friends lying dead on the floor as Hunter D made his way toward them.

Yal swings his swords downwards from above as Talon thrusts towards his father's stomach, Hunter D blocks Yal's attack as his whip turns into a single spiked baton. He uses the other to block Talon's attack rising both of them to above and over the back of his head causing the weapons to lock together.

He smiles.

He brings the weapons from behind his head to in front of him, he jumps and spins side ways, this unlocks the weapons and causing the brothers to fly towards the walls. Hunter D lands on his feet as TG members begin to help the brothers, with their weapons in hand, up.

A few TG members begin to try to escape through the door which the other man is blocking. He quickly kills any that approach him easily while still remaining between the doorway.

Yal and Talon regain to their feet and attack once more, Yal leads the charge as the TG members back away trying to find another way out. Yal attacks first swiping from his right to his top left. Their father blocked the attack knocked the weapons from Yal's hands, both blades stuck into the ceiling above his head.

Talon attacked with his bladed staff, Hunter side stepped Talon's first attack and cut the staff in two forcing both piece to also piece the wooden ceiling.

Yal and Talon stare at their weapons briefly and quickly look back down at their father, he smiles crudely at them once more, he quickly punches them in the stomach, they fly towards a wall at the back of the room. Yal hit his head knocking him out.

Hunter D quickly jumps up to the ceiling and rips out one of Yal's swords and half of Talon's bladed staff, he then throws the weapons at the brothers just as they hit the wall. Talon's weapon went into his left shoulder pinning him against the wall. Yal's pinning his clothing under his right against the wall, Hunter D then quickly throws Yal's second blade pinning his clothing under his left arm to the wall.

He then jumps towards them again killing any member to get in his way.

He stops inches away from Talon's face, 'I thought you were gunna kill me the next time we met Talon? Change your mind?'

He pulls away from Talon and goes for the other half of Talon's bladed staff and uses it to attack the remaining TG members, unlucky enough to still be alive. After quickly slaughtering the unlucky ones he walks back over to the brothers.

'I still see you both still pay a tribute to your dead brother. You both carry fabric stained by his blood on your weapons and you, Talon, use a part of his favourite t-shirt as a bandana, for shame.'
'Hunter D, Burn this place down' ordered the man that stood between the door way

Hunter places one finger underneath the bandana and pulls it away from Talon's head.

'Let's save this little reminisce for another time, shall we?'

He walks to the centre of the now blood filled room, pulls out a light and sets fire to the bandana. He drops it and walks towards the door. The other man, throws something into the room by the fire, a small container of PHOENIX that begins to leak onto the floor. Two men leave and close the door behind them leaving Yal and Talon for dead. The small container quickly reacts to the fire, causing a small explosion with in the room, small bits of the fuel fly onto and burn the two brothers, scaring them both on their cheek like rain drops as the room begins to fill with black smoke.

'Were your sons the ones with the crystal?—' said the man, '—No? Find the other. He must have it. Don't worry about the other he's infected I should have control over him soon enough, NOW GO!'

Hunter D disappeared into the night, the man disappeared, disappearing into the growing crowed that came rushing to attempt a rescue or to help. What they rushed into was not a burning building but a burning slaughter house, blood was smeared all over the walls and even parts of the ceiling, the floor was covered with the dead bodies and limbs of the Trans-Gression.

'What the hell!' yelled out Co Hobson, just reaching the gate of the Karves.

Bright orange flames forced their way out of the building releasing think black smoke into the air, as many villagers rushed to collect water to stop the fire from spreading to close by houses. Co Hobson forced his way through the crowd to the entrance, once inside he felt sick. Not because of the deadly black smoke hanging from above but once again his brothers and friends were dead, all of them lying in pieces.

Villagers were already slowly helping the knocked out brothers, Yal and Talon, from the wall. Co Hobson rushed over to help and dragged them both from the burning slaughter house.

He dragged them two hundred yards away from the burning wreck, both of them were breathing fine but Co Hobson still demanded the villagers to stand back.

'Who did this?' he asked them, the brothers didn't reply but the villagers did,
'A man that attacked them last time and a man with white hair'

A man with white hair? The man that fell into PHOENIX? The scenario replayed in Co Hobson's mind from ten years ago.

'It looks like they're housing PHOENIX, rather than making it' said Marko.

Marko is leading the way followed by Co Hobson and another man behind him, they're walking on a narrow one man cat walk twenty feet above large metal containers and pipes connecting to one another, inside the containers is the fuel.

'How can this be? Shouldn't they be making it rather than digging it up?' said the man
'I don't think they're digging it up either . . . something strange is going on here' said Co Hobson
'Stop right there!' yelled a man

They turn round to see a man armed with a SMG.

'And you are?' asked Marko

The man smirks and then suddenly whistles, three more men armed with SMGs came running and stood side by side with the other.

'We're FOX'
'FOX?'
'Fouilleur Of X-tal, created two years ago by master Hillweller. Created for one purpose . . . defeat the Trans-Gression'
'Looks like we just captured their leader, I guess we won't be needing that Special Forces team' said another to his stooge.
'We have any options?' whispered Marko to Co Hobson
'Just one . . . RUN!'

They began to run along the flimsy catwalk, to reach an exit. The FOX members open fire, bullets sprayed everywhere and soon they began to run along the catwalk to catch them. As the weight began to mount many of the bolts broke away for buckled under the weight. A single bolt was hit by a bullet just in front of the third member of TG, the catwalk section gave way under him. He may of been able to jump it if another bullet didn't just hit him in the left shoulder just as the bolt gave way. The man fell into the PHOENIX. Co Hobson stopped and tried to turn back to help as the FOX members charged towards them, but Marko pulled him away and they fled the area.

Two weeks later.

It was a dark night in Karves, the moon was shining and no one else was in the streets except two members of TG and Co Hobson. They are walking towards the hideout, the wind suddenly roared, footsteps echoed from the rooftops.

Before Co Hobson even realised it something was falling towards him. A man with long white hair, white as the moon, stood by Co Hobson, the man suddenly and violently grabs Co Hobson by the shoulder, spins him around and then grabbed him by the throat, raising him into the air with one hand.

'You!?' said Co Hobson
'YOU left me to DIE, I've come to REPAY you COMMANDER'
'It wasn't my fault . . . I . . . I'
'You fled. Never attempted to help me'

The man raises a weapon to Co Hobson's throat, a long slightly curved katana blade. The moon light reflected from it showing his cloths. Everything was black leather, gloves, boots, trousers and vest. A necklace hung from around his neck, but Co Hobson couldn't make it out.

'Because of YOU I . . .—' He turned his head away from Co Hobson and looked towards the moon as if it was talking to him '—Planet? Elemental Crystals. WHY SHOULD I CARE . . .—' He turns back to Co Hobson '—you're right, NO KILL HIM! No!'

He let go and immediately disappeared in the moon light.

'Is everything okay? My follower?' asked the Priest

'Huh—' He looked up, realising he now resided in the chapel with the remain TG members, '—Priest, I was just . . . lost in thought and wondering about the others that travelled with us. Are Yal and Talon okay?'

'I fear they've seen worse but they could do with every little help they can get at this moment'

'How did I get here?'

'Oh? You were brought in by the villagers, you looked to be in shock'

'. . . Perhaps I was. I hope the others are okay'

'Ah the others I hope they are alright also, after all they are my sons, as well'

'We are all sons of god, Priest'

'Of Course. If you and any other Trans-Gression members need a place to stay you may stay in the chapel'

'Thank you Priest'

"I arrived back at the inn, in Karves sometime after midnight, with Emily on my back. As I entered the village nothing was on my mind other than the sound of Emily calmly breathing.

It was if I was in a trance, just wanting to get to the inn no matter what. I overheard the villagers talking of something that just recently happened. I didn't take too much notice it sounded all like mumbling to me."

The women by reception was a sleep again, he crept behind her to get a key, the same room he was in before, and sneaked upstairs and into the room.

Some time passed before Emily awoke, during the time Varin just stared out the window like his brother once did turning to look at her sleeping peacefully on the bed. One question appeared from time to time in his mind.

"Is this a dream?"

She awoke, tears began to stream from her eyes again, 'Varin?'

He turned from the window immediately and sat down beside her, 'I'm here'

'Where are we?'

'We're in Karves'

She says in shock, 'Karves City? but . . .'

'But this is Karves Village'

'. . . How? When did this happen?'

"Karves, Rebuilt in the year 2399, after being destroyed by PHOENIX in the year 2259." Well that's what the monument says when entering the village"

'2199? Is that the date?'

'No, the date is April 6th, 2609'

She tried to search for words, as Varin once did, she soon gave up as more tears took over.

'Where the hell am I? How did I get here, what about my parents, family, friends—' she cuddles Varin, still crying '—I feel so alone, so vulnerable in this place'

'Don't worry—' He places his arm around her shoulder, '—I won't let anything happen to you.'

'You promise' her tears seem to stop as she raises her head towards Varin

He turns to look her in the eye, 'I promise'

A smile seems to grow back onto her face, 'I'll hold you to that'

Varin's mind suddenly wondered about his brother, had Sylvia reached Windor yet? Or had they died in the cold on their way? Or had they been attacked by a Fiend? Or . . . ?

'You still do that I see' said Emily, Varin turns to look at her once more, '—still off in your own world'

'I have a good reason this time. My brother Drogun, I met him in this world. He didn't die as I thought all along'

'Your brother? If he's alive here that means your father must be. Right?'

He didn't reply and his mind once again wondered to his brother, until Emily spoke once more

'You know, this kind of reminds me of when we were younger. You looking out for me.'

'Yeah I suppose it does'

'I never stopped loving you—' blurted Emily suddenly, '—I was angry when I first saw you at the PTC, because I was hoping to never see you again to get over you. But I couldn't help but still feel for you, I cried myself to sleep every other night . . .' she went to continue but Varin cut her off.

'P. T. C? Wha?'

'Shenma's Police Training Centre. You remember that right?'

'. . . I . . . I think so, I remember someone. Ren?'

'He was our instructor. How could you forget?'

'I can't remember a number of years, all I can remember is the Karves Incident and then suddenly I wake up here'

'You used to have a journal, what happed to that?'

'I don't know.'

Varin goes quiet again, enjoying the moment of seeing Emily again.

'Don't go into your own world again'

'I . . . every time I went into "my own world" I wasn't thinking about the past, most of the time I was thinking about us. What type of house should we get, kids, where to live . . . When I should ask your hand in marriage'

'I . . . I had no idea. I assumed you kept thinking of your brother and father. You never opened up to me'

'You never asked.'

'I hope you don't mind, but I need to go to sleep. I feel a little tired from all that crying'

'You always did cry a lot, that's one of the reasons why I helped you when we were younger'

2257, Karves Primary School.

A four year old child, with red hair is crying in a corner of the playground, next to the building. Two older bullies aged six are calling her names and forcing her to cry more.

'Carrot top!'

'I didn't know carrots can cry haha'

'She probably has a bad case of Ginger-vitis'

Teachers are round the playground but they don't give a damn about their students to stop this. A five year old blonde haired kid in the distance has had a enough and takes matters into his own hands.

'Leave her alone!—' he yelled to the bullies, they turned to face him, '—pick on someone your own size'

'Oh no!—' they said sarcastically, '—Not the all mighty Varin Vargon'

'Just leave her alone before . . .'

'Before what?' they begin to punch their hands

'Before his older brother, decides to join in to make it a fair fight' spoke an eight year old Drogun, walking towards the group. The two bullies raise their arms and a state of fear begins to show on their faces.

'. . . No, no it's okay Drogun . . . we were about to leave'

They smile nicely at him and run off before giving Varin one last evil look. Varin walks over to the red haired girl as Drogun begins to walk towards Varin.

'Varin, if you have any more problems with them just call for me. Bloody cowards have to go for someone weaker. younger than themselves.'

Varin didn't pay too much attention to what Drogun said, Drogun noticed and decided to leave.

'Are you okay?' asked Varin to the red haired girl.

She attempts to stop crying before answering.

'What's your name?' asked Varin

'My name—' she breathes in through her nose to try to calm herself before finishing '—Emily'

She extends one of her hands, he grabs it to pull her up. They smile at each other and spend the rest of the school day walking and talking to each other.

"I got into a fight with those guys later after school on my way home, Drogun wasn't with me at the time. But I wasn't as weak as I looked, my brother had the reputation as a brawler around the school even though he never got into fights, but he did show me a few things at one time or another.
Let's just say they will never think I'm weak again."

Varin is walking to his home by himself down a narrow alley way only big enough for one person at a time to walk down near the back of a few houses. The right walls that made this passage were the back bricks of houses and to the left was a zigzag shaped metal wall same height as a garage would be.

'Hey Varin!' shouted a young boy

Varin turned round as soon as he heard his name, it was the bullies again.

'Your brother isn't here to protect you this time—' they both walked toward Varin, '—We're gonna do it our way'

Varin didn't speak, he lowered his backpack and removed his jacket. The bullies smiled amongst themselves and rolled up their sleeves, before moving in for the kill like a flock of vultures.

The first, swung with a right hook. Varin caught it as it came towards him, placed it behind the bullies back and pushed him towards the zigzag metal wall. The second came and went to punch straight with his left at Varin, but Varin held the first bully as a shield. After blocking the shot he threw the first bully to the ground behind him and attacked the second.

He was still in shock that he hit his friend before he realised Varin was coming for him, Varin grabbed his arm that was still out stretched. He then threw his knee into the second bullies ribs. Winding him, the bully staggered against the fence and crashed to the floor.

The other bully however got back to his feet, blood was coming from a small scar on his nose from the wall. The bully attempted to stop the bleeding with his left hand as he went to swing at Varin with is right.

Varin once again grabbed his arm and this time, thrown him over his shoulder, the bully landed with a terrible thud. Varin walked over towards his stuff. The second got to his feet but decided to flee, he yelled out the other bullies name as he began to run.

'Craig, come on let's get out of here . . . . WILKINS!'

Varin and Emily are suddenly snapped from their reminiscing by a flash of lighting that laminated the room, bringing them back to the present year of 2409. They finally see the rain on the window.

'Weren't you once afraid of thunder and lightning?' asked Varin

'Yes I was, until . . . we broke up. Then I wasn't afraid no more. Because . . . because I had to look after myself. No one to protect me anymore . . . You know Varin I . . .'

Varin stopped her from continuing. He looked at her, staring right into those eyes blue eyes, they both leaned in and kissed.

CHAPTER 15

Rýnaðaer Vaeres

NIGHT SEEMED TO disappear with a click of a finger. The sun had just rose and many villagers opened their stores and began to go to work for the day. The sun had already dried all that remained of the rain. Birds were cheeping outside of the window.

Varin wiped the sleep from his eyes took a quick look towards the window and turned to awaken Emily.

She wasn't there, panic began to swell within Varin, the bed sheet looked like they had been ripped from the bed. He got out of his bed and noticed that the room looked like a struggle took place, the door had been broken with the handle looking like it was about to fall off any second. He ran towards the door and down the stairs, the receptionist was still asleep, he ran out through the double door and looked round, not a sign, not a clue, no one saw a thing.

'EMILY! I can't lose her I just found her . . . EMILY!!'

"I thought that it happened while I was asleep, I later found out I was partly correct"

The night soon leaves the elvish lands, the Elven village of Windor begins to wake. Lush large green fields surround the village, but the village ready for anything, protected much like Karves Village, with high wooden walls. A walk way is built upon the wall and is used as a look out by guardsmen constantly protecting the village, twenty-four seven. Each guardsmen carries a lance, roughly carved from a tree and for the blade is a sharpened stone, sharpened so much it almost gives a shine like glass. It is tied to the wooden lance.

Each guardsmen also wears a wooden helmet and wooden body armour. Many of the guardsmen have short hair to reveal their long pointy ears, as a proud and noble race.

One of the Elf guardsmen sees something in the distance, he yells in Elvish, 'Something approaches, call Elder Kai'

The guards seem to suddenly beam into life as they scurry from the lookout point to the centre of the small village in search of Elder Kai, leader of the Windor tribe.

In the centre of the town is not a monument or a house but a tepee similar to the Cherokee design. The guardsmen rushed in and there sitting in the centre, mediating, was the elf Elder, Kai. Unlike most of the other elves the elder's hair is long and white, his hair tied in a brad hidden behind his ears. Wearing proudly a skin of one of the fiends in the area, the colour is blue but the skin is not of a Togu. It's of something much worse from these lands.

'Elder—' The guardsmen lowers his head, '—I . . . I'm sorry but something approaches from the north'
'Is it a Fiend?' replied the elder, still with his eyes shut
'We . . .'
'Oh . . . It's Drogun—' spoke the elder, '—I can see him, he's hurt—' He suddenly opens his eyes, '—OPEN THE GATE!'

The guardsmen run from the tepee towards the gate they begin to yell at one another, 'Open the gate! Fist Of Fire returns'

As the tired Togu and Sylvia approach the slowly opening gates the words of the Elven guardsmen are heard.

'Odael si kari! Rýnadaer vaeres'

The Togu runs through the gathering crowd of elves, one of the elves is standing in the Togu's path, the Elder. He slowly raises his hand and sharply puts out the palm of his hand, the common sign for stop.

The Togu slides to a stop in front of him. then he says

'Kyr kos (good girl)—' he then looks up to Sylvia and asks, 'Arwenamin, Sut naa lle?'
'W . . . What?' asked Sylvia
'Oh I'm sorry, what I said was "My Lady, how are you?—' he turns to the other elves and says in elvish, '—Get Drogun in my quarters immediately'

They grab Drogun from the Togu and carried him into the Tepee.

'Where are you taking him?' she jumps down, and struggles to find her feet for a second

'He needs our help, he needs rest'

The Elder walks into the tepee following Drogun, along with a few others, two guardsmen step out from within and stand guard outside, not allowing anyone in.

Sylvia attempts to gain access but no luck.

'Sorry my Lady. You cannot enter'

She is grabbed by a female, 'My Lady come with me, we'll take care of you'

She is led by the arm into one of the wooden houses near the Elder's tepee to shower and sleep.

Inside the tepee they began to remove Drogun's robes and clothing, scars mark his body almost like burn marks. He laid still almost lifeless, only the faint sign of breathing gave his death act away.

'Leave us' ordered the Elder.

Everyone leaves, he seals the tepee shut after the last person and kneels on the ground near Drogun. He begins a chant, an ancient pray, as holds his hands out above Drogun's body.

The Elder now began to glow like Drogun once did, flares of light began to fly from the Elder towards Drogun as if he was absorbing them. Every time a flare was to touch his body, he word arc his body almost as if it was painful.

This process continued all day until dusk.

～◦◦◦◦～

The Togu slept in the front room of a wooden house, the house was given to Sylvia to use as she stayed in the village. Lying next to it was a bowl half filled with water which was most likely once used as a salad bowl.

Sylvia slept in the master bedroom. Her once proud purple dress, now ragged and dirty, hung on a line near a small fire place. Beside the bed lying on a chair was a gift from the female villagers. A white dress, which is much lighter in weight, but tougher, than her old dress.

When worn the skirt of the dress hangs to one side, down to an inch or two above her ankle on her left, the other side barely reaches her knee and unlike her previous dress this one has no sleeves. The elves also gave her a new pair of boots, black, as well as a pair of fingerless gloves, also black.

Someone knocks on the door, waking Sylvia from her sleep. Sylvia quickly gets up and puts on her gifts from the villagers. The person that knocked entered the front room of the house, the Togu wakes as a young girl, no more than the age of fourteen enters. She lowers her head as she enters but keeps her eyes looking up towards Sylvia.

She then begins to try and speak, 'D . . . Drogun. I . . . is . . . is, awak . . . ke'

Sylvia smiled and approached the girl whom began to head for the door freighted by Sylvia's approach. She then waved "come" but didn't say a thing.

Sylvia stood there as the Togu stood beside her, rubbing it's head against her hand.

'Stay here girl, I'll be right back'

She left the house and saw most, if not all, the villagers crowding around the Elder's tepee. The Togu didn't listen to Sylvia's command and left the house also with a yawn, it blinked as it came outside into the dark and sighed in annoyance, seeing the large crowd all surrounding Sylvia as she marched her way through the crowd

The Elder was dragged from the tepee, held from under his arms by two guardsmen. He was physically drained from saving Drogun's life.

Drogun now twitched from time to time on his bed of hay, almost as if he was suffering from a bad dream but he was clearly awake. A blindfold was placed over his eyes as he lay still on the bed.

'You may see him now my Lady' said the little girl.

She moved through the crowd as they parted way and entered the tepee.

'Sylvia . . . ?—' he said as she entered, '—you brought me here . . . thank you'
'. . . you're welcome—' she replied in shock, '— . . . how did you know it was me?'
'The Elder told me that I was brought here by an Eilaer' before she had a chance to ask what an Eilaer was Drogun spoke again, 'Sylvia, please take this note—' he stretched out his hand and between his two fingers was a small folded piece of paper, '—Please. Take this to Varin and the others. And please bring them back here.'

She grabbed the note and was about to open the fabric door

Drogun spoke once more, 'Thank you, for bringing me here. I owe you one.'

She stepped outside without saying a word, she whistled and the Togu immediately dived through the crowd to be by Sylvia's side. The crowd disbursed making a path to the gate as it rushed past, mainly because the Togu knocked them over.

The guardsmen barely had enough time to open the gate.

She and the Togu just managed to get through the barely open gate and headed out into the large green fields and off towards; the desert, the snowy mountain top and the short mountain climb down, through the forest, over a ocean and finally to Karves Village.

"No problem . . . right?"

'How are they Mr Hobson?' asked the priest

Co Hobson has been in the chapel all day along with the two still unconscious brothers, Yal and Talon. Co Hobson at first didn't hear the Priest, is hands linked together holding his head up watching the sleeping bodies of the twins at his feet as his thoughts laid elsewhere.

The priest coughed to gain his attention, he staggered from his day dreaming and took to his feet, standing up to speak with the Priest.

'How are th . . .' the Priest asked again, but this time Co Hobson answered before he could finish.

'They are still perfectly fine, Priest'

'Here have some water, you've been watching them all day'

The Priest pulls out a small flask from his under his robes and offers it to Co Hobson, he takes the flask from the Priest.

'Thank you' he says with a big swig.

'I'll be leaving shortly to accomplish some tasks outside of these walls, perhaps I will see you on my travels?'

'I'm not too sure I'll travel anymore . . . not after this'

'What of your friends? Have you heard anything from them?'

'No, they were never . . . never really part of the TG. They probably went on to do their own things rather than help a dying cause'

'Never give up hope, they may return. Hope is the one thing we humans have'

'Even if it's a fouls hope, Priest?'

The Priest smiles and walks towards the double doors of the chapel, he opens the doors and steps outside but he suddenly stops and turns.

'A fouls hope is better than no hope'

He slams the doors shut behind him. Co Hobson speaks to himself, 'What help is hope, if it's delusional hope'

"*I spent all day around Karves trying to find someone that saw Emily, a shred of evidence that said she went that way, or this way. I found none, had it been a fiend that attacked I once thought, stupid but anything could of happened or was it somebody from the town or had she just left on her own accord . . . ?*"

Varin saw someone leave the chapel, 'I haven't asked him yet', he thought to himself. He ran towards the man and asked, 'Father, have you seen a . . .'

The Priest cut him off, 'You are a friend Hobson, Yal and Talon's?'

'. . . Yes I am'

'They're inside the chapel, you should pray for your friends my son. They will need them'

The Priest continues to walk.

'Need them for what?'

The Priest stops and turned, 'Because they were involved with that incident not too long ago'

'Incident?'

'. . . Are you an idiot son?—' He clears his throat, '—Someone attacked the TG and burnt the place to the ground, your friends are lucky to be alive'

Varin's jaw instantly drops with shock, not once noticing the burnt down building all day. He ran into the Chapel.

'You're welcome son.' says the Priest sarcastically to himself as Varin closes the door.

For a second or two Emily left his mind, he only cared for Yal and Talon but as he closed the doors behind him she instantly came back to his mind. His hand reached for the door to leave and continue his search until Co Hobson spoke.

'Priest? . . . Hero!? How is your brother?"
'To be honest I don't know, Sylvia took him with the Togu. How . . . how are they?'

Varin moved closer to the three.

'Yal and Talon? They're fighters they'll wake soon'
'What happened?' asked Varin
'They were attacked, all the TG were, everyone but myself and these two were killed. The TG is no more'
'You can't give up'
'Why can't I, many of us died today. SPARK has won, they're not playing around. I should of killed them when I had the chance'

The door creaks open, the Priest has returned with a bottle of clear liquid in his hand, 'I have something that may help'

He approaches the brothers and removes a drip from the lid, he places it over the top of Talon's wound and squeezes it three times to allow three small drips to drop onto the open wound.

'Is that . . . ?' said Co Hobson

'Phoenix Tears—' spoke the Priest cutting Co Hobson off '—it should heal them soon enough'

'Erm . . .—' mumbled Varin '—What are Phoenix Tears?'

'Phoenix Tears basically a mix of antibiotics and plasma to help sick or injured people, some people call it a potion others call it Phoenix Tears because of an ancient myth' replied Co Hobson

'And that myth is?' asked Varin

'That the tears of a Phoenix have healing powers. Of course Phoenix's don't exist, even in this crazy world where monsters exist. Monsters like SPARK, monsters like that white haired man.'

The Priest looks up at him.

'White haired man? you mean that Thorn guy?' asked Varin.

The door suddenly and violently blasts open, the Togu pounces into the chapel revealing Sylvia with note in hand.

'Sylvia!—' cried out Varin, '—Where's Drogun!?'

She hops from the panting Togu and says, 'He's at the Elven village. He wanted me to give you this letter'

She handed it over to Varin, Varin first wished not to except the letter fearing the worst had happened to his brother but he reluctantly took the letter and read it out.

CHAPTER 16

The Prophecy of Old

"VARIN, YAL, TALON, Sylvia, Hobson.

Myself and the people of this world need your help, Ten years ago I was given the task to look after five Crystals, Elemental Crystals. Each one representing the four elements and the human element—Earth, Wind, Water, Fire and Heart. These Crystals could give the user a power similar to that of a god, with each crystal the elves could control that element. It was they would create the mountain that parts the land of the elves and the rest of the world with the use of the Earth crystal. They realised however if these fell into the wrong hands, chaos would bring the end of the world.

The crystals were then placed on a platform one hundred feet above the elven village of Windor for safe keeping but one night we were attacked by a single man, he killed many in his path to reach these crystals, the ones in the platform had no idea what was heading their way. The man seemed to come out of nowhere, through the mist he attacked. Three people were on that platform myself, my master and his apprentice at the time."

Ten years ago,

A dark night, the moon light shining, the wind howling. One hundred feet above the elven village of Windor, the safely guarded oval shaped platform at it's the centre, placed against a wall, rested the five Elemental Crystals. Green for Earth, a sky blue for Wind, dark blue for Water, red for Fire and pink for heart. Around the platform was a columned railing, stopping those from accidently falling from it at night. In the centre, around the Elemental Crystals laid a number of columns.

They each crystal began to shine and glow brightly but not because of the moon light. Silence seemed to grow even more quiet as the wind stopped.

'Apprentice!—' yelled Kai, soon to be Elder of Windor speaking in elvish, '—Do you hear that?'

'I hear nothing Master Kai' replied Ka'dul the Apprentice.

'Drogun, how about you?' asked Kai

'I hear little to nothing Kai'

'I don't like this, it's too quiet, Drogun signal to the village to make sure everything is okay'

Drogun nodded and moved to the rim of platform, he raised his right hand to signal with a flame from his hand. The wind suddenly picked back up and something fell from the moon towards him at first it was a dark figure. The figure revealed a curved shining weapon in the moonlight, unsheathing a katana, and thrusting it towards Drogun.

Drogun quickly reached for his weapon, an Iron sword, he blocked the attacker. Drogun was however forced to the floor, the man stood above him, Everything was black leather, gloves, boots, trousers and vest. A necklace hung from around his neck but Drogun couldn't make it out. A man with long white hair, white as the moon stood above Drogun.

The man smiled, he thrust his curved katana downwards to impale Drogun. Ka'dul thrust his lance towards the attacker, the attacker quickly turned and cut the sharp glass like rock away from the wooden lance, the blade fell from the platform towards the ground.

Drogun rushed to his feet as the master approached the attacker with his weapon, Tur-anion the Patriot, the attacker blocked the attack and jumped to the other end of the platform. A grin stretched across his face. Kai stumbled and fell to the floor, his left leg was cut, blood dripped from the attackers blade.

Ka'dul ran towards the attacker with his bladeless lance.

'Ka'dul no!' yelled Kai

He suddenly stopped in his tracks five foot away from the attacker. The attackers blade was through his body. Blood began to ooze into his mouth, he spat it into the face of the attacker. The attacker suddenly ripped the blade from his body, grabbed him as he stumbled forward. He grabbed Ka'dul's shoulder and threw him into the night sky until gravity took over.

'NO!' yelled both Kai and Drogun.

Again a sadistic smile stretched across his face.

Drogun rushed towards the attacker now, the attacker rushed towards him.

He swung his blade to the left from his right, the attacker swung his also the same way. The attacks weapon cut through the blade as it did he turned on the spot while lowering to the ground, faced Drogun again at waist level and stabbed, impaling Drogun's right knee, cutting through him like a piece of paper.

Drogun placed one hand behind his back and begun try and concentrate as something began to glow in Drogun's hand. The attacker didn't notice and instead looked towards the Elemental Crystals. Heat streamed from the growing fire ball as the attacker began to turn around. He suddenly revealed it to the attacker. The attacker panicked, he removed the blade and jumped back as Drogun fired. Burning the attackers attire.

The attacker stood on to columned railing as Kai got back to his feet and ran towards the attacker. The attacker took a step back and fell from the platform.

'Drogun are you okay?'

'I'm fine'

'Who was that man?'

'I don't know, his hair was white like the moon, stained with the blood of . . .'

'A "Blood Moon" . . . can it be?'

"—We came to call him Holfast, which means Blood Moon.

By the next morning I returned to the ground to find most of the village had been killed. Even the Elder at that time was killed and Kai was soon voted to be the new Elder. But something else happened that no one could of seen. THE prophecy began, the prophecy that speaks of death and destruction, the end of the world. I know this may sound like crazy talk but please come to Windor, I'll explain more once you arrive."

'He's right ya—' said Yal groggily awaking from his long sleep. He began to cough and gasp for air, '—It does sound like crazy talk. Now I know I'm not the most level headed person here but that is some crazy—' the church bells ring, no one hears what he is saying as he continues until they eventually stop, '—Penitentiary stoop! Am I right?—' the others stare at him as he asks, '—What?'

'Anyway how can we getting there?' asks Varin

'We?—' says Co Hobson, '—There is no we anymore Hero'

Co Hobson rises to his feet. He begins to make is way towards the chapel doors.

'But if it's true what my brother says, the planet will need yours and the TGs help'

'Don't you get it! The TG are no more, go home Hero!'

Sylvia runs in front of Co Hobson and stretches her arms out to bard the door, stopping him from leaving.

'Varin's right, the planet needs the TG's help!' yelled Sylvia to Co Hobson.

"At the time I didn't know why she was doing it, she wasn't even a real member of the TG. Yet she was demanding the fight to continue against SPARK. Co Hobson wanted to hear none of it but she talked him down and turned his view around on the situation. There was something about Sylvia at that moment that reminded me of . . ."

'She's right Commander—' spoke Talon unsteadily waking from his sleep, wound now fully healed '—As long . . . As long as there are TG members around the fight must go on to save the people of the planet'

Sylvia lowered her arms as Co Hobson turned to face Talon.

'But what she and Drogun are speaking of is saving the entire planet not the people' replied Co Hobson, slamming himself in one of the benches.
'The people are part of the planet, we fail if either go' said Yal.

No one spoke, the only sound was from the wind slowly forcing the bell to sway from side to side. Co Hobson now buried his head into his hands.

'How can we save the planet?' asked Co Hobson

'Wasn't that the point to the TG?—' replied Varin, stepping closer to Hobson, '—To stop PHOENIX! To stop SPARK! To stop the death and destruction to the planet? At least that's what I thought it meant. I don't know about you guys but I'm going there to see my brother and to save the planet if need be'

'Varin wait—' said Yal, '—I'll join you'

'As will I' spoke Talon

'Same here' said the cheery Sylvia.

Even the Togu stepped forward to join in but Co Hobson sat there, not sure of what to do.

'Shall I join them?—' he thought to himself, '—What about the others can they be replaced or even avenged? Can the TG be rebuilt again?'

'Okay—' yelled out Co Hobson, now raising to his feet, '—I will join you, for Trans-Gression. Down with SPARK!'

He put out his hand, Yal and Talon placed theirs on top of his repeating his words 'For the Trans-Gression. Down with SPARK'

Sylvia does the same and says the words once more. Varin not sure what to do, looks around the group, they all look at him and each have the same expression on their face, 'Join in.'

Varin places his hand atop of Sylvia's cold soft hand, 'For the Trans-Gression. Down with SPARK!'

'And how do you suppose you can get there?—' spoke the Priest standing by the chapel entrance, the door now closing behind him.

"He wasn't there before, in fact I don't remember seeing him after he placed Phoenix Tears onto Talon's wound. He just disappeared and reappeared. No one can do that"

'—I have something you may be able to use, an Airship. I believe it's very primitive even before the 20th century. Though it's not very big it should be able to take you from Karves to Windor with some ease.'

'What's it's fuel?' asked Co Hobson

'It is fitted with two small propellers and it's balloon is filled with Helium. It is what I use to travel to other chapels that need my services but the planet is far more important than how a simple old man travels' replied the Priest

'Thank you father' said Varin

The Priest lowers his head to Varin, while removing a scroll from his robe. He passed the scroll of paper to Co Hobson showing the location of the Airship along with some instructions on how to control the airship, titled 'Learn to fly.'

The scroll was old, torn and stained from all its years in service, a dark red lingered on one of the corners of the scroll probably from wine.

'You think . . .—' paused Yal, '—You think that Crystal that we collected is one of these crystals that Drogun speaks of?'

'Good question, perhaps . . . we could speak with the Professor? He after all looked at the crystal' said Talon

'The airship isn't too far away from the Prof's place, we could drop by' spoke Co Hobson

'Let's get going then' said Varin charging from the Chapel.

"Where did the Priest go again?"

The Togu, Sylvia, Varin, Co Hobson, Yal and Talon left the safety of the village to the surrounding, infested forest.

The forest is quiet, nothing but the gentle sound of the wind blowing amongst the trees and the crack of old branches by the group as they march their way through the forest.

'I don't like this' spoke Yal

'Don't like what?' asked Varin

'The quiet'

'The quiet?' asked Sylvia

'It's too quiet—' said Talon, '—They're afraid of something'

'What can monsters be possibly be afraid of?' replied Varin

'Bigger monsters' answered Co Hobson.

Varin suddenly trips over a log lying on the floor, the others continue on, he turns to see what he has tripped over. Lying under a small pile of leaves is the lifeless carcass of a fiend, a Shori. A white furry animal half a metre in length with black stripes along it's body.

Varin gasps in horror, the brothers turn on instinct Yal unsheathing his weapon. The Togu growls as Sylvia slowly approaches the body of the Shori, as well did the others surrounding it. The others pull out their weapons.

'It's a Shori, they have a tenancy to pretend to be dead to fool their pray' whispered Talon.

Varin slowly stood up and reached for his revolver, meanwhile Yal slowly removed the leaves over the top of the Fiend.

They all suddenly took a step back, but it didn't move it continued to lay there. The Togu began to sniff the body. It was dead alright. They turned back onto the path heading towards the Professor's cabin no more than a mile away now.

More bodies of Fiends began to pile up, each with a similar wound, a stab through the rib cage or the slicing off of a limb, even the trees weren't save from the fight that took place, countless trees were cut down or showed sign of a battle mark.

Talon placed his weapon away and pointed to a point just up ahead.

'There. The Professor's cabin'

'Finally. Maybe he could tell us what this is all about' spoke Yal

'As well as the crystal' said Varin

They approached the cabin, putting their weapons away. Knock, knock.

CHAPTER 17

Defying Fate

'ELDER, SOMETHING APPROACHES in the sky' spoke an elven warrior

'A Fiend?' asked Kai, Elder of Windor.

The warrior shrugs.

'Bring it down, whatever it is' commanded Kai.

The warrior nods and leaves the tent.

Drogun rises from his bed within the tent, still covered with bandages across his torso and right arm. He stands face to face with Kai.

'Master, what if that thing is my friends?'

'Drogun, there has not been any flying machines for hundreds of years. It's most likely a fiend'

'And if it's not?'

Kai never spoke his look said it all, 'They will die'

Drogun rushed out of the tent.

Elven archers took to the walkway with bows and arrows as the streets cleared. Orders barked amongst the lieutenants and soldiers, 'Get into line! Aim for the Fiend'
'Sylvia is that Windor?' asked Yal
'I believe it is'
'Looks like they brought out the welcoming party' spoke Yal
'Then why do they have bows?' asked Co Hobson
'Prepare to fire!' yelled the general

Drogun ran towards the front of Windor to see the approaching target. The airship which the Priest lent to Varin and the others, now only half a mile away.

'FIRE!'

A female scream emitted from the airship.

'NO!' yelled Drogun.

The archers did not hear in time, a volley of a hundred arrows headed towards the airship. Drogun threw out his left hand in the direction of the arrows, fire erupted from his hand almost like a river stretching towards the arrows creating a wall between them and the airship. A few arrows got through the wall of fire.

'Grab onto something!' shouted Co Hobson to the group.

A arrow hit one of four ropes holding the wicker basket to the balloon, serving it from basket. Varin fell towards that end, he managed to grab a hold of the side of the basket as an arrow passed him. Something began to drip in front of his left eye and stain his shirt.

"I didn't care at that moment, my only intention was to hold on"

Another arrow hit, this time it struck the back of the balloon. Air began escaping and it began to plummet back first towards the ground. A meter from the ground Varin let go just before the airship hit the ground. It hit the ground with such force the basket flung everyone away and ripped itself from the basket. Ending up only a few meters from the town.

Suddenly the sound of many bows stretching was heard by Drogun as he still stood in shock.

'STAND DOWN!!—' he yelled towards the archers, '—Fire another shot you'll see I'm far worse than hell!'

'Drogun!—' yelled Kai, '—I'm sorry, but this was their destiny. You know that, you've seen for yourself, What the prophecy says'

'It says they die in the crash but . . .'

'But what Drogun?'

'Hope. The prophecy speaks more . . . and in them, my friends, my Myradi. While there's life, there's hope!'

'Death cannot be defeated, only defied, but never questioned. If they do survive they will die soon after'

"I walked away from my Master to help. The others looked at me. I felt their eyes on the back of my head, but I didn't care.

They all knew the prophecy and the words that my Master spoke of, it's not their authority to mess with fate. Nor is it mine . . . but I will"

Still in pain from his muscles, Drogun limped to the crash site. As he approached the basket he saw the Togu alive and well, standing over Sylvia, gently licking her face trying wake her. She wasn't moving or breathing. He limped as fast as he could to her but was stopped by a hand reaching out from under the balloon grabbing at his foot, Co Hobson.

Drogun looked down and back up to see Varin next to Sylvia with deep cut from an arrow over his eye with the blood staining his hair and cloths. He started to perform CPR as Drogun helped Co Hobson with his broken leg and arm, drag Yal and Talon from under the balloon.

Yal was unconscious but breathing very faintly. Talon's arm was broken. Sylvia began to breathe once more.

Varin picked up, as she laid in his arms, and Drogun carried Yal the same as Talon helped support Co Hobson with his good arm. They marched back towards Windor. The Togu took the lead as still the elves stared, no one helping. All of them just watching in silence.

"A few hours passed, Sylvia still laid asleep. I placed her and the others in the closest house that would allow us entry. The Togu cared for her in one of the bed rooms while I tried to cool the others down."

'What the hell is their problem!—' yelled Co Hobson, '—They could of killed us! and they did nothing to help'

Co Hobson continued to pace up and down, even when injured he couldn't sit still, wood splints and bandages held his left leg in place, as did one on his right arm. Bandages covered his ribs. The Ninja Twins both sat leaning by the wall. Yal now awake was sitting on a stool with a bandage around his head.

Varin sat in the corner away from everyone. He had an small dressing over his cut eye, a bandage around his right arm and his fingers taped together on his left hand.

Drogun stood leaning against the wall closest to the main entrance and windows in silence as the other continued to argue and sigh amongst themselves.

'Why did they attack us!?' asked Yal looking towards Drogun. He remained quiet

'Why didn't they help us?—' asked Co Hobson, '—DROGUN!'

'GOD DAMIT DROGUN!' yelled Talon

He quickly grabbed one of Yal's swords and throw it at Drogun. The sword hit the wooden wall beside his face, he didn't flinch. Drogun grabbed the handle of the sword ripped it from the wall and walked away from the wall. He stood in the centre of the room, he pulled out his sword. Suddenly he throw Yal's sword into the air, he swung his blade and placed it back away. Yal's it the floor and fell into three pieces.

'Hey!'

'Enough!—' commanded Drogun, '—I've had it up to here of you three bad mouthing these people! There is a reason for what they did, which will be explained in due time. But for now just wait . . .'

'Wait!?—' asked Co Hobson, '—wait . . . for what! Those dagger ears nearly killed us, they injured your brother and you just stand there as if nothing happened, you're just as bad as those pointy eared freaks!'

Drogun suddenly erupted with anger. Co Hobson was slammed to the wall, something sharp was pointing into his neck, he looked down and saw Drogun's 'Tur-anion' pointing into his neck.

'I know what happened, I knew it was going to happen but at least I tried to stop it, these people are my family, they have ancient traditions and beliefs. You can't imagine what these people have been through over the generations for you and the rest of mankind. Now shut up and wait.'

He removed his blade from Co Hobson's neck and placed it away, a sudden pain stroke him.

"It's only a headache"

A loud bump came from the bedroom. The door opened, the Togu strolled out followed by Sylvia, she began to lean against the door and looked half asleep.

'The wait is over, let's go' said Drogun

He made his way to the door and opened it as the others rose to their feet.

'Hey what about my sword?' asked Yal

As they exited onto the streets, the elves stopped and continued to stare once again. The streets became quiet,

Drogun led the group looking towards where he's going but the others looked around at the staring elves.

Drogun handed them each a stone weapon and wooden armour that he stole as they walked for another twenty minutes in silence, entering a forest.

'Drogun, where are you taking us?' asked Varin
'To see the Wall'
'The Wall?'
'It has all the answers you'll ever need. For all of you'
'How can a wall have answers for us?' asks Co Hobson
'It foretells of a prophecy. One of which you are all involved in—' replied Drogun, as they continued now into a thick jungle, '—I do not believe it was by chance that we all met. We are all linked to PHOENIX in some way, even the one that has been following us.'
'The Togu?' asked Sylvia in confusion
'No.'
'Who do you mean then Drogun?—' asks Yal, '—I have not sensed someone following us'
'He's been following us awhile now. He's fast but impatient, a couple of times he's got a head of us. In fact—' Drogun looks around, '—he's a head of us right now. But he doesn't know where we are going and I believe—' He cuts through several vines and standing in front of him is an ancient pyramid, '—we're here. This is the first time any non-elven tribe people have entered these grounds so stick close to me."

They walk towards the pyramid, in the centre was stairs leading to the top but Drogun went nowhere near them, he instead whet to the side of the pyramid where from west to the east was a passageway with an ancient language written into the stone.

They all, except for Drogun, entered with aw on their face. He then ripped a piece of fabric from his jacket, he then got his sword and wrapped it the around the sword and finally set the piece of fabric a light before passing it towards the others as they walked further into the passageway. He raised his own hand and created fire with his palm and uses that as his torch. He began to search the inscriptions.

'Here it is . . . now, the language is every ancient and so isn't fully translated'

'In what way might I ask?' asked Sylvia

'It's all translated we just don't know what a couple words are, they could mean one thing or another.—' replied Drogun, '—Okay I'll begin.

In the year 2399, the five crystals that control shall be lost in the darkness of night with a blood moon rising,—We figured these crystals control and power the planet, Fire being the earth's core, Water the oceans, tides and so on—

Once gone the planet shall be thrown into chaos as the planet slowly dies.

—Now this is where it gets a bit fussy—Two brothers of Fire and Ice shall step forth and the Kildarfu shall be the chosen one to collect all five and return them before the year 4000.

—It gets a bit more hazy,—Without all five collected a great evil will doantatie—We're guessing summon—and a meteor shall fall to destroy the decaying planet.—We guess this great evil is blood moon or in elven Holfast—

With the five collected the chosen one shall become—this part is really unreadable but it then later goes on to say something about someone becoming a god, we guess that's the evil and how it summons the meteor.'

'You said this will answer our questions but it hasn't!' says Talon

'This is just the beginning, the rest from here on talks about "the selected" to aid the chosen one to collect the crystals and basically everything that has happened up until now, and something about a child of heart'

'What happens later?' asks Sylvia

'Something about a war, the heart and death . . . well more death. According to these walls you all should of died when being shot down by the arrows—' Co Hobson suddenly reacts with interest, '—You were all meant to die, that's why they did not help. They were afraid if they changed fate they'd bring a curse to their village.'

'Now what do we do?' asked Varin

'We return, it will be getting dark soon and then we will continue on our journey and if you're willing to join me, collect the crystals.'

Drogun looked amongst the group.

Sylvia smiled and nodded, 'I'm with you Drogun'
Varin was next to join him, 'Same'
Yal and Talon nodded
'Are you all nuts!?—' said Co Hobson, '—You all think, we could save the world? By hunting down these Crystals? You know how nuts that sounds? If we have until the year 4000, why not let someone else worry about it, how can this thing refer to us?'

Drogun turned and walked a little further down the passage before coming to stop. He shone the light on one final inscription.

Co Hobson looked, as Drogun read it aloud.

'The commander of those against moral principle, shall witness the rebirth from the ashes of a fallen bird—' Drogun pauses as Co Hobson backs away slowly, '—It mentions you and you witnessing the birth of our enemy, Holfast.'

Co Hobson pauses for a while, not sure what to say or do.

'Okay . . . I'm in'

CHAPTER 18

Chosen

THEY RETURN TO the elven village of Windor. The main gate opened, two rows of six elven warriors led by an older elf and a veteran of many battles. Masar. Marched towards the group. Each elf armed with a bow, a quiver of twenty arrows and a sword. Each wearing thick plated wooden armour as if they were prepared for a war.

'Rýnadaer?—' asked Masar, Drogun nodded as he looked around at the other men, '—pyndrel tol'

'Drogun, what did he say?' asked Varin

'They're placing us under arrest—' replied Drogun, '—for denying fate'

'They won't take m . . .' spoke Co Hobson before Drogun stopped him

'Stand down Commander—' Drogun turned to Masar and said to him, '—we'll go quietly.'

The Masar began taking each of their weapons as the other elves led Drogun and the others back into the village. The Togu began to growl at the elves walking towards it.

'No, girl. Calm down' commanded Slyvia

The Togu stopped growling and allowed the elves to place the collar around its neck.

"They lead us through the village, most of the elves came out to watch almost as if it was a parade or a walk of shame. We came to a building slightly larger than the other buildings. We entered and saw their armoury of spears, swords, bows and shields, to the right was a small doorway leading down some stairs into a dark wet dungeon. Their jail cell. Masar stayed at the top of the stairs as we were led into the three cells"

Co Hobson, Talon and Yal entered the cell furthest away from the stairs. Drogun, Varin and Sylvia entered the middle and the Togu entered the last vacant cell. The warrior elves locked the rusty cells and left. A familiar face came down the stairs carrying woollen blankets.

'My old friend, Domere' spoke Drogun in elvish

His friend didn't speak, until the door leading to the jail was closed.

'Here Drogun take these—' he handed the blankets through the cell '—there's not much else I can do. There is talk, talk that the Elder and the council has lost faith in you and the prophecy. They intend to jail you for life and get other people to collect the crystals.'
'What about the protectors? The guardians of the elements will attack them, only the chosen has save access to the crystals.'

'They plan to send the most skilful of warriors . . .—' I sudden noise came from above, the Elder has arrived, '—I must go.'

Before he goes he places a number of things upon the cabinet beside the stairs.

'Drogun—' called Varin, '—What was . . .'

The door swings open, Masar stands in the doorway. He waits until Domere pass him and begins to make his way down the stairs, staring into the eyes of Drogun, with a grin across his face and his warrior armour clanging together. He comes to the cell which Drogun is in.

'You know, this is your third strike mongrel—' said Masar in elvish '—you should of been thrown into here sooner but because you are supposedly "The Chosen One" they let you off and now they deem you unworthy of that title.'
'You never believed I was the one and I agree—' replied Drogun, Masar's smile getting bigger '—my brother is The Chosen One'

The smile dropped from Masar's face.

'Now, now Drogun. Do you think anyone will believe you? Especially since you've committed; theft, murder, denying fate and don't forget that he was prophesied to die? The council will make their decision, and not even the Elder can make them change their mind. If . . . he was on your side'
'And what of you? have you lost faith in me?'

'I lost faith in you the day you killed my first son and allowed my second, Ka'dul, to die.—' Drogun didn't speak, he moved his eyes away from Masar's, the smile returned to Masar's face, '—Oh what is this? The fearless protector of Windor gone quiet . . . Togu got your tongue?'

'Enough Masar' said Kai, the Elder, from the top of the stairs

'Elder, I'm sorry I . . .'

'Leave us Masar'

'But I . . .'

'I said leave!'

"And so he did as he was commanded. Although leaving he went back up those stairs like a dog with a tail between its legs."

'You have some nerve coming back here Drogun, after taking some elven weapons for your friends, defying fate and the prophecy—' said Kai, '—We have lost faith in you Drogun, over the years you've caused fires, killed many of our people and now. You've stolen and defied fate'

'Oh my god, I understood that . . . hey I know elvish' said Yal

'Yal he was speaking in our langue' said Co Hobson

'I do not deny the deaths I have caused. And I do deny fate, fate is in our control, the control of the people, not some higher force.' replied Drogun

'Is that you belief?' asked the Elder

Drogun nodded. The elder moved away from the cell, back towards the stairs.

'Very well. I'll inform the council that our chosen one has lost his faith'

'I'm not the chosen one. I believe my brother is. He's got to be the brother of Ice'

'Drogun, you were brought here from a young age, you were and are trained for this, you are The Chosen One.'

Varin didn't pay too much attention, he was distracted by the small pool of water beside him. He removed the bandage to see the scar, a scar he's seen before, but a face he remembers from the past.

~~∽∾∾∾∾~~

2269, atop the rooftop of the SPARK Corp. Building in Shenma City.

Co Hobson finished speaking over a radio as Varin kicked the door open, aiming his gun at Co Hobson

'Freeze!' yelled Varin

Co Hobson casually turned, 'Hello HERO . . . it won't be long now . . .'

'Until your bombs detonate? I got friends disarming them now they're the top of the class in bomb disposal' said Varin with a cocky look on his face.

That was until Co Hobson grinned, which suddenly changed as quick as it appeared.

'No, Hero. It won't be long until PHOENIX destroys us all'

Varin then took one sudden step forward, 'There's nothing wrong with PHOENIX! It's our energy and it's the only way to survive and you wish to take that away. You wish to kill human kind?'

Co Hobson turned his back to Varin, paused for a second and began to speak once again, 'Back in the twentieth century they had fossil fuels and alternative resources—' he then turned round and continued speaking, '—And if you recall, 2259, the great city of Karves was totally destroyed. Only three hundred people survived out of a population of thirty thousand and the same thing will now happen to Shenma, the deaths of all these people will be on your shoulders!—'

Varin then moved his eyes away from Co Hobson, keeping no eye contact and began to think to himself, 'I was seven at the time, how could I remember?'

'—What's a matter hero!?—' Varin looked at Co Hobson and kept eye contact with him while Co Hobson was finishing his comment, '—the guilt crushing your shoulders? Well since you came this far you might as well take me in and take another life . . .—'

He held out his hands together, ready to be cuffed.

'—only kidding Hero'

The sound of a familiar Apache helicopter reached Co Hobson's ears and so he quickly reached inside his pocket, pulled out a small round silver ball, he threw it to the floor, releasing smoke.

Using this as a smoke screen for his escape. Something fell from the helicopter that now hovered above Co Hobson.

The Apache took some more height as Co Hobson grabbed what fell from the helicopter, a ladder.

Co Hobson left Varin a parting message as he disappeared off into the distance, 'You have some skill Hero, hopefully you'll live before the PHOENIX rises'

The smoke cleared away and Varin ran to the edge of the building watching Co Hobson disappear into the distance.

'Damn lost him . . . GODDAMNIT!' cried out Varin.

He leaned slightly over the edge of the building, he stands there for a little second longer and turns, upon turning he hears a strange noise. Suddenly a man is standing in front of him by the stairs.

Varin is quick to react, 'Freeze!'

The Stranger casually walks across the roof, but upon hearing Varin's command he stops and then turns to face him, he stars at Varin for a second and then laughs.

The Stranger then suddenly stopped laughing.

'MaKe Me . . . VaRIn'

There was a mark on the floor where the Stranger, assumed Varin, was hiding. As he looked at the man he quickly made a mental note of what he looked like.

'He has long white hair . . . no older than twenty five, red eyes and the cloths that look new but strange, all black, all leather.'

Upon the Stranger calling out Varin's name, Varin was quick to reply, '. . . How you know my name!?' he said pointing his gun at the Stranger.

He then laughed again and walked off to the right and disappears into thin air, another burn mark appeared where he once stood.

Varin stood in shock.

"How could a man do that? Just disappear into nothing?"

A few seconds after he disappeared two more men came from the same location the Stranger appeared, one man was wearing a black hooded jacket, Varin was unable to see his face.

The next man looked no older than twenty, he had blonde spiky hair and ice blue eyes also had a scar above his left eye. These two men also disappeared at the same spot where the other stranger disappeared. Varin, blown away at what just happened, put his gun away into his holster, and sighed.

'I knew it wasn't going to be a quiet day.'

'Varin . . . ?—' asked Yal, '—Is he okay?'

They turned to see Varin sitting in the corner, shaking and covered in sweat. The puddle of water next to him had turned to ice.

Drogun walked up and crouched beside him, he grabbed a hold of Varin—it hurt him as he held his little brother, he shook Varin trying to snap him from his dream.

'Varin! Stay in this time, stay with us.'

It seemed to do the trick, Varin awoke from his vision of the past gasping for air.

'It was me? All those years ago? I saw myself . . .'

The Elder places one foot on the bottom step of the stairs and turns to Drogun, 'See what you do to those around you Drogun, you've turned him to madness. You were my best student . . . but I'm afraid my child, your time has passed'

The Elder left and ordered no one else to enter the jail. Co Hobson still sat in the corner closest to the gate, starring at Drogun's back as Drogun stood still by his cell gate.

'Hey Drogun—' called Co Hobson, '—Why don't you use your power to melt these bars?'

'The cells are heavily enchanted to stop anyone using magic upon them'

'So how do we break out?' asked Yal

'I have no idea.' replied Drogun, he turns his back to the gate and leans against it.

'Drogun—' said Yal, '—We have a question to ask you.'

'Yes—' said Talon, '—It's about that night at Skyspear. Did you go to see the Professor?'

Drogun moved his eyes away from Talon and stared at the floor in front of him.

'No.' he replied
'Why not?' asked Yal
'I knew what the crystal was, I knew its purpose'
'Do you still have it on you?' asked Talon
'Yes'
'We got a device from the Professor, the device could aid us in searching for the rest of these crystals. We just need to borrow that one for a second.'

Drogun hesitated for a second, but then reached his hand inside his pocket as Talon walked towards him the bars.

"Something wasn't right, my head began to burn up. A voice echoed but it wasn't my voice, they wanted the crystal whoever it was."

Smoke rose from Drogun's pocket and pain grew on Drogun's face. He quickly pulled it from his pocket and passed in to Talon. His hand continued to smoke as he yelled out in pain and dropped to his knees.

His black jacket became a flame and began to burn away, the rest of his cloths burnt has he fell towards the floor. Within seconds it ended, the jacket now ash and Drogun unconscious.

'Was that the crystal?' asked Varin

'The crystal is the element Water . . . maybe it reacted against him since he has control of fire?' replied Talon, looking just as confused as the others.

Sylvia placed one of the blankets over Drogun's naked body. No one else knew what to do, imprisoned and without an idea how to escape. It soon became darker as the sunset.

"Hours seemed like minutes, before long it was close to midnight and getting colder. Sylvia laid curled up with me to keep warm. The others huddled over themselves. I stayed awake most of the night to keep an eye on Drogun. My eye shut for a second and before I knew it, it was day light . . . Drogun was gone, the Cell gate ripped from its hinges. The door at the top of the stairs was open and a noise came from above."

Varin quickly reached his feet and ran to the top of the stairs. In the armoury stood Drogun now clothed, placing a lid on a barrel, a barrel who's lid was slightly askew due to an elf's head was popping out of it.

'I borrowed his clothes' said Drogun

Drogun was wearing black baggy cargo trousers, a black t-shirt and a dark purple denim like jacket a size too small for him.

'How did you open the cells gate?'

Drogun searches his clothing's pockets for keys

'I didn't, I woke and found it open'

He finds the keys and makes his way down the stairs. He hands the keys to Varin and goes to wake Sylvia. Varin suddenly remembers about the cabinet, he turns and sees on the cabinet are weapons, one for each person.

For Yal, two katana swords each with two blades attached to the hilt.

For Talon, a long white metal staff that could be folded up and used as three nun chucks connected by a chain.

For Varin, a Cavalry Pistol from the 17th Century with no gun powder or bullets.

For Sylvia, a white scythe made from a light metal, that too can fold up like her old one.

Each weapon possess a magic secret, the same that Drogun's possess. Amongst the pile of new weapons is Drogun's blade and another blade.

'Sylvia, Sylvia wake up'
'D . . . Drogun—' she opens her eyes and gives a small smile hearing Drogun's voice, '—Thank god you're okay'

Varin meanwhile opens the cell gate to the Togu. The Togu immediately goes over to Sylvia, knocking Drogun out of the way as Varin goes to open the next cell gate to Co Hobson and the Ninja Twins. Drogun helps Sylvia from the ground as the others stand beside the stairs.

'Grab a weapon' said Drogun, pointing to the weapons and so they did. Each of the grabbed their own weapon leaving just a sword, similar to Drogun's.

'Co Hobson why don't you take it?' asked Drogun
'I'm fine with my own fists' he replied

'I'll take it then—' said Varin, '—since there is no ammo for this gun'

'Okay good, I'll just quickly say these weapons have elven magic in them. Like my sword, it can disappear until I call for it?' asked Drogun

'It disappears? I assumed it was just under you jacket' replies Sylvia

'Each of these weapons is full of elven magic, you place it on you somewhere and it disappears until you need it and then it will take physical form once again. Varin, yours on the other hand creates ammo, once you fire, it create another round instantly reloading the weapon for another shot. Your sword on the other hand does not contain magic so you'll need to keep that on you at all times.'

'Sorry to cut you short Drogun, but we need to get out of here first' said Co Hobosn

'You're right. The only way to get out of here however, is to fight our way out" replied Drogun

'What? couldn't we sneak out?' asked Yal

'We wouldn't have a chance, we're near the centre of the village and its high noon, we'll be spotted in seconds'

'What are we waiting for then?' asked Varin

Drogun nods, placing his weapon on his back, it vanished, as he led the group up the stairs before coming to a stop, crouching by the door.

Varin was the last up, he saw a leather case with a strap long enough to wrap around his thigh, he picks it up on his way towards the others and begins to tie it around his right thigh.

Drogun nods to the others, they nod back. Each get their sword ready, Drogun reaches for his and it appears where he placed it. He begins to reach his hand out towards the door handle and throws open the door.

They run into the streets, Drogun makes eye contact with a female elf holding laundry. She drops the basket and yells for the guards.

'Don't kill them' ordered Drogun

The non-warrior elves ran from the street into their houses, grabbing their children and pets as they ran. Within seconds the streets were empty but filled with the sound of armour clanging together. Above the houses on the lookout, elven arches began to take positions, the sound of the bows tightening now filled the streets.

'Stay low and keep to the buildings' ordered Varin

"Only one chance to escape. Through the front gate, five hundred warriors to fight, two hundred arrows to dodge. Against seven of us. Without killing one of our attackers. We should get some sort of reward"

A dozen warriors with spears and swords in hand ran towards the group yelling. The group quickly stood up, revealed their weapons and spread out.

A spearman ran towards Co Hobson. The spear was now a foot away from Co Hobson, he stepped to the side and grabbed it with his left hand yanking in the spearman, he swung his right fist connecting with the spearman's face as another warrior approached.

Two swordsman ran towards Drogun. The first swordsman swung his sword to the lower left from his right, Drogun swung his sword in the opposite direction to knocking the guard away. Drogun raised his sword over his back as the second swordsman attempted to attack him from behind. Drogun blocked the attack and struck him with his elbow as another warrior approached.

A swordsman ran towards Varin. Varin held his gun in his right hand and sword in left as the swordsman attacked. Varin not knowing how to use a sword properly took aim with his gun but then remembered what Drogun said. The elf swung his sword for Varin's face. Varin ducked under the blade and stepped to the side of the warrior, he then elbowed him in the rips and wacked the butt of the gun into the back of warrior's head. The warrior dropped to the floor unconscious as another warrior approached.

A spearman ran towards Talon. Talon stood in his fighting stance prepared. His opponent ran towards him with spear in hand aiming for his torso. The spear was three foot away from his body when Talon finally reacted, he used his new staff as a high jump pole lifting him up and over spear. Directly below him now was the spearman, as he began to fall Talon raised his staff high into the air and struck the spearman from behind by rendering him unconscious. Talon turns to see another warrior approach as he turns his staff into the three nun chucks.

A swordsman ran towards Yal. The swordsman strikes downwards against Yal but the swordsman's sword is stuck between the two blades of one of Yal's katanas. The spearman attempts to attack Yal, but using his other blade Yal cuts the sharp metal away from its wooden base. Yal then uses his stuck blade to throw the warriors sword away, as he turns Yal kicks the man into one of the buildings and then delivers another kick, this time to the spearman knocking him to the floor.

Two spear man ran towards Sylvia, charging at full pace. She stood her ground and waited until the spears were just close enough, she attacked. She began to spin her scythe cutting away at the spears, now making them nothing but harmless sticks. The two warriors stood in shock as Sylvia made her next move, using the butt of her scythe to hit one of them warriors around the side of the head on her right, but by doing this she left her self-open. He prepared to attack but was stopped by Drogun, giving him a punch to the ribs with his free hand.

Drogun ran towards another attacker.

CHAPTER 19

𝔅anishment

'FIRE!'

The sound of the bows released echoes in the streets.

'Get inside quickly' yelled Talon

The group ran into the two buildings on the side of the street creating an entrance for themselves, followed by the six remaining warriors. Drogun, Sylvia and the Togu entered the building on the right, followed by two swordsman and a spearman. Varin, Co Hobson, Yal and Talon entered the building on the left, followed by three swordsman.

Drogun, Sylvia and the Togu slowly backed themselves into the corner of the room as the men approached. The Togu growled and seared at them as a cocky smile stretched across their face. Drogun stood in front of Sylvia and looked as if he was waiting for something to suddenly happen.

"As I stood there starring at these guys, a countdown begun in my head. 3 . . . 2 . . . 1."

He suddenly moved, he ran to the Togu and jumped onto it's back. The spearman raised his spear as the Togu charged forward, Drogun raised his sword. From behind Drogun a number of objects ripped through the roof, arrows. The warriors smirks suddenly changed into shock as the arrows missed Drogun and came for them. The spearman lowered his spear slightly, Drogun swung for the spear cutting it away from the wood as the arrows hit the warriors. They instantly dropped to the floor, hitting it harder and faster than Drogun dropping from atop the Togu.

They laid on the floor in pain, the sight almost sadden Drogun, it would of if it didn't make him smile. The three of them returned to the streets as did Varin, Co Hobson, Yal and Talon. And they continued their march towards the front gates.

Above the front gates, one hundred archers awaited them.

'Run, keeping going' yelled Drogun

What remained of the three hundred, plus, warriors gave chase as the neared the front gate.

'Drogun! Archers' yelled Co Hobson.
'I'll take care of them. The door it's closed, Varin use your ice!' yelled Drogun once more.
'What?' replied Varin
'Your ice use it!'
'I have no idea how to'
'Concentrate on the door!'

Drogun raised his sword above his head and put the sword horizontal. Above the archers was the sun without a cloud in the sky, as they got closer to the range of these archers he tried to reflect the sun back at them to temporarily blind them. The archers tightened their bows more at they drew closer.

'Ready . . . aim . . . fi . . . ARGH' yelled one of the elven officers

Drogun managed to blind them as they were only a few hundred yards away from the gate. Some archers tried shooting missing the group by far.

Suddenly a cold wind blew as if it were summoned, it froze some of the archers where they stood but more importantly the door began to turn to ice.

"How the hell did I do that, I thought to myself . . . it was kinda cool.
. . . No pun intended"

'Nice work Varin. Now shoot it' said Drogun

Varin pulled out his pistol and took aim, he pulled the trigger and a bullet flew from its barrel. He waited a second and pulled again, to his amazement another bullet did erupt from the barrel of his gun, he pulled the trigger a number of times shooting in a door for the group to run through. He sped up to take the lead and jumped at the door, kicked down the door he had created. It slid a couple feet away from the ice gate as he stood crouch a top of it. The others ran through. Drogun lowered his sword as the group ran as fast as they could to escape. The archers turned.

'FIRE!!'

Drogun stopped and turned hearing the commanded, one hundred arrows came straight for them. He held out his hand, nothing happened.

'What the hell' he said to himself. He tried again, not even a flicker or spark of a flame. The arrows grew closer. He tried harder and for the first time was scarred.

A foot away the arrows began erupting into flame, not quite what he wanted but as each arrow began to slowly turn to ash, the group continued on.

A foot from Drogun most turned to ash or hit a few yards away from him. One however was coming straight for him with no time left for him to evade, it flew to an inch in front of his eye and turned to ash.

The archers reloaded and the three hundred or more warriors began to spew through the ice door. He turned and ran to catch up to the others.

Some Elves are however faster runners than humans, the group ran from the archers range but the warriors soon court them up. The group were soon stopped by a band of four warriors racing ahead of them. They were soon surrounded. They pulled out their weapons once more, Varin pulled out his pistol.

'What are you doing?' asked Drogun
'Don't worry, I don't intend on killing them' replied Varin

Ten warriors all carrying swords approached the group, suddenly one yelled and stepped out from behind another, 'DROGUN!!'

'Masar'

Drogun ran towards him, he did not watch the other elves or even notice them. He just focused on Masar. Varin raised his gun and rested it on his other arm. He took aim and shot each elf in their shins that stood in Drogun's way. The five remaining ran towards the group.

Masar and Drogun's blades clashed together as they both showed their strength against one another.

'I've been waiting for this day Drogun!'

'As have I Masar—' Drogun gave an evil smile, '—After all you taught me how to use the sword and now it's time the apprentice defeated the master'

Drogun shoved Masar back and their battle began, each blocking each other's attacks, both evenly matched. They clashed their swords together again. Suddenly a shadow was cast over them, they looked towards the sun and saw a figure of a man falling towards them. The figure revealed a sword and broke their struggle between the two apart cutting Masar's arm off in the process. The man dusted himself off, as Masar laid in pain holding what remained of his arm.

'Nice to see you gentleman again' said Thorn

'What the hell are you doing, I could of taken him'

'Sorry I believed I was helping'

The small band of elves were defeated, by the army march forth was not. Their war cry got the groups attention. In the distance standing upon the walkway at the village of Windor, a elf yelled, 'ENOGUH!'

His voice echoed to Drogun and the others. The army of warriors stopped as the man began to speak once more,

'THERE HAS BEEN ENOUGH BLOOD SHED ON THIS DAY.

DROGUN, AS ELDER AND YOUR MASTER I BANISH YOU, AND YOUR FRIENDS, FROM THESE LANDS AND PLACE A BOUNTY UPON YOUR HEAD. YOU HAVE FAILED AS MY PUPIL. BRING ME THE INVALDEL.'

The army continue to run towards the group.

'I'm sorry my master' Drogun dropped to his knees.
'Drogun, I know where we could escape to—' said Thorn, '—we have to go through more elven territory but we could make it to the Continent of Ruins"
'Which way is it?' ask Yal
'To the north, towards the disappearing bridge'
'Drogun we've got to go' said Varin

He rose to his feet as the ground shaked under the running footsteps of the army as the group ran towards the north, towards the disappearing bridge that could take them to The Continent of Ruins but first they need to lose the army.

'Run towards the jungle' said Drogun, he began to run.

Drogun led the way, running past the approaching army, to the jungle. Before he reached the first leaf of the jungle he stopped allowing the others to pass him. Drawing his weapon as the army approached. Each warrior prepared their weapon. Drogun tightened his grip on his sword.

Suddenly he swept his sword across in front of him, a fire begun in front of him, stopping the warriors a meter away from himself. He put away his weapon as the fire began to spread and became a circle around them. Drogun smiled as he turned away.

"Luckily they soon lost us in the jungle, thanks to Drogun slowing them down with that circle of fire. But it didn't stop us from running. We continued to run until night fall, staying clear of any villages. News spreads fast in the elven lands."

Drogun helped keep the pace, knowing how the elves could capture them if they were to slow at any point. They soon reached the half-way point through the elven lands before resting.

One member of the group is still awake, Sylvia.

The group laid huddled around a small fire, off in the distance is a village, two miles from the group. Sylvia is keeping awake by watching the village in the distance, watching small bits of flaming light as she writes a passage in her diary.

Sleep begins to take over her, her end begins to dip as her eyes close for a second, a second later she opens her eyes, the village now a flames.

'Guys, GUYS!' she yells and stands up
'Wh . . . What!?' asked Co Hobson

They all awoke, except Drogun, all of them stood in shock as the village burned. Sylvia awoke Drogun, he slowly reacted and reached his feet, as if he never slept the entire night.

'My god shall . . . shall we help?' asked Yal

'No—' said Thorn, '—it could be a trap'

'A trap!? those people could be really injured or worse—' said Varin, '—we gotta help right, Drogun?'

'They're only elves.—'Drogun stopped for a second, '—I mean we must help, let's go.'

Set off and reach the village as soon as they could, but not fast enough to help anyone. By the time they arrived the village was consumed by the flames, leaving nothing but ash and smouldering wood in the village. They searched the streets of life, for hours on hours they searched hoping to find survivors but all they found was the charred remains of elven women and children.

"What kind of monster could have done this . . . ?"

They continued their search until day break and soon they had to move on, towards the north. However the further they travelled, the more villages they found burnt down to the ground overnight. Some containing many corpses, others without a single sign of life that once belonged there. Each village was the same, destroyed by flames from the centre of the village and most of the villages looked like they weren't prepared for the attack, others looked like they tried to put up a fight but failed, arrows laid throughout these village as well as swords and burnt armour.

Unable to bear the burden of not been able to help, they travelled as far and as fast as they could in a day hoping to get ahead of the arsonist to stop any more attacks. Even if it lead to them being captured by the Elves and their returned to prison until their death.

They arrived at night fall to the village of Vodos, this one had yet to be attacked, they entered knowing fully well what would happen but they went in anyway and immediately confronted by warriors with spears in hand pointing to the throat of each member of the group.

'What are you doing here?—' spoke the general in elvish, '—Are you here to burn down our village as well, Fist Of Fire?'

'We didn't do it, we came here in hope of stopping the attacker' replied Drogun

'Why should we believe you, everyone knows you can control fire' said the general

'But you know I am bound to an honour code, much like yourself. Please Aiskins, allow us shelter here to stop the attacker. My old friend.'

'. . . Very well, old friend. I trusted you when we were young men and I still do despite what the Elder speaks of you—' Aiskin turned to his warriors, '—Stand down!'

They removed the spears from the group's throats.

'Please follow me.—' said Aiskins, '—We'll give you a room at the inn were you may stay the night but you must be gone come morning.' Aiskins turned once more and began to walk.

Drogun turned his head to the group, 'It's okay, we may stay the night'

It was close now to midnight. Outside of the inn two guards were posted to watch over the group, they stopped anyone from entering or leaving. Following the group round was another two guards. The entire group were sitting or standing around a small room. Drogun stood closest to the windows, looking out, as usual, wrapped in a blanket complaining of the cold.

'What the hell is going on?—' asked Co Hobson, '—In the past five days we've seen seven or more villages burnt down. Is someone sending us a warning or are we just at the wrong place at the wrong time?'

Talon is standing with his arms crossed thinking, sitting near to Drogun is Sylvia keeping a watchful eye over him as the Togu chews on a bone from a leg of editable fiend by his feet. Thorn is sitting away from the group, sitting by himself on another table playing with the device given to them from the Professor.

'Maybe this is our father' replied Yal, unsure.

'No, our father is a murder but this is not his thing. Something much worse is going on here' said Talon

'Sss . . . So cold' says Drogun to himself.

'What's a matter with Drogun?—' asked Sylvia, he doesn't reply, so she turns to the group, '—He's been acting like this the last couple of days'

'He's probably just got the flu, he just needs to stay warm although it quite warm already here' replied Talon

'How do you get this thing to work?—' asked Thorn angrily, annoyed by the machine '—The stupid thing won't work. It only picks up that water crystal'

'Give it here—' replied Yal, he takes a look, '—maybe we're out of range of any other crystal, ya?'

'It's meant to show each crystal on the entire planet' replied Talon

'Maybe the things are underground or something?' said Varim

Something beeps on the screen for a short second and disappears.

'What was that? Something just flashed, it was pretty close' said Yal

'Give me it—' demanded Thorn, Yal picks up the device and drops it onto the floor under the table. He picks it back up and gives it to Thorn, '—nothing there now'

He places it away into his pocket.

CHAPTER 20

Arsonist of Vodos

ANOTHER HOUR PASSES, Thorn asks bored, 'No sign of an attack yet?'

'Not yet—' replied Co Hobson, '—I think we got a head of the arsonist, he should be attacking this place tonight'

'What if you're wrong Commander?—' asked Drogun, '—What if the arsonist doesn't'

'Then we'll wait until they show themselves'

". . . A voice, I heard. A voice in my head . . ."

Drogun suddenly collapses onto the floor, still shaking.

'Drogun! Drogun' called Sylvia, trying to wake him.

The guards stood there unsure of what to do.

'We got to take him to his room' said Varin

They placed Drogun upon the Togu, who now stopped chewing the bone. They followed it to Drogun's room as Varin demanded the elves get a doctor or some kind of medic, they did not understand a word he said. Thirty minutes passed and each member of the group went to a separate to sleep. The two guards placed themselves outside of Drogun's room, ordered by his friend Aiskins to be considered the most dangerous.

'Brother, where are you?'
'I'm right here what are you talking about?'
'You're not my brother!'
'I'm not? Could of fooled me'
'I don't trust you, my brother died along with my father'
'Father? what are you religious? You should go to church.'
'What?'

Lightening stroke, illuminating the area, it was a rooftop, a rooftop he's seen so many times.

'The boundaries have been vaporised,—' said a hooded character standing upon the highest peak of the roof, a peak similar to a lightning rod, '—right from my eyes. If everyone jumped from a bridge, everyone dies. And this flood of ones and zeros . . . man, we got no ties, we got no heroes.—'A blonde haired man begins to cry, '—Do you remember, when you used to laugh, and do you remember when you felt? It seems all these days you do is cry. Crying at the hand you been dealt. Crying at the hand you been dealt. I ask you, if a tree falls and no one's around, does that fallen tree make a sound? Hell yeah, the waves still can be found. The waves still can be found. You see these waves, they start, just where the light exits, it's a feeling that you cannot miss, and it burns a hole, through everyone who feels it, these waves will permeate, they will dominate and they will confiscate everything and this world and the next world. Everything.—' The crying from the blonde haired man grows louder, '—Listen to me. Take your tears, put them on ice, I swear I'll burn this city down. It's time to end our crusade way, and face the powers that I can't even imagine!'

The hooded man jumps from the rod, revealing a sword. The rod is stroke by lighting as the hooded man falls towards the unarmed blonde haired man. He stops his crying and looks at the hooded man falling towards him.

'FIRE!' yelled Yal

Varin heard the yell from two rooms away, waking him from his dream. As he reached his feet he heard the floor boards out past his door creek as the others ran past and down the stairs. Varin took a quick glimpse outside and saw a hooded man in the streets walking calmly down the streets as the elves run amongst the streets in a panic.

'The arsonist?' Varin thought to himself.

Varin quickly turns, opens the door and runs down the stairs. Rushing onto the street he finds the others, commanding and helping people flee from the streets to safety as some of the villagers tried finding water to stop their homes from being destroyed by the flames, pushing the small or weaker to the ground. The entire town was already a blaze lighting up the night sky.

'I saw the arsonist, they're around the side heading towards one of the bigger buildings' said Varin

'A big building?' replied Talon helping an elderly man from the ground.

'That building is the gun powder stock house' said the elderly man.

'What? why do elves have gun powder?' asked Co Hobson

'It doesn't matter we need to stop him' said Thorn

"Him . . . How did he know it was a guy?"

'We need to help . . .' spoke Talon before getting cut off by the old man

'No worry, son. Go and kick his ass'

Talon gave the man a small nod and set off with the group, running towards the building, the Togu quickly began to lead the way.

'Where is Drogun?' asked Varin

'I saw him before his happened, he said he was going for a walk. He said he didn't feel too well' replied Sylvia

As they drew closer, with each step they drew closer to revealing their weapons, only Varin hoped to be the first to reach the arsonist.

As he ran with the others towards the north hoping to reach the gun powder stock house before the arsonist, the flames reminded him of a time where he first felt pain, the day of the incident, the day the world changed for him, for everyone once living in the great city of Karves.

He remembered the burning flames close to his skin, the suffocating smoke choking him. The screams of others, a light and a shadowy figure with a hood. As well as what remained of the train which his brother and father were on. Nothing but the flames and smoked now consumed the train rather than the everyday people going about their everyday lives, all that ended that day.

Varin snapped himself from his day dream, a couple hundred yards from him was the arsonist heading towards the gun powder stock house. Anger, sorrow and pain from that day enraged him and so without thought he raised his gun, aimed at the arsonist and pulled the trigger.

'No . . .—' yelled Yal as he knocked Varin's arm, but the bullet still hit the arsonist, '—What the hell are you doing?'

The arsonist was shot in the knee but he continued on wards to the stock house as if nothing had hit him.

'We're supposed to stop him and bring the guy to justice, not execute him' said Talon as he and the group ran to catch the arsonist.

Varin stood there for a second, 'Sorry' He then ran after them.

The arsonist now noticed them coming, he passed his arm out in front of him creating a wall of fire to slow, he smiled and continued as the group still approached.

Sylvia jumped atop of the Togu as they drew near the wall, it jumped the fire landing safely on the other side. The Ninja Twins led the way running through the wall, burning their cloths slightly in the process. As he ran, Varin began concentrate on the wall of fire, it slowly began to die down as he reached the wall.

"He was becoming good at that."

Two houses down was the arsonist and the stock house. He entered the building.

The Togu lead the way once more with Sylvia on top, it soon reached the stock house. With her weapon at the ready, she jumped from the Togu towards the door. She slashed it once as she flew towards it, cutting it in half, she smashed her way through coming to a stop a few feet from the entrance. The Togu entered but continued further in without her, seconds later the group entered.

All was quiet.

They take a quick look around while guarding the door, the stock house was set up much like a barn would be with ladders leading to another smaller floor. All around them was countless barrels of gun powder and from what they saw there was more on the next level of the barn as well as a window, but on the floor next to them was blood, blood leading to the ladder.

'Where's the Togu?' asked Yal

'Twele, her name is Twele' said Sylvia

'Twele must of followed him' said Varin take a step forward

Suddenly a growl and a whimper of pain fell from the floor above, the Togu was attacked. It, fell kicked, from the upper level and cut by a sword around its left eye. Sylvia put down her weapon, which disappeared, as she crouched to see the pain stricken Togu. Pain, fear and a realisation expression appeared for the first time on its face. The group including the Togu then looked up to the higher level and saw the arsonist standing on the edge, covered with the blood of the Togu.

There was also blood on his long leather coat, from where Varin shot him in the knee. The coat was similar to the one Drogun once had.

The arsonist jumped from the higher level to the floor and as he came to land he slowed as if he was floating. He landed not far from Sylvia and Twele, as he did he placed his arms behind his back and lowered his head. The hood of his coat covered his face, nothing could be seen other than his mouth and the evil smile he gave to the group.

"Where's his blade? He must of had a blade to cut the Twele . . ."

Suddenly, the sound of something sizzling echoed in the stock house. He gave an even more wicked smile and fled towards the window on his left. Where he stood was a trail of gun powder leading to the barrels close by. The arsonist jumped through the window as the group realised what happened, Twele although injured got back to her paws and limped as fast as it could as Thorn forced his way past the others running for his life. All of them fled. Except Varin.

"I froze that gate, and calmed that fire . . . maybe I could get it to work again"

And so he remained in the room with the trail shorting with every second, he stretched out his arms and concentrated in hope to freeze or put out the flame before the place became rubble.

But unlike before, flashes of memories came to his head. An image of him in the train station of Karves City, an image of him been attacked by Craig when they were younger, the image of Co Hobson telling him he will cause the deaths of millions. The image of him standing outside the prom alone like he has always been.

'NO!' He yelled as the trail ended at the barrels.

The place exploded with such force it blew the roof off the building, the explosion caused the surrounding buildings to break away losing sides or even their roofs. Every window in the village cracked or broke apart and the flames spread more. Debris from the stock house fell down onto the village, creating holes in roofs, destroying parts of already weakened buildings.

When the stock house exploded it knocked Yal back causing him to hit his head off a rock as he landed, Talon was hit by a piece of the wall and knocked out as well. A beam flew towards Sylvia but the injured Twele jumped in front of it, taking the full weight of it to protect Sylvia. The force of the beaming hitting them caused them both to fly a few feet back winding them both. Co Hobson was blown through a house, a beam fell and trapping him under the rubble.

Varin was forced towards the wall of the stock house, he went through it and laid in pain on the ground, winded but conscious. He earned from the distance the echoes and cries of pain from the other villagers, and that sound—the sound of something burning just ever so close.

He looked up at the night sky, now with an even more orange tint as the arsonist walked over to Varin. Something sharp suddenly was point at his throat, a sword. Varin stared at the arsonist as he stood above him now raising his sword to stab Varin. As he did light reflected from the sword illuminating the arsonist's face as they starred at each other.

'Drogun!?'

As if woken from a dream Drogun shuck his head, he lowered his weapon and dropped it to the ground causing it to disappear, he stumbled back away and fell on his backside in shcok of what he was going to do. He removed his hood and knew what he had to do. He got back up and took a few steps away from Varin and suddenly realised the great pain in his knee, almost falling to the ground because of it, but he continued to walk, dragging that leg behind him as he walked back to the south, back to Shenma City. The skies opened up, and rain fell putting out the raging fires.

Darkness returned to Varin.

'Hush little baby—'
'So you travel once more, back to Shenma . . . a choices needs to be made'
'—don't say a word—'
'A choice to be a warrior of light or a warrior of darkness'

'—mama's gonna buy you a mocking bird.'

'What do you choose, Drogun?'

'My decision is my own elder'

'You no longer speak with respect, you should praise me for I am your father, your only family'

'No! you may of took me into your arms but you did it unwillingly.'

'. . . So . . . you've became a warrior of darkness?—'

No reply.

'—When a warrior of light attempts to extinguish the darkness, he succumbs to it. Becoming the very thing he despises. He becomes the hated. The darkness, the enemy itself.'

'If the lamp of the body is the eye. If therefore the eye is good, your whole body would be full of light . . . but if your eye is bad, your whole body will be full of darkness. If therefore that light in you is darkness, how great is that darkness . . . Answer me Elder. ANSWER ME!'

"Something suddenly jumped from the darkness, a creature . . . no a man . . . his hair was white like wool . . . holding a sword flying towards me"

Varin finally was awoken from his dream by the Twele nudging his head. It was purring softly as he woke, and getting to this feet. The Twele then ran towards Sylvia lying on the floor still winded.

'Sylvia are you okay?'

She gasped for air first before she replied 'I'm . . . fine'

He reached out to help her from the floor, 'I'll help you up'

As she rose to her feet she yelled from pain, she placed her right arm over her ribs as Varin wrapped her left arm around him.

'Where are the others?' she asked
'I don't know—' he replied, '—Twele can you find them?'

Twele turned and began to search the rubble around them for the others.

'She has a name you know—' said Sylvia, Varin turned with a question written on his face, '—her name is Twele, meaning protector"

They moved towards some rubble which Twele was looking around for the others.

'When did you give her the name?'
'Today, I just thought since we met, she's protected me so I thought it would suit her.'

They both went quiet for short time as Twele scavenged the area.

'Varin . . . about that night at Skyspear. I'm sorry . . .'
'Skyspear, oh the kiss. I completely forgot about that.'
'Oh . . . well . . . erm . . . I'
'Don't worry about it'

"My heart belongs to another. Always has. Always will. Emily."

'You see the letter was for your brother . . .'

'My brother, shit the fire—' He looked back to the building that once was the stock house, '—Drogun did this . . . he is the arsonist'

Twele began to purr once more to get the attention of Varin and Sylvia. As they came over Twele back removing bits of metal and wood with her teeth. Underneath they found Yal, breathing fine.

'Yal, YAL!' yelled Varin

Yal slowly woke, he opened his eyes and quickly closed them once more, 'Ah . . . the light' he said slowly.

'Light?' Varin looked up to the sky, night began to turn into day.

'It's only two in the morning, why is there sunlight?' said Sylvia

Varin helped Yal to his feet, almost falling over with Yal, as Twele searched once more.

'Where's Talon?' asked Yal

Twele once again purred for their attention and once again began to remove the debris from over someone's body.

~~~∞∞∞∞~~~

A lieutenant of the Elven Army of Window enters the tepee of Kai, the village's Elder.

'Elder. Sir, sorry to disturb you . . . the night has become day'

'That generally happens at dawn lieutenant'

'. . . but sir, it's not dawn'

'What?—' replied the elder, '—How can this be? It's not time'

'He's ready sir'

'No this cannot be.—' he says rising from his bed, he stands at his small desk looking over the notes spared out, 'It's far too early for him to be ready . . . but the recent chain of events, they must of forced this.'

'Sir, how could Drogun becoming a warrior of darkness invoke Blood Moon to resurface?'

'It's been prophesised, I must see The Wall. Where are the Togu Riders?'

'They've located the group'

'Excellent, take me to The Wall and give them the command, Order 67'

CHAPTER 21

The Brothers of Fire & Ice

THE VILLAGERS HAD now packed and left the city, going north, leaving the remains and ashes of Vodos behind. The group rested as Varin prepared.

'Talon are you okay?' asked Yal

'I could be better' he replied

'We need to go' said Varin

'Go . . . go where?' asked Talon

'To Shenma City'

'Why?' asked Yal

'Drogun was the arsonist. He's heading to Shenma City'

'How do you know this?' asked Talon

'He was talking to Kai the elder. I saw it in my dream'

'Varin. It was a PHOENIX DREAM, you only dreamt it. Drogun will be around here somewhere' replied Talon

'NO. It was him I saw where he was going, I saw the path of destruction that he left in his wake and what he plans to do'

'What did you see?' asked Yal

'I saw more villages burnt to the ground, I saw power lines running from Shenma destroyed. I saw what he plans to do to the people that work at SPARK. He plans to kill them all, to litter the floor with their blood and bodies. I need to stop him.'

Varin begins to walk off.

'What about Thorn and Commander Hobson?' asked Yal

'. . . What does your gut tell you?' replied Talon, he to begin to walk, following Varin.

Yal began to walk, hanging his head. Sylvia raised her arms to climb upon Twele, she yells in pain. Yal and Talon stopped.

'What's wrong?' asked Yal
'My ribs' she replied

Talon ran over and placed his hand gently onto her ribs. She yelled once more in pain.

'They're broken. Sylvia, you can't come with us . . .'
'But I want to'
'I'm sorry you can't, not with that injury. Continue to travel north, you should meet up with some Trans-Gression members from the other continent. They'll look after you. Take the Twele.'

'But I want to help you guys'
'You can't, not until those ribs heal'

They helped her upon Twele and she and the Togu went. She ran up to Varin.

'Bring him back'

He nodded and with a kick, they sped off again running past Varin and then turning to the north, tears trickling down her cheeks.

'Be save my love'

If the dust settling Yal and Talon soon joined Varin, and began to leave the village.

'Varin, it'll take days to reach Shenma City. How can we reach that on foot?' asked Talon
'I don't know but we must, Drogun has already passed Windor' he replied
'In two hours?—' replied Yal '—That's impossible'
'Where's the nearest village?' asked Varin
'Ten miles west of here' replied Talon.

As if from nowhere three riders upon Togu's surround Yal, Talon and Varin. Each carrying a sword and bow and heavily armoured like the Togu's they ride. The group reveal their weapons.

'Finally caught up with us have they?—' said Varin '—took them long enough'
'Let them make the first move' said Talon

One of the riders dropped his Togu, Yal prepared his weapon but the rider did something that any of them was expecting. He kneeled before them.

'Heroes, take the beasts and ride to our salvation'

The others then climbed from their Togus and kneeled, unfortunately neither Yal, Talon or Varin knew what they spoke. They placed their weapons away.

'We don't understand' said Varin

The elven rider handed Varin a scroll. He unrolled it and read what was written upon it was;

"Order 67"

Nothing else written upon it, he begins to search the paper and then suddenly more words appeared to merge.

'Take the Togus and ride to Shenma City and kill Drogun.'

The words disappeared once more as Varin rolled up the scroll. Varin annoyed by this walked past the three kneeling riders and jumped on the Togu of the first rider. Yal and Talon followed closely, stopping to thank the riders and rode off into the distance heading south, to Shenma City.

'Varin?—' spoke a voice inside his head, '—I am Kai the . . .'
'Elder I know, how are you able to do this'

'Each village Elder can do to speak to one another or to someone else.'

Within a few minutes they pass three burnt down villagers, seven miles apart from each other.

'Varin, these Togus have been trained for speed. You should be able to stop your brother before it's too late'

'Too late for what?'

'There's a part of the prophecy which we never showed Drogun . . . this was only possible if certain events were to happen, such as your arrival here and if you were to survive the fall from the sky. Two possible outcomes are about to happen as a result of the warrior of light becoming the warrior of darkness and fighting the brother of Ice. One, the brother of fire kills the brother of ice, thus entering the world into darkness. The other, the brother of ice kills the brother of fire, ending the darkness. However each will bring the destruction of the planet'

'What?'

'You saw what he did, he tried to even kill you, I've seen into his mind and your mind. You want to kill him'

'No. I want to stop him and although you may read my mind you cannot read my soul.'

'You think he's still of light. Shame . . . you were I only hope. Now we have no one.'

The Elder ends his talk with Varin as an Elven Priest leads him to The Wall deep within the jungle. They climb the stairs entering the room.

'We're here Elder.'

'Is this it here?'

'I believe so'

Varin and the brothers have now entered the snow fields getting closer to the mountain ridge.

'Priest what does it say?' asked Kai
'It says what has already happened and about to happen.

Night shall turn to day. Storms will begin above a grand city, wind and lightening shall control the skies.—'

Varin and the brothers are now at the ridge, the Togus begin jumping from one rock to the other downwards as above a storm begins to brew above Shenma City, thunder, lightning and winds. The land around Shenma begins to darken from clouds, tornados begin to touch down in areas of the city through junk and scrap into the air. Lightning begins striking buildings, setting some a blaze.

'—Upon this time a great evil shall resurface from hiding and binding, a blood moon. A warrior of light attempts to extinguish the darkness, thus succumbing to it. Becoming the very thing he despises. He becomes the darkness, the enemy itself.—'

Now the group are at the gates of Shenma City, the power has been knocked off from the freak storm above. The Shield and the electronic gates are offline. The group continue charging forward and onwards towards SPARK.

'—The great evil will search for the elemental crystals as the chosen one is districted by his own evil corruption.—'

They are now at the doors of the SPARK Corp. building. The storm above Shenma seems to be strongest around the building as if this was the centre of it all.

'—The brother of fire, shall fight the brother of ice. Darkness shall fight the light. One shall die, both endings will bring the destruction of the world and the coming of evil. It has begun.'

They enter the building, the remains of workers, blood and ashes, litter the lobby. They approach an elevator, even the elevator was stained with signs of death. They take it to the top floor, the floor they been to before, the main office of SPARK. The doors open, the windows of the floor implode scattering glass everywhere.

'The storm seems to be getting worse, ya' said Yal
'Must be Drogun's doing, we need to stop him' replied Varin

They open the office to see Thorn with his father, Diamant, dying in his arms.

'He . . .—' said Thorn, '—Drogun, killed my father. He's waiting for you on the roof'

He pointed towards the balcony, a trail of blood leads from his father the floor to the balcony. They step onto the balcony and follow the trail that climbs a ramp to the roof, a floor above the office.

'Where is he?' asked Yal as they looked around the roof.

'Brother, where are you?' asked Varin

A fire stars around Yal and Talon forcing them back.

'Varin!' yelled Talon

He turns to see the fire, forcing them back towards the ramp. He tries to concentrate, he can't focus. Drogun is on his mind, concern for his brother.

'Brother! . . . Drogun where are you'
'I'm right here brother, what are you talking about?' replied Drogun

"I know this, I've seen this in my dream"

'You're not my brother!' said Varin
'I never said I was, I lied this whole time'
'The Drogun I know, wouldn't of killed countless numbers of the defenceless. He would of protected them. I should of realised my brother died along with my father'
'Father? What are you religious? You should go to church.'

Lightening stroke behind Drogun, the light illuminated the area. It was a rooftop that Varin has seen once before in a dream.

'What are you doing here Drogun?'
'The boundaries have been vaporised,—' said Drogun standing upon the highest peak of the roof, a peak similar to a lightning rod, '—right from my eyes. I have been given a power to do anything'

'Then why? Why use it to harm people?'

He smiled, 'If everyone jumped from a bridge, everyone dies. And in this flood of ones and zeros . . . we have no heroes. We got no ties . . .'

'What are you saying Drogun?'

'I hate you!—' he screamed as thunder echoed, '—You killed mother, it's because of you she died.—'

Tears begin to swell up into Varin.

'—Do you remember, when you used to laugh? And do you remember when you felt? It seems all these days you do is cry. Crying at the hand you been dealt. Crying at the hand you been dealt. What happened to the people you loved Varin? They died because they were linked to you. Mam, Father, Emily, Karves, the TG. All because of you.'

'I . . . I . . . my fault . . .'

'Yes because of you, everyone around you dies. I see even Sylvia didn't survive you'

'No . . . no, I am not at fault here. Everyone makes their own destiny, and Sylvia made her choice yet still lives.'

'She lives? Huh, I guess that kiss wasn't so deadly after all'

'Kiss? You saw? How . . . ? the light, you were the one that cast the light upon us?'

'Yes . . . I saw you kiss her and I was the one to cast the light'

'. . . Why? Were you jealous?'

'SHE WAS MINE! I'm a damn hero Varin, do you know how long I've done this and been alone. A hero deserves a reward and the least I get is not even a thank you'

'A true hero doesn't expect a reward'

'Haha . . . then I ask you, if a tree falls and no one's around, does that fallen tree make a sound? Hell yeah, the waves still can be found. The waves still can be found. You see these waves, they start, just where the light exits, it's a feeling that you cannot miss, and it burns a hole, through everyone who feels it, these waves will permeate, they will dominate and they will confiscate everything and this world and the next world. Everything—'

The tears become more overpowering on Varin as he knows what's coming soon.

'—Listen to me. Take your tears, put them on ice, 'cause I swear I'll burn this city down and show you the light.'

'Drogun, I know what you plan to do next, we can't do this. BROTHER LISTEN TO ME!'

'I don't remember saying I was your brother.—' Drogun begins to laugh as the storm above becomes more violent. It begins to rain, '—It's time to end our crusaded way, and face the powers that I can't even imagine!

Drogun jumps from the rod, revealing his sword. The rod is stroke by lighting as he falls towards the unarmed Varin. He stops his crying and looks at Drogun falling towards him. Varin bends slightly and unsheathes his sword from his right thigh, blocking Drogun's falling attack. As Drogun's feet touch the floor Varin kicks Drogun away and pulls out his gun with his spare right hand.

'Drogun, I don't want to do this, but I will if I must'

'You must!' snarled Drogun

Varin pulls the trigger, three times but each bullet is blocked by Drogun's sword. He again jumps to attack Varin from above, Varin rolls out of the way. He quickly gets back to his feet as Drogun turns and swings wildly at him. Varin turns his blade down to block a low attack, he quickly raises back up to block high as fast as he could. He's seen what Drogun can do with the blade, he knows what could come next.

Yal tried to rush into to help, but is grabbed by Talon. 'Yal no, this is between them.'

'What?—' asked Yal, '—You know Drogun is good with the blade, we need to help Varin.'

'There's nothing we can do.'

They continued to cross swords as Yal and Talon looked on. They threw each other a punch, a kick or an elbow whenever they could. They crossed swords once more trying to overpower the other.

'Murderer!' yelled Drogun, face to face with his brother.

Varin forced Drogun back, as he stumbled back a few steps Varin reached for his gun and pulled the trigger four times before Drogun came back with an attack of his own.

Drogun stood up and smiled as the bullets flew towards him, his long leather jacket seemed to fly from his body catching the bullets. As they pierced the leather, the holes begun to turn to flames instantly burning the jacket and turning it to ashes. Drogun walked through the ashes unscathed.

Drogun swung his blade more wildly catching Varin's clothing and flesh with his sharp blade, he now stood in his face again, giving Varin a right hook.

Varin retaliated with a head butt and a knee to the stomach of Drogun. Drogun dropped his weapon, grabbed Varin by the waist and threw him over head. He dropped his weapons as he entered into a roll and stood back up with his back to Drogun.

They both turned to face each other and ran at each other, a few steps away they began to prepare their attacks. Varin launched with a right hook, Drogun spun raising his arm to block the attack, as he turned to face Varin once more he jabbed with his own right.

Varin caught the punch but stepped back as he saw Drogun prepare for more, he continued to spin and this time with an elbow from his left, Varin blocked it again using is left forearm. Pain shot up his arm but he had no time to breathe as Drogun span back the other way now with a number of haymakers and with that he saw his opening. As he turned to face Varin he closed his arms in close to protect himself before sending out a jab again, Varin ducked under the jab and struck with an elbow to the stomach of Drogun.

He staggered briefly until Varin gave him a side kick into his chest, knocking the wind out of him once more. He fell onto his back a few feet away, as soon as he hits the floor he flips himself back onto his feet again. He punches low catching Varin of guard hitting him in the stomach before delivering his own kick to Varin.

"The kick moved so fast if you were to blink you'd of missed it."

Varin falls and lands on his back a few feet away, he quickly rolls backwards and gets back to his feet, he runs to Drogun again. Drogun takes a step forward as the both prepare to punch each other in the jaw again.

Drogun stares heartlessly at Varin, almost with a sick grin of pleasure on his face at the pain he's inflicting on his brother. They both strike each other at the same time and both were equally matched. Suddenly an evil idea seemed to spark in Drogun's eyes. Flames seemed to grown from his shoulder and work their way down his arm to his fist.

The fireball exploded in his hand upon contact Varin, the force set them both back flying—Drogun quickly flipped over hand landed on his feet. Varin came to a sudden stop upon hitting the steel girder of the helipad.

Varin got back to his feet, slowly watching the silhouette of Drogun slowly approach him, highlighted by the flames behind him. Varin regained his breathe and entered into his fighting pose once more as Drogun did the same. Drogun smiled once more, leaning towards him slightly, before he knew it Drogun was already in mid-air and already a few feet away as he spun in the air about to kick. Flames erupt and follow his feet striking Varin on his left bicep as he tried to block the attack, he stumbled back a step as his arm fell numb.

He retaliated with a kick of his own, missing Drogun, as he missed he leant in with that left leg to give him another blow from Varin's elbow, he blocked crossing forearms. Drogun then swiftly punched Varin in the chest causing him to take another step back. He tried again with a few other punches but the feeling had quickly come back to Varin's left arm blocking most of Drogun's attacks. Drogun spun once again but this time Varin wasn't going to allow him a chance to attack, Varin reached back with his right leg and kicked out Drogun's feet from under him. The power alone spun Varin on the spot, as he turned back Drogun had placed his hand on the floor and his foot were flying towards Varin's chest. Varin blocked and fell to the ground as Drogun's other foot swiped his feet from under him.

"It took me by surprise but I didn't have much time to recover as Drogun had already leapt into the air, flipping towards me feet first."

Varin rolled out the way narrowly missing Drogun as he came crashing down, Varin quickly got back to his feet, he side kicked Drogun in his leg as he rose to his feet. Varin quickly delivered a roundhouse kick to the staggering Drogun, hitting him in the face causing him to stumble towards a maintenance shed a few feet away. Varin was already behind him ready to launch another punch, as it approached Drogun ice began to flow from Varin's shoulder to his fist creating a solid glove. Drogun ducked out of the way as Varin's fist struck the brick corner wall of the shed, the ice and the bricks wall shattered as Varin spun on the spot ready to attack again.

He launched the same fist again, Drogun blocked it, he launched the other, Drogun evaded it and pushed him back. Before he took another step back Varin threw a kick, Drogun evaded this to by spinning past it coming to a stop with his back to face with Varin. He twists his torso and grabs the off balance Varin by his shirt and throws him towards the maintenance shed a few steps away. Varin lands feet first horizontally against the shed, Drogun looks up at him in shock as he jumps from it and wraps his legs around Drogun's head, the force alone causes them to spin as Varin flips backwards placing his hands on the floor and throws Drogun towards the steel girders of the helipad.

As he flies towards them fire flies from him causing the girders to bend and melt away. The once raised helipad falls to come level with the rest of the rooftop as Drogun emerges from a burning hole in the helipad. A small radio tower falls from the helipad, Varin jumps over it and flies towards his brother, as Drogun powers up a fire ball.

He launches the erratic fireballs at Varin, who flips in mid-air avoiding them before crashing down as Drogun leaps back. Ice seems to spread from Varin's fist as it crashed causing sharp spikes of ice to come piercing through the ground, Drogun narrowly avoiding them. He flips in the air and lands on his feet as Varin now rises and begins charging towards him. He quickly prepares to kick Drogun with his right leg, Drogun steps back, he spins and swings the other around as Drogun now steps to his left away from Varin, the second kick misses. They begin to parry each other's punches until Drogun eventually lands with three swift kicks with his left leg, the first two Varin manages to block as Drogun aimed high but it left him open for the third.

It hit Varin in the chest, he backed up as Drogun aimed high once more, Varin quickly raised his guard but Drogun was able to kick it away with ease and that's when Varin noticed something, fire began to spread down Drogun's right leg. He launched his right leg forward aiming for the chest as a blaze of fire streaked behind his foots path, Varin side stepped attack scorching his clothes slightly in the process.

He raised his arms to block another attack from Drogun but couldn't move fast enough after feeling the heat of the flames against his skin from that last kick, Drogun span into the air again kicking Varin forcing him back and with that he took more steps away until he was a few meters away.

They now stood the complete size of the helipad away and Drogun suddenly began to move his arms around, preparing a powerful fireball. Varin lowered himself into his fighting pose until he saw Drogun prepare cast the spell by stretching out his hand. It cast a light bright enough to be seen from outside of the city.

Varin flipped over head touching the floor with his hands the ground froze over and as he raised his hands into the air the ice followed creating a thick wall of ice between him and Drogun.

The fireball left from Drogun's hand as Varin erected the wall.

The giant ice wall than began to hurl itself towards Drogun as the fireball hit, reflecting fire away. Drogun continued to cast the fireball, causing fire to fly from his hand like a continuous flame until the wall due closer, he stopped casting and paused for a brief second before jumping the entirety of the wall. Below he saw Varin as he came down with a boot out stretched to greet his younger brother. Varin blocked the kick causing him to slide back from Drogun, who landed perfectly fine two feet away.

Varin scissor kicked forward, Drogun blocked it and ducked under Varin's now approached left fist. Varin began to swing more rapidly and wilder fists, Drogun smiled mockingly at him dodging each fist and blocking the next three after that.

Again they stood as equals, blocking and dodging each other's attacks, neither landed another attack on each other for the next few seconds of the battle.

Varin had Drogun stepping back now, seeing a chance he attempted a spinning mid-air kick as Drogun has done a few times with succession, he performs it perfectly but Drogun back flips away creating some distance between him and Varin.

Drogun quickly gets back to his feet, an aura of flames surrounded him—the fight wasn't going the way he had planned, he thought it would be over by now and that just made him angry, the thought that he could be beaten by his younger, weaker, brother.

He ran to Varin, jumped into the air and performed a bicycle kick striking Varin repeatedly in the chest, before landing he kicks out one last attack, striking Varin in the head. Varin spins on the spot relying from the blow and also preparing a spinning fist. Drogun dodges the first and strikes Varin in the ribs with his right followed by an uppercut with his left as Varin huddled over on himself, Drogun spun and dropped to on knee as he sent out both arms into Varin's stomach forcing him to land on the other side of the roof.

Varin quickly gets back up ad takes a step forward but suddenly drops to his knees and coughs up blood.

A voice echoed in Varin's head, 'Varin, it's Kai . . . you must do this. Light must prevail over Darkness'

'I can't—' replied Varin speaking out loud, '—he, he's too strong.'

'You must! For your love, for Emily!'

'Emily . . . ?—'

Varin slowly rises to his feet, staggering slightly, he looks up to see through a sea of haze Drogun now rising, his vision altered by that uppercut. He stands still, he closes his eyes and breathes in heavily to regain his composure as he prepares for battle once more.

Drogun laughed to himself.

'—For Emily!'

Drogun begins to run towards Varin, he now stands a few steps away preparing to punch Varin with a huge grin on his face as Varin remains still.

The fist flies towards Varin's face now only an inch away Varin suddenly grabs the fist pushing it past him as he spins past Drogun. The grin on Drogun's face quickly turns into shock and then rage with the miss, he kicks up his leg as he stops himself. Varin blocks the kick and offer's Drogun his own kick to his back, Drogun bends underneath and quickly raises to give a back fisted punch to Varin.

Varin blocks the attack with both hands and then launches his own left first forward into the stomach of Drogun, whom blocks the punch and then spins to try that back fist punch. This time Varin steps back and blocks Drogun's other punches that he throws forward. Angered slightly Drogun then kicks up ward with his right, quickly followed by his left launching him off the ground. Varin dodges them, even the third kick that Drogun rapidly threw forward trying to hit Varin in the face.

At that moment Drogun then swung his right fist headlong into Varin's waiting grasp, Varin swiftly landed his elbow into Drogun's ribs and bowed, spinning, under Drogun's arm and punched upwards towards Drogun's bicep. Breaking his arm.

Drogun pulled his now useless arm away, stumbling back because of the pain but continued to attack throwing his good arm out wildly casting quick blasts of fire point blank at Varin. Varin blocked and dodged each blast and threw out his own fists, attempting to blast Drogun with shards of ice. Even with one arm, they were both equal, block and dodging each other's attacks but Drogun was panicking and backing away with each attempt and miss until Varin caught a hold of his arm and threw him over head.

Drogun flipped in the air, landing on his feet and jumped back into the air, he prepared another powerful fire ball as Varin jumped into the air after him. Drogun cast it forward, hitting Varin as he grew close but something happened, it didn't affect him Drogun stopped and saw Varin was covered in ice like an entire body of armour. Fear shot across Drogun's face as Varin now grabbed a hold of Drogun's shirt collar and punched him in the face. The impact caused the ice around Varin's fist begin to crack.

Drogun was stunned but suddenly realised he and stopped falling after the second punch, he had crashed down onto a column of ice that now held them thirty feet above the rooftop. He looked back up to Varin.

'Do it you coward, kill me or I promise your bitch will be the first to go'

Blood now poured from Drogun's lip and nose, yet he smiled, a bloody vicious evil smile.

'Emily . . . No!!' yelled Varin, as he began to strike Drogun in the face.

With each vicious strike of anger the column broke by another foot, the crack is Varin's ice armour quickly spread to the rest. Half way down the armour broke but Varin didn't care he continued, by the time they hit the ground,

Drogun landed with a thud, Varin's fists were bloody raw but yet he continued to punch with all of his might.

'VARIN!' yelled Yal and Talon. Both of them ran over to pull Varin from Drogun
'Enough, that's enough.' said Talon
'I loved you. I love mother and father. I love Emily—' yelled Varin, '—I love her, you cannot deny me that. I would do anything for her, I would never do anything to put her life in danger'
'What about the people of Karves' said Drogun, lying of the floor already showing scares of the battle.
'I murdered no one'
'But you will me, after all that's what the true prophecy says . . . RIGHT ELDER!?' yelled Drogun. He then begins to laugh.

Varin steps away, picks up his gun and blade, and walks back over to Drogun, dragging the sword. He raises it to Drogun's throat.

'Varin no' said Yal upon deaf ears.

Now standing above Drogun with sword pointing at him, he begins to think in over.

'No . . . You're not worth it'

Varin begins making his way towards the ramp as Yal and Talon stand aside to let him through. The rain begins to stop and the skies clear to show a beautiful day as Drogun begins to laugh.

'Hahaha . . . That's your one weakens . . . Your emotions, your human emotions. They are after all the weakness of all mankind. Haha, it's so funny, even the elven word for little brother, Myradi, can also mean weak one. Haha, you know, you'll have to kill me one day.'

Varin continued to walk down the ramp with Yal and Talon close behind, 'Drogun, never come looking for me or the crystals. Or I will kill you.'

CHAPTER 22

Revelations of the Past

THE THREE OF them go slowly back down to the office and enter from the balcony. Standing beside the body of Thorn's father is Commander Hobson.

'Commander—'said Yal, '—How did you get here?'
'No thanks to you!' he replied pointing a gun to the head of Yal
'Commander?' asked Yal
'Primrose, we have company.'

Up from a few steps is Thorn. Co Hobson switches on a radio in his pocket.

'What's going on here?' asked Talon
'Hmph . . . thought you would of figured it out by now—' said Thorn, '—allow me to introduce myself. I am Primrose Hillweller, son of this dead geezer and now new owner of SPARK Corporation.'
'. . . You killed your father?' asked Varin

'Yes. I just killed the fat fuck when that psycho stormed in here demanding something before he snapped and went outside.'

'Commander what's going on?' asked Yal

'You were always the slow one Yal. I've sided with the enemy.'

'Why?' asked Talon.

'Twelve years ago . . . Primrose woke me from my sleep in that pod over there. He realised who I was but he made a proposal to me . . .'

Twelve years ago,

Co Hobson rested in a sleeping pod alongside the Hillweller family, planning to awake a year before them, something is wrong however and he begins to wake three years before them. A red light inside the pod begins to flash as he slowly awakens.

The pod door is suddenly flung open, smoke begins to cover the area but he feels something cold and sharp against his throat, staring at him is a man he recognises but has yet to meet.

'Commander Hobson I presume. I am Primrose Hillweller'

'How . . . how'd you know I was here?'

'I didn't, I planned to awake early to undermine my father . . . none of the less. I have a proposal for you'

'. . . I'm listening'

'Establish a new Trans-Gression or die.'

'What makes you think I'd do what you want . . . ?'

'I know you're not a foolish man, and like any man you crave power. I wager once you destroyed SPARK, you'd take control yourself'

Co Hobson didn't reply

'I thought as much, all I require of you is to create a new TG to distract my father as I create a new group for something much more important. I'll happily give you all the money you want . . . Commander'

~~~

'He then rewarded me with money, my weight in gold. I lived for a king as I created the new Trans-Gression blinding his father's vision of the new group, FOX'

'FOX—' continued Primrose '—Fouilleur Of X-tal. Meaning Seekers of Crystal. Or as I like to call them puppets.'

'He even created the twelve members of Cognition using bioengineering from help of a friend.'

Primrose turned his back to the group

'Their true purpose was to hunt down the elemental crystals of this planet'

'WHAT!—' yelled Dicembre, '—Cognition are . . . just . . . puppets?'

Primrose turns back and see's Dicembre, the leader of Cognition standing by the door.

'Dicembre—' smiled Primrose '—You were a brilliant experiment, although I'm a little surprised you hadn't worked out already . . . no matter I now process all but two of the elemental crystals and this device should help me find the remainder'

'The device from the Professor?' asked Talon

'Yes the one and the same.'

'Is that why you joined us?' asked Varin

'Not really, I knew I had to keep an eye on you all, specially you Varin Vargon . . . you're an interesting fellow as I've been told by a mutual friend. Anyway as this room is getting a little crowded I think it's time I left'

'I . . . you mean 'we' right?' asked Co Hobson

'No Commander . . . I—' Primrose suddenly removed a gun from his pocket and shot Co Hobson. A perfect shot between the eyes. Co Hobson dropped his gun and drops to the floor, '—a bid you all adieu.'

Primrose then runs back up the stairs and hits a switch revealing a escape tube.

Dicembre runs to the control panel, looking for something to stop Primrose's escape. He hits a button and reveals another room at the back.

'Dicembre, leave.' commanded a familiar voice

Dicembre pauses, nods as the group hear sound of four footsteps on a metal floor. Dicembre leaves expression on his face as if he's seen a ghost. A man steps out of the room, a familiar face, and stands next to the death body of Co Hobson.

'Nice to see you again Varin—' said Craig, '—Who am I kidding, I fucking hate your guts'

'Craig Wilkens . . . the bully from Karves . . . how . . . ?'

'Shut the fuck up, you always did talk a lot. Why won't you ever fucking die? Every time we met I try to kill you but it doesn't ever work! WHY?'

'What are you talking about?'

'Maybe the PHOENIX Poison from that day messed with your memory, oh well let's start from the beginning of why I'm so much better than you and why she should have been mine. I am the son of the founder of SPARK Corporation—' he holds out his hands as if expecting a round of applause, '—Tell me what year do you think it is?'

'2609'

'Ha ha ha. Oh daddy you were such a genius, the year is actually 3997. In the year of 2359 my father a poor man, found PHOENIX and created SPARK. But in 2399, there was a problem and the PHOENIX spread throughout the world causing an incident no one has ever seen before, some at the time compared it Chernobyl incident. PHOENIX infected people turning everyone into their opposites causing what is now known as PHOENIX Poison. My father fixed this problem by cleansing the world and rewriting history. He told those that were partially infected the year was 2210 and being the genius that my father is told everyone that the fossil fuels had all been used causing global warming and freak storms, wiping out half of the planets population along with them'

'And ever since then SPARK has been ruling the world with an iron glove' said Varin

'That's right Varin'

'VARIN!' shouted a female voice

Craig ran back into the metal room, removing a gun from his jacket pocket and slaps someone in a chair with it.

'You do that again I will kill you—' Varin rushes over to stand next to Hobson's body s, '—Don't come any closer, or you will be just as dead as that fucker next you.'

'You said you tried to kill me before, what do you mean?' asked Varin

'2259, well your 2259.'

'The day of the Karves incident?'

'Bingo. I was the one that created that 'incident'. My intention was to kill you, but alas I was a young boy and so I miscalculated the power of the blast and instead I took out the city, not bad for a test run.'

'What? You destroyed a city to get to me.'

'Sort of it was meant to be you and your family. I knew that day you were going on a trip, so I planned to destroy the tube station to wipe you and your family out. I got into a SPARK Corp. building and caused it to cave in on itself. Making the blast. You know it's amazing where you can get into when your father is the most power being on the planet.'

'You always were full of yourself'

Craig marched up and pointed the gun against Varin's head.

'And you and your family were always trying to play the hero. You saved the day when I was bullying Emily and then when I try to get payback your brother has to save the day. Luckily on that day I got half my vengeance back. After that I laid low and watched you both from a far. Remember the day of the prom? . . . Of course you do, the day Emily broke up with you. After that I thought I'd let you live your life knowing you can't have her, the women you loved. But you remained in the picture, you followed her to the PTC and became an Police Officer because of her. Am I right?'

'Yes. I love her, I know I never told her but I do love her.'

'Why are you saying it in a present tents? Why not past? . . . You know she's alive? You're the guy that we grabbed her from'

'What?'

'Yes I see now, that was fun. If only I realised sooner, you wouldn't be alive now. I did wonder why she was calling your name as we dragged her from the room.—' he suddenly stops and grabs the person from the chair, '—Recognise her Varin?'

'Emily!'

'Right, ten points. Don't come any closer little Vargon. You know, should both know actually, that I loved Emily once, that's the reason why I brought her to this time. But she doesn't love me—' he then suddenly throws Emily down the stairs to Varin, he then took aim with his gun and shot her as she fell, '—So no one shall have her!—' he pauses for a second as her body hits the floor, '—Now, the second time I tried to kill you was the police st . . .'

Varin jumped to the ground to pick up the gun that fell from Co Hobson's hand, he quickly took aim and shot Craig as he was talking.

'You destroyed the building next to the police station to kill me, and so you saved Emily for yourself. And doing so . . . brought me here, you should know my brother, Drogun is also here, in this time and I intend to find my father. You're quest for vengeance failed! You failed!'

Craig dropped to his knees, dropping his gun in shock.

'I . . . brought you here? but how I . . .'

Varin pulled the trigger again and Craig fell back.

'Choke on it!' screamed Varin, pulling the trigger over and over firing another five shots before stopping.

Craig laid on the floor, he began to choke on his own blood and the life began to fade from his eyes. But Varin didn't notice, he kept pulling that trigger as tear began to swell. He finally dropped the gun and fell to his knees beside Emily. He turned her body, she was still breathing, and rested her head in his arms to speak to her.

'Varin you came—' she said, '—I knew you would come'
'I . . . I—' Varin began to search for words. '—I love you.'
'I love you too Varin' she now began to tear up
'I should of said it sooner . . . I'
'Don't. It was meant to be this way'
'You were always one to believe in fate'
'It brought me to you didn't it—' she coughed, coughing up blood, '—don't look at me Varin'

Tears now stream down their cheeks.

'I see again in your eyes. That thing that made me fall for you . . .'
'Weakness?'
'Strength.'
'Varin!—' she begins to search for his hand, '—I can't see . . . it's dark.'
'I'm here'
'Cold . . . so cold'

He wraps his arms around her, tears begin to fall onto her head as her own tears fall onto Varin's arm.

'I love you . . . Emily'

She stops breathing, he repeats himself again.
And again.
And again.
There was never a final reply.

'Varin . . .—' said Talon placing one hand on his shoulder, '—it's time, we should go'
'What now? what can we do now?' asked Varin
'I don't know . . .' said Yal
'The TG's dead without it's leader'
'Well not quite, Yal and I are now the highest ranking officers'
'. . . I'm not sure I want to carry on'
'What about the prophecy, ya?'
'You need to carry on Varin. If it's true what Craig said, we don't have much time left to find the other Crystals'

'How am I meant to protect the planet if I can't protect the ones I care about? First Drogun turns and now, Emily . . . my Emily . . .'

'Varin. I know how you feel . . . our father, Raiden, killed our brother as a result of PHOENIX Poisoning but you must continue to fight, it's what the fallen would want.'

'. . . Perhaps you're right'

Varin lowers Emily gently. She was still smiling, in her final moments she looked happy in his arms.

'We should leave' said Varin

"And so they did. They left the tomb that the building has now become. Leaving the city of Shenma, in silence. The Ninja Twins unknowing what to say to Varin. They headed towards Skyspear to allow Varin to rest."

The wind blows calmly on the rooftop of the SPARK Building. Drogun final moves, spiting blood rising to his feet, he bends over to pick up his blade. As he stands back up, he hears something suddenly land behind him, he turns to see.

'What . . . how? You . . .'

'YOu reCkoNISE me?'

'How could I forget an evil, such as you . . . Holfast'

'So, U arE ONe of THE ElvEs'

'No I'm human'

'EiTHer WAy . . . You shALL tASte MY steEL'

'Here Togu, here! Come HERE!' yelled Yal.

The three Togu's were playing around just outside the city limits. One of the three Togu's heard Yal's call and tone. It didn't like it. Ran towards him

'See just need to be firm with them' he smirked

It jumped up to him, knocking him down and pining him to the ground. It growled and snarled an inch away from his face.

'Ha . . . huh . . . nice kitty' said Yal nervously.

Talon began to laugh, as the Togu climbs from him, allowing him to get up. He reaches his feet and begins to laugh as well, it even puts a smile on Varin' face.

"Yal being jumped on by the Togu cheered me up, but my thoughts remained of Emily and all the moments we shared."

CHAPTER 23

The Beginning . . .

"AT LEAST UNTIL . . ."

The SPARK Corp. building suddenly exploded in a finale of smoke and flames, sending out a wave of destruction across the city. Other buildings fell and collapsed, homes were destroyed, innocent lives lost as SPARK came crashing down upon itself.

However something, something came from the rooftop, someone in all black. A man. They all noticed at the same time as the man flew towards them and then changed direction heading towards the south.

'Drogun!?' asked Yal
'I don't think it was . . .' said Talon.
'I'm going after him' replied Varin

He then jumped onto the Togu and headed towards the direction of the man. The Ninja Twins whistled for their Togus, whom quickly came over and followed Varin.

Anger swelled now deep inside Varin. What Co Hobson once said to him, on that rooftop along ago was true. The people of Shenma lives depended on him and when they needed him, he wasn't there. The death of those people now weighed heavily on his shoulders. He knew one thing, he had to kill him for justice.

He had to kill his brother.

They raced forth, covering many miles following the shadow of Drogun. They raced through the forest surrounding Shenma City, or at least the ruined remains of Shenma. Beyond that was the open fields, leading to the wastelands.

They quickly reached the fields, keeping Drogun in sight.

'Something's wrong' said Talon

Varin didn't answer, luckily Yal was just as clueless as he was.

'What is?'

'These fields are often swarming with Fiends . . . where are they?'

'Hunting? Gone to the ocean for a drink?'

'They're hiding from something. We've seen this before remember? The Professor's place'

"I had forgot about that meeting with the Professor until then . . . I thought he was some crack pot but now it was all making sense."

More bodies of Fiends began to pile up, each with a similar wound, a stab through the rib cage or the slicing off of a limb, even the trees weren't save from the fight that took place, countless trees were cut down or showed sign of a battle mark. Talon placed his weapon away and pointed to a point just up ahead.

'There. The Professor's cabin'
'Finally. Maybe he could tell us what this is all about' spoke Yal
'As well as the crystal' said Varin

They approached the cabin, putting their weapons away. Knock, knock.

'Enter' called a muffled voice from inside

The group, Varin, Yal, Talon, Co Hobson, Sylvia and Twele, entered the cabin. It was small but almost cosy, a small bed laid against the wall in front of them, that looked like there hadn't been anyone sleeping in it for the past week. The rest of the room was full of electronic gadgets and jars of liquid, some containing unpleasant things.

'Professor? Where are you?' asked Co Hobson
'I'm in the back here conducting SCIENCE!'

A small curtain separated them from "the back", they approached as the Professor's silhouette splashed across the curtain from sparks, from something he's working on.
Co Hobson goes to move the curtain.

'Don't touch, mwhehe'

Both Co Hobson and Yal stopped. Talon looked at the guilty look on Yal's face.

'. . . I wasn't going to touch anything' he said with a unsure grin.

'Professor, we really need to speak to you as quick as possible' said Co Hobson
'Just a second . . . EUREKA!' cried out the Professor

The device that the Professor was working on came to live with a number of bleeps and boops. It then suddenly exploded, setting the Professor's hair on fire. The others prepared to move in and help as the Professor ran around franticly searching for the fire extinguisher, he quickly found it spraying himself and the device. Covering himself and the area in a cloud of smoke.
He came stumbling from beyond the curtain coughing.

'Professor Valiant Shirriff, at your service'
'Excellent to see you again Shirriff' said Co Hobson

He looked no older than they were, on the street Varin thought many wouldn't of even realised he was a Professor without his lab coat and stethoscope. His hair was long and greasy, coming just past his ears. Around his head he wore goggles that seemed to have a swirly pattern on the lens and were mirrored. He was just as tall as Varin.

'We call him Professor Insano' whispered Yal to Varin.

'What can I do for you and the TG? Want more of my brilliant SCIENCE!?' asked Professor Shirriff almost breaking into maniacal laughter.

'Possibly but we have a few questions—' replied Talon, '—also did Yaris come by?'

'Ah yes that lumbering oath, he's the one that broke my clock that you saw me repairing'

'How did you get a clock to burst into flames?'

The Professor shrugged.

'None of the less, did you find anything out about Varin here?' questioned Talon

Varin looked at him confused.

'Sorry Varin, ya. We gave your Police badge to the Professor to find out if you were from the past.'

'Oh so this is the boy. Well may I please say—' the Professor grabbed and began to shake Varin's hand, '—it is a pleasure to meet a time traveller please tell me how'd you get here?'

'He's not sure Prof' said Co Hobson.

He looked slightly disappointed as he let go of Varin's hand.

'We worked out for ourselves awhile back than that Varin was the real deal, but what else did you find out'

'Oh, I got a full file on him from the old Shenma records' replied the Professor pointing at his computer

Even Varin was a little curious about what was on his record and there it was his entire history with the Shenma Police laid out in front of him. He passed a simulation based in Gade City with flying colours and stopping real Trans-Gression members in the process with two other cadets in training, Cadet Craig Benson Wilkins and their squad leader Cadet Emily Goredell, together they formed Squad A.

'The first time we met Hero—' said Co Hobson, '—I remember it well, an unsure lucky bunch of cadets stopping us. We got a little too cocky I guess'

The file went on to state due to their team work the group remained together for a number of years in Shenma. There was one final entry at the bottom about Varin's next run in with TG.

"A riot broke out on the streets of Shenma with Trans-Gression members storming the SPARK Corp. building leading to an assault onto the roof. And that's where I last met Co Hobson on the roof of Shenma—that memory never left me waking me like a nightmare"

'You do sound like quite a hero Varin' said Sylvia.

'After that battle all reports end, which seemed odd to me so I began to wonder and with the power of SCIENCE! I found out that the . . .'

The Professor was suddenly cut off by Co Hobson 'The station was destroyed, Trans-Gression were blamed—' he paused but only to look at Varin, '—I can assure you we had nothing to do with that. With the Police gone, SPARK tightened their grip on the city creating their own law enforcement group to control Shenma, amongst the confusion that's when I entered the building and sealed myself in one of their pods.'

"That must have been around the time Craig grabbed Emily, sealing her in the pod to bring her to the future . . ."

'Excellent find Doc . . . I mean Professor' said Yal
'Did you find out anything about the crystal that Drogun brought?' asked Sylvia
'Who? And the what now?'
'Drogun and the crystal?'
'. . . No, no one brought me that'
'What but he said . . .' spoke Yal.

"Drogun never went to speak to the Professor that night, and that's when he saw Sylvia and I, kiss . . . but where did he go all night then?"

'No matter—' said Talon, removing something from his pocket, '—I happened to have a fragment of it here, it must of chipped off when we were chased by the Guardians'

Talon held out his palm with the small fragment lying in the centre, the Professor quickly grabbed a machine and scanned it.

'The computer shall give us all the information we need through the magic of SCIENCE!' said the Professor excitedly before breaking out into a quiet maniacal laugh.
'You'd think he'd get bored of science with the amount of times he says it' jokingly said Yal.

'CRYSTALLISED PHOENIX!' yelled the Professor suddenly throwing his arms up, knocking the fragment from Talon's had.

It flew into the air, spinning towards the back of the room, the group stood in disbelief. All except for Varin, who saw it begin to fall towards him. He reached out and grabbed it as it landed in the palm of his hand.

He looked at it, it glowed, as the others came over except for the Professor. It then seemed to crack and then melt into Varin's hand, he felt a cold tingle down his spine as it did.

". . . That must be how my magic abilities awoken? But why then, why not when I held the entire crystal earlier? Sounds more like coincidence that I'm just lucky than the Brother of Ice, a chosen one, a hero"

'This is amazing, this is incredible yet there it is, clear as day—' spoke the Professor, '—the crystal has power and according to this it can be used to control H_2O, not just a simple spell to cast H_2O but true magic. So strong it can control water.—' he began to search for papers to write down notes as he continued rambling to himself, '—According to these readings it gives off minuet traces of radiation, enough to track it maybe find more?'

'Ergh Professor, I think we might have a problem, ya?'

He turns to see the group standing around Varin, staring at his palm.

'It melted into his skin' said Co Hobson

'Give me a few moments—' he turned back face his computer picking up papers and notes before pushing past the curtain, '—I'm going to make a crystal finding device.'

"Over the next few hours Professor Shirriff stayed in the back creating the device, it seemed to last forever with his banging, sawing, screwing and welding. Every now and again he'd even break out with a cry of 'SCIENCE!' or just a maniacal laugh, eventually he emerged with the device in hand. With that we said our thanks and left."

"We never learnt what happened to the Fiends, but whatever seems to have happened to the same Fiends here, was it all Drogun's doing."

The sun began to set behind a smoking mountain, thirty miles up a head. An active volcano rested to the south of this continent and it seemed this is where Drogun was heading to.

From this distance Varin could still see Drogun enter through the crater of the volcano. Finally he had come to a stop, Varin kicked the Togu more and it quickened.

They soon arrive at the bottom of the volcano, the heat from it quickly rose through the ground scorching the Togu's paws as they leap from rock to rock.

The Togus stop as they land on a long path leading to a vent once used and created from a previous eruption many years ago.

'Varin, now might be a go time to get of the Togu' said Talon

'They look pretty tired ya' added Yal

He couldn't of agreed more looking at the Togus panting with their tongues for air and water.

Varin gave a nod and dismounted from his Togu and lead the way into the volcano. He was soon followed down into the conduit, a circular walkway sprawling down. The sprawling walkway led down twenty floors to the magma chamber even from this height he could make out that in the centre, high above the lava, was another small path leading to a small platform holding a red, ruby crystal. But no sign of Drogun

The further they went down, the more the air become harder to breathe, each breathe seemed to hurt.

They quickly grew tired until they saw a man was beside the pedestal holding the crystal, a man with white hair.

'DROGUN!' yelled Varin, the anger inside now at a boiling point.

He began to sprint downwards to the path. He reached the pathway and there stood the white haired man, back facing Varin.

'Yal, you're blade' said Varin, holding out his arm.

Yal and Talon reached the path, they stopped for breathe. Yal quickly passed Varin one of his blades.

'I warned you Drogun, that I would kill you—' said Varin, sword in hand and walking closer to the man, '—if we were to meet once again. Now it's time for you to pay!'

Varin slashed the blade down from over his shoulders. The man revealed his weapon blocking Varin's attack with ease while still facing and starring at the ruby crystal.

'I aM NO DrOGun. I aM kNoWN—' the white haired man finally turned his head, '—Holfast.'

He knocked the sword from Varin's hand, and grabbed him by the throat. The sword landed on the narrow pathway a few feet from them as he lifted Varin slowly from his feet.

'R yoU THe CHoseN 1?—' asked Holfast. Varin tried to speak but could not speak, '—CoME fOr THe crySTAl I C, THIEF!—' his grip tightened as Yal and Talon react by revealing their blades, '—We've met bEForE U & I, something about the past . . . Hmph, No mATTeR. If U ArE nOt THEN you wILl DIE!'

'NOOO!—' yelled out a voice from the top of the spiral walkway, the man jumped, '—Brother!' yelled the man, Drogun.

Holfast threw Varin to Yal and Talon, they caught Varin but with the power Holfast threw him they were flew back towards the wall winding them. Varin looked up grasping for air to see Drogun reveal his sword to attack the defenceless Holfast whom was still staring at Varin. He suddenly smiled and raised his long katana towards the falling Drogun, whom was now a meter away.

'Argh!' yelled Drogun.

Varin reached his feet to see Drogun pierced by Holfast's katana through the left section of his chest and the shoulder blade.

Holfast smirked as he held Drogun over the pathway, he began to retract his blade using his over free hand to push Drogun away. Drogun twitched and cried out in pain. He suddenly removed the blade from Drogun and watched him land to the floor on his knees.

'BeG, bEG for your life'

Drogun crawled away towards Varin.

'Oh, what's this?' said Holfast

He climbed up to Varin's ear and whispered into his ear, shock and confusion appeared of Varin's face as the smirk of Holfast grew into a smile. Drogun then handed Varin his sword before, backing away and rising to his feet. He then back up to the edge of the path.

'Holfast . . . you're a fool, always have been, always will. With my death, someone much more powerful than me shall rise in my place and put your ass where it belongs. My brother, Varin.'

He then leant back, spreading out his arms and he began to fall, he smiled to Varin and Holfast as he fell towards the molten magma below.

'DROGUN!' yelled Varin as he stretched his arm over the edge.

Yal and Talon pulled him back as Holfast began to laugh.

Tears swelled as Drogun disappeared from sight. Everything seemed to go silent until the laughter of Holfast reached Varin's ears. Rage now returned to Varin as the forth coming tears disappeared into vapour. Varin quickly rose to his feet with Drogun's sword in hand. He grips the hilt tightly I hand. He then begins to run towards Holfast, yelling as to stop Holfast's laughter. Varin swings.

The laugh and smile quickly changed to a blank expression as Holfast disappeared with a flash and a blink of an eye. His laughter echoed.

Varin began to look for his enemy, nowhere to be seen. He turned back towards the pedestal that once held the elemental ruby crystal of fire. It was no long there.

'Face me coward!' yelled Varin tears again in his eyes.
'You R NOT wORThy' replied Holfast.
'Damn you . . .'

Varin dropped to his knees, tears now dripping down his face from the loss of his brother and the loss of Emily. Three drops fell from his face, one fell to the ground and the other two fell onto his arm, they hurt. He looked to his arm and saw the two drops turn to ice.

"They became a permanent reminder to myself of that day."

Yal looked at the device they received from the Professor to see two crystals moving away from them as Talon approached Varin.

'Varin, I'm sorry . . . but we need to leave . . . the Volcano is becoming unstable'

Rocks began to loosen and break away from the walls, the lava below began to slowly rise up. He quickly jumped back to his feet. With a nod they began to run, Yal leading the way back up the spiral path way as rocks around them began to crumble away.

With the speed, the Ninja Twins quickly made their way up the levels faster than Varin. The Lava now had reached the platform and seemed to speed up and more rocks and even the spiral walkway broke away and fell.

The path fell away just ahead of Varin, but his mind seemed clear with the thoughts of what Drogun said to him echoing within.

'Brother, I love you. It was good seeing you again, finally I'm not alone in this world.—'

Varin pushed out his arm, repairing the gap with steps of ice.

'—I'm sorry, sorry for everything that's happened. Everything we did as kids, everything I've done now—'

He heard the fizzle as the ice he created melt away as the lava rose a few levels below him now.

'—I'm lucky to have you as a Brother. Here take this . . . and one last thing'

A few more levels up Varin saw the exit, not far now but neither was the lava. Suddenly the ground beneath him began to shake and give way, he got a few steps forward before the path finally gave away. Varin fell reaching out his hand the grab the edge of the path—he narrowly missed it but just as suddenly someone grabbed his hand, looking back up he sees his saviour the Ninja Twin, Talon.

'Quit hanging around ya, Varin' said Yal

Varin groaned from the joke as the lava laid not too far off from his heels. Talon also groaned as he pulled up Varin. He quickly rose to his feet and they continued to run with Yal taking lead once again. They reached the exit but it wasn't over yet the Lava wasn't too far behind. Yal whistled and the three Togu came running. Each of them jumped atop the backs of the beasts, gave them a kick and fled the area.

The volcano erupted through the vent narrowly missing the Togu's tail that Varin was riding. They road forth a number of minutes and miles as the volcano lit up the sky in the distance, before coming to a stop near a spring of fresh water. They jumped down from the Togus, as they strolled towards to water for a drink. The group knelt near the water and began to wash their faces clean from the soot and ash.

'Whoa that was close ya . . . who wants to do that again?' asked Yal.

They stood back up as both Talon and Varin looked at him and smiled.

'Count me out, I'm just thankful it's over' replied Talon

'It's not over—' add Varin, '—it's only the beginning. Holfast is out there, searching for these crystals we can't let him get his hands on them'

'He has two of them, I looked at the device the Professor gave us. He has two'

'If the prophecy is correct and he's the True Evil, we need to the find the other two before he does'

'Where should we begin?' asked Talon

'The Continent of Ruins, a lot of that continent isn't mapped, could be a good place to hide away the remaining crystals, ya'

Varin climbed atop of his Togu, 'Then that's where we'll head.'

Talon climbed back on his Togu, 'We'll have to avoid the Elven lands'

'Good, I don't fancy being shot at again ya' said Yal as he climbed upon his Togu, almost falling from it in the process.

The Togus began to slowly walk towards the north

'Varin. If I may ask what did Drogun say? Before he . . .' asked Yal

'He said . . .'

"Here take this . . . and one last thing . . . I will return."

To be continued . . .